WHEN THE MOON IS FULL

The bass rumbling in Seth's chest was unmistakably a threat, and I noted his eyes had shifted from a deep hazel into an amber color similar to my own. Sean and Dillon pulled me back to shield me from him, and I had to stand on tiptoe to see over their shoulders what happened next.

Between one blink and the next, Seth was shifting. He cried out a challenge before his human vocal cords were too changed by the shift to allow for speech, his last words trailing off into a long, drawn-out howl. "You're dead! You're all dead, unless you yield to me!"

I watched, fascinated, as Seth's chest deepened and his arms grew thick with muscle. The crack of bone and sinew adjusting and reforming was sickening, but fortunately didn't last very long since he'd forced a quick change. The fur that sprang out of his skin was a shade of deep brown a little darker than his hair, covering sleek muscles and a powerful frame that would rival Chaz for size if he had shifted, too. No wonder Seth thought he was badass. Still, size didn't necessarily mean one had smarts or skill or experience, things Chaz had in abundance.

Seth wasn't go__ ___ wolf either; he was assuming the half-and____ ____ __ __ __ be stuck in again tonigh___ ____ _____ es— once the moon

If he survive___

Books by Jess Haines

HUNTED BY THE OTHERS

TAKEN BY THE OTHERS

DECEIVED BY THE OTHERS

Collections

NOCTURNAL
(with Jacquelyn Frank, Kate Douglas,
and Clare Willis)

Published by Kensington Publishing Corporation

DECEIVED BY THE OTHERS

WITHDRAWN

JESS HAINES

AN H&W INVESTIGATIONS NOVEL

ZEBRA BOOKS
KENSINGTON PUBLISHING CORP.
http://www.kensingtonbooks.com

ZEBRA BOOKS are published by

Kensington Publishing Corp.
119 West 40th Street
New York, NY 10018

All Kensington titles, imprints and distributed lines are
available at special quantity discounts for bulk purchases
for sales promotion, premiums, fund-raising, educational or
institutional use.

Special book excerpts or customized printings can also be
created to fit specific needs. For details, write or phone the
office of the Kensington Special Sales Manager: Attn. Special
Sales Department. Kensington Publishing Corp., 119 West
40th Street, New York, NY 10018. Phone: 1-800-221-2647.

Zebra and the Z logo Reg. U.S. Pat. & TM Off.

ISBN-13: 978-1-4201-1189-7
ISBN-10: 1-4201-1189-2

First Printing: July 2011
10 9 8 7 6 5 4 3 2 1

Printed in the United States of America

ACKNOWLEDGMENTS

David—I owe you a soda.

Ellen—you are, as always, awesome. Thank you so much for all your help!

Eve—thank you for "loaning" me Christoph. I promise not to abuse the privilege—too much.

Chapter 1

My hands shook as I put my pen to the contract laid out before me. The *Notice of Mutual Consent to Human/Other Citizen Relationship and Contractual Binding Agreement* that would permanently cement my relationship with Chaz.

If he'd sign it too, that is.

"Shia?"

The pen left a streak behind when my hand jerked. I looked up, quickly shuffling some other papers over the contract to hide it amidst the clutter on my desk.

"Yes?"

Jen, H&W's receptionist and bookkeeper, peered into my office over the rims of her glasses. She eyed the papers like she knew I was hiding something, but was too tactful to say anything. "What was the name of that crazy guy who was here a month or so ago? The one you didn't want to take calls or appointments from?"

I wrinkled my nose. "You're talking about that tall, blond guy, right? His name is Jack."

She nodded and disappeared around the corner. Curiosity piqued and the contract momentarily forgotten, I rose from my squeaky office chair to lean against the doorframe. Jen was on the phone, her feet propped up on her desk while she wrapped up a game of solitaire on the computer.

"No, sir, I just checked, and she's in with a client. I'm sorry, but I'm not about to interrupt her meeting. Like I said, you can leave her a voice mail, or I can take a message."

I frowned, folding my arms as I watched her multitask her game and the phone call. Jack's calling wasn't a good sign. The man was a member of the White Hats, one of those crazy vigilante groups who go around destroying any supernatural critters that cross their paths. The first time I'd met him, he'd threatened me at knifepoint to attempt to get me to join his cause. The second time around, he had walked into my office in broad daylight and held a gun on me because he thought I was working for vampires. Aside from being a few beers short of a six-pack, he was bad news, pure and simple.

"Like I said, *sir*, she is not available." Jen's tone had turned professionally icy, and I strongly considered giving her a raise. She was doing an excellent job of putting off the pushy creep. "You're free to leave a message with me or call back another time." She paused, listened to his reply. Soon she was nodding along to whatever he was saying with a sly, triumphant smile. "Yes, I'll see she gets it right away. What's the message?"

Swinging her feet off the desk, she opened up

an e-mail and clattered out Jack's message. She saw me out of the corner of her eye and made a face, though she kept her voice cool and polite on the phone.

"Yes, I'll get this to her as soon as she's free. Thanks for calling Halloway and Waynest Investigations."

"Thanks for getting rid of him," I said as soon as she plunked the phone down. "That guy is nothing but trouble."

"No kidding. I'll forward the message since he left a phone number, but I don't know if it'll mean anything to you. All he said was, 'tell her this time it isn't us.' Any idea what he's talking about?"

I frowned, brows furrowing. "That's all he had to say? 'It isn't us'?"

"Yeah."

"I have no idea."

Shaking her head, she turned back to her computer and sent me the e-mail, my preferred form of message. Sara was much more organized than I was when it came to keeping track of Post-it memos. My desk was a rattrap clutter of dust bunnies, chewed up pens, and scattered business cards that should've been filed away or organized somehow long ago.

"If he shows up here looking for me while I'm out of town, call the police. He's a nuisance."

"Okay," she agreed, not bothering to look away from her game. Shrugging off my uneasiness, I turned back to my office, but she stopped me with another word. "Oh, Shia?"

"Yes?"

"I almost forgot. Some guy named Alex or something left a message on the main voice mail for you last night. I forwarded it to your phone."

I'd ignored my calls earlier so I could avoid any new emergencies getting piled on me before going out of town. Which Alex might have attempted to reach me before I left? Alex Mills, the insurance agent? No, he was out of town on vacation. Alex Temps, the client I tracked down a stolen antique for a couple weeks ago? No, no, he had bitched about my rates from start to finish and hadn't been in the least grateful when I completed the job. He'd already paid, shortchanging me by a hundred and fifty bucks, the stingy bastard. I doubted I'd ever hear from him again. Who could it be?

Wait a minute. "Alex" calling me right around the same time as Jack the White Hat?

Oh, no. No, no, no. That could only mean one thing.

Stifling a shudder, I made sure to keep my expression calm and blank. I didn't want to upset Jen. If she'd listened to the message more closely or caught me looking upset she'd realize who it was, too. Her wounded, disapproving looks were the last thing I wanted to deal with right now.

"Thanks, Jen. I'll check it out."

"No prob."

I closed the door, moving back around my desk and moving the files aside so I could review the contract one more time. My concentration was shot; my good mood soured. A White Hat and Alec Royce had both tried to get in touch with me, and I had no idea why.

The clock on my computer read 3:15, which meant I still had a little over two hours before my boyfriend Chaz would pick me up for my first real vacation in months.

Being stuck recuperating in a hospital or taking time off from work to wait for the effects of a vampire's blood bond to wear off does *not* count as a vacation, by the way.

Sara was supposed to keep an eye on my apartment and my messages while I was gone. It was only for a few days, but that was more (voluntary) time off than I'd taken in quite a while. Her boyfriend was letting me borrow one of his laptops so I could keep an eye on my e-mail and stay in touch. He'd threatened to sic his familiar, a tiny black mouse named Bob, on me every night for a week if anything happened to his coveted Fragware 5000. I'd sworn up and down I'd treat it like my own. Seriously, who wants a *mouse* crawling on them in their sleep? Ugh.

Anyway, things should've been winding down. My current clients had been given the message that I would be out, and Jen was supposed to refer everything to Sara until I got back. Jack and Royce's surfacing again changed all of that.

I frowned down at the blinking message light on my phone, strongly considering waiting until I returned to town to listen to it. Alec Royce, like Jack the White Hat, was straight up bad news. He was wealthy, good-looking, and had made a couple of halfhearted attempts in the past to seduce me away from Chaz. We should've been able to go our separate ways since I'd saved his life and he'd returned the favor by saving mine.

However, the guy was a vampire, and I should've known better than to think that he'd forgotten about me over the last month. He'd used threats and coercion to get me to sign a contract that bound me to him by letter of the law, and then later he bound me to him in a much more tangible way—by blood—in order to save my life. While I was grateful for being saved, the method he used to get me out of the clutches of Max Carlyle still gave me nightmares. The remembered taste of his blood on my lips made me shiver, and not entirely in a bad way. Disgusted and horrified as I was, it had been an electrifying experience to feel so needed, so safe, so complete, while under his sway.

As you might imagine, I'd done everything possible to keep the hell away from him since then.

I thought when I changed my cell phone number that it might keep him and some of the other undesirable elements of my past from contacting me, but the number to my office was plastered all over the Yellow Pages and the Internet. I wasn't thrilled to know he wanted to talk to me again, but having him call me was marginally better than having him show up here at my office or, worse yet, at my apartment.

Grumbling under my breath, I lifted the receiver and punched in the password to listen to the messages. There were a couple others I had to wade through before Royce's smooth, cultured voice came on the line.

"This is Alec, and I'm leaving a message for Ms. Waynest. Shiarra, I just wanted to make sure you know that whatever happens while you are out of town is not my doing. If someone tries to make it appear otherwise, I'd appreciate being informed so that I can take action. I hope all is well with you, and enjoy your vacation."

Well, that was confusing. Both Jack and Royce were telling me they weren't responsible for whatever was going to happen while I was out of town. First and foremost, how the hell did Royce find out I was traveling? I didn't post my itinerary on the ten o'clock news. Second, what were they so worried about?

It wasn't unusual for Royce to cover his bases. Though he hadn't tried contacting me since I'd run away from his home after the blood bond wore off, it wasn't entirely out of character for him to make efforts to keep his name out of anything potentially nefarious. If he was worried that something might upset some plans of his or make him look bad, he'd take action.

Jack's covering his ass didn't make any sense to me. We hadn't parted on the best of terms. Actually, the last time I'd seen him, I was walking out of the White Hat Super Secret Ninja Hideout after announcing that I felt safer with the monsters than I did with the hunters.

Yeah, I do need to brush up on my people skills a bit.

Regardless, it didn't matter. Whatever it was they were worried about couldn't possibly be any worse than what I'd already been through. Fighting mad sorcerers and psychotic vampires was not on the to-do list while I was on vacation. I was anticipating a few awkward moments, since this trip was intended to help me get to know Chaz's unofficial family better, but that shouldn't have been enough to make either Royce or Jack stir themselves into giving me some kind of warning.

Chaz and I had been discussing doing something like this for a while. The biggest problem with our relationship was that Chaz is a werewolf. He's the leader of the Sunstriker Tribe, one of a few packs that live in and around New York City. The Moonwalkers have the biggest pack in town, and they'd laid claim to Central Park, along with a bunch of the parks and reserves all up and down Long Island. That meant the Sunstrikers and many of the other smaller packs had to head out to places like Caumsett State Park, Blue Mountain Reservation, or even as far as the Catskill Mountains when getting together as a group to run as a pack or to hunt. All that travel just to avoid difficulties with the Moonwalkers.

It was pretty inconvenient for the smaller packs. Not everyone can explain away needing to take three or four days off from work every month around the full moon without people getting suspicious. So, as one might imagine, the parks and preserves not claimed by the Moonwalkers were always coveted and fiercely protected. Sometimes the smaller packs got into skirmishes with each other, vying for the same hunting grounds on the full moon. It generally didn't get so out of hand that humans, like me, got caught up in their problems. However, if Chaz and I stayed together during the height of the lunar cycle, I would need to be prepared to have lots and lots of furry critters around.

This vacation was our "trial run" to see how I might handle having a whole crapload of shifted Weres around me during the full moon. We'd drive up to the lodge in Hunter tonight, and the daylight hours would be devoted to getting to know the people who made up his tribe. Friday, Saturday, and Sunday night, the moon would be full, and I would get to see them together as a pack. I'd have to be careful, though. Tempers would be short, and some of them might change before the full moon.

No doubt, this would be one weird four-day weekend. I was reasonably certain I could handle it. As long as Chaz was with me, I would be fine.

To be honest, I was more excited about the prospect of staying in a cabin out in the woods with Chaz than about seeing a bunch of furry people running around in the dark but, hey, I could deal with it.

Though I was awfully nervous about the contract I'd been in the process of signing when Jack called. While we had resumed dating, Chaz and I hadn't slept together since he'd revealed what he was. Legally, he couldn't touch me. Even sleeping in the same cabin would be pushing it—but I was tired of how careful we had to be, and of how distant he was with me after both Royce and that psycho vampire, Max Carlyle, had temporarily bound me to themselves by blood. Offering to sign a *Notice of Mutual Consent to Human/Other Citizen Relationship and Contractual Binding Agreement* with him should make him sit up and take notice that I wasn't going anywhere, that I truly wanted to be with him, and that I trusted him again.

My worry was whether or not he trusted *me* enough to sign it, too.

This little camping trip seemed like the perfect opportunity to make things right between us. We'd gotten a good group discount at a small resort up in the Catskills. It was too early for snow but too cold to tempt many vacationers. Plus, now that school was back in session, tourist season was officially over. Chaz had assured me that the guy who owned the property wouldn't have any problem with the Sunstrikers—he was also a Were. One well-known among the supernatural community for having bought a bunch of forestland out in the mountains and cordoning off his borders to keep out hunters and tourists, which helped any packs staying with him know exactly how far out they could safely range on the hunt.

It was hard to picture anything going wrong. After all, I'd been introduced to Chaz's pack before. We'd even gone out to dinner or the movies with a few of them. The only other time I'd seen the entire pack in one place was when we showed up to fight David Borowsky, the crazed sorcerer who meant to enslave all of the Weres and vampires in New York using a weird magic artifact. Sure, they were dangerous, but since I was the pack leader's girlfriend and had helped save their furry butts, as long as I didn't do anything too stupid they should be able to hold their hungers and tempers in check.

What could go wrong?

I pondered these things while I stared at the contract. Screw it. I tucked the papers away in my bag and followed Jen's example, amusing myself with a card game while I waited for the clock to tick by and Chaz to come pick me up.

Chapter 2

I wasn't pleased when a familiar face showed up at the office an hour before Chaz was expected to arrive. Though I'd been strenuously ignoring anything going on beyond the haven of my office, I couldn't help but overhear Jen arguing with someone outside. I figured if it was that important, Sara could handle it.

Then Jen's voice rose, loud enough that I couldn't mistake who she was speaking to, or who he was here to see.

"Mr. Pradiz, I'm afraid you're going to have to come back next week. Nothing has changed since I told you over the phone an hour ago that she isn't available. Now would you *please* leave?"

Oh, for fuck's sake. "Mr. Pradiz" was the tabloid reporter who had splashed my personal life across every newspaper in town while I was busy trying to stay alive. He'd been following me from a distance ever since Royce scared off one of Max Carlyle's minions who'd come to kidnap me. We had an uneasy understanding that I'd give him the scoop behind the supernatural hoopla that always seemed to blow up around me as long as he left me the hell alone and let me come to him when I had a story. I didn't like him following me around, but all he'd agreed to was keeping his distance and not approaching me or my friends in public. For him to show up here, now, couldn't be good news. Whatever he wanted, it could wait until I got back to town.

I groaned and heaved myself out of the squeaky office chair, cracking my office door open and peering out. Jim's clothing was neat, but nondescript, his skin bronzed by hours in the sun and blond hair fashionably tousled. Aside from the tiny digital camera peeking out of his shirt pocket, he didn't seem to be armed with anything other than a complete inability to take a hint. The avid interest gleaming in the reporter's hazel eyes when he spotted me instantly put me on my toes.

He grinned, showing whiter than white teeth in a practiced look that might have been attractive had I not been overexposed to the charms of far greater predators—such as Max Carlyle and Alec Royce.

"Ah, so you *are* here! Ms. Waynest, just a few quick questions—"

"No."

"It won't take but a minute—"

"*No.*"

His eyes glittered with impatience and something else I didn't want to explore too deeply, that ingratiating smile wilting around the edges. "Don't be so quick to turn me away. You haven't even heard me out yet."

"I don't need to. You've been shadowing me for over a month—so if you haven't found whatever the hell it is you want from me yet, I'm sure it can wait a few more days. I'll get back to you after my vacation. Hell, I'll even give you an exclusive if you can promise to stay the fuck away from me until then."

"An exclusive?" he said, one bleached blond eyebrow arching high. "My, my. You must be desperate to hide something from me."

"Fuck you."

"Thanks, you're not my type," was his deadpan reply. I frowned, and his smile returned, brighter than ever. "All I'm interested in is a story. I hear things are heating up around you. I want to know why."

"Tough. You can wait 'til I'm back. Please, Jim, I promise I'll talk to you if you just leave me the hell alone until Monday."

"Tempting as the offer is, I'm not sure I can take it. But I'll tell you what—here's my card. Call me when you figure out you're in over your head."

He gave me a shit-eating grin as he flicked the card at Jen and sauntered out of the office. She muttered something uncomplimentary under her breath about his theatrics and slid the square of paper off her desk and into the trash. I was tempted to call out for him to stop and explain himself, but the idea of souring my vacation worrying about whatever he was after was deterrent enough to keep my mouth shut.

Jen tapped her nails lightly on the desktop, scowling after his retreating form in the beveled glass. "Shia, I know it's none of my business, but you should really figure out what's going on and get these people to leave you alone. They all seem like bad news."

"No kidding."

"He's not the first one to stop by."

That put a chill down my spine. "Who else was here?"

"Some other reporters. A girl with blond hair who looked like she was packing some weapons, and who was wearing a White Hat pin. She tried to trick me into telling her where you were vacationing, but I got her out of here without letting anything slip. Oh, and some guy named Devon said he'd swing by once you got back into town. That one was cute." The hopeful way she looked at me at the mention of the ex-White Hat didn't ease the frown from my features. Not one bit. "Anyway, they all wanted to see you, but none of them wanted to leave a message or wait around. I told them all you'd left already so they wouldn't keep bothering us."

"Thanks, Jen," I said, retreating back into my office. "You did the right thing. Don't worry about it; I'll handle whatever it is they're so worked up about next week."

I shut the door and leaned against it, closing my eyes. Something big must be going down, but whatever it was could happen without me. I wasn't going to put my vacation on hold—not for reporters, not for vampires, and *definitely* not for White Hats—even if said White Hats weren't card-carrying, pin-wearing members anymore.

The world wasn't going to end if I put this on

ice. Royce and Jack would've had more to say in their messages if they thought some big bad thing was coming to town. I'd just put it all out of my mind for the weekend.

A touch of paranoia made me scribble down a list of who had tried to reach me before I settled with grim determination in front of my computer again. Contacting those people would be my to-do list—as soon as I got back.

Luckily, Chaz arrived early, only fifteen minutes or so after I'd immersed myself in the shiny distractions of the Internet. Jen eyed him appreciatively over the rims of her glasses while he examined some of our new brochures. She gave me thumbs up as I lugged my suitcase out of my office. Eager to get out of town and brimming with excitement now that I could leave all my worries behind for a few days, I grinned and winked back.

Chaz is a personal trainer, so his schedule is fairly flexible. Handy for when he needs to handle pack business. It also means he has a delightfully ripped physique that only hints at the incredible strength he has as a Were. His baby blue eyes sparkled with laughter when he saw me struggling with the suitcase I'd packed. He immediately came over to give me a distressingly chaste hug and to take up the handle in one hand, lifting the heavy bag with ease.

"Hey, love, let me get that. Ready to go?"

I smiled and got up on tiptoe to give him a peck on the cheek. "Of course. I've been dying to get out of here."

"Don't forget to leave me your keys," Sara called from her office.

I slapped my forehead and dug around in my purse while she tore herself away from the skip-tracing program she was running to see us off.

"Thanks for watching my stuff while I'm gone. No road trips to California while I'm out." I grinned as I tossed her my car keys.

"No worries of that," she said, laughing as she caught them. She slid her hands into the pockets of her jeans, following us out of the office and down the stairs. "Too much work to do. I can't wait 'til Thanksgiving rolls around. Your mom cooking again this year?"

"Heck yeah. Hopefully my dad's lightened up by then. Mom's finally talking to me again."

My parents had both nearly had heart attacks when they found out I was associating with Others. After my stint in the hospital from being beaten to crap by a Were, they'd given me ten kinds of hell about how I was living my life. When they found out I'd contracted myself to Alec Royce, they'd come within inches of disowning me. Thankfully, my mom was coming around and had decided I wasn't about to sprout horns and a tail or drag the minions of the Devil to the dinner table with me on family outings. The jury was still out with my dad.

"You're his only daughter," Chaz said, frowning. "I don't think he'll be able to stay mad at you too much longer. Besides, you're alive and unhurt. Doesn't that count for anything?"

"Not where Others are concerned. He's not very liberal about that sort of thing."

Sara clapped me on the shoulder. "Don't worry about it; he'll get over it Remember that time he bailed us out after the party at NYU? He was only pissed off for about two weeks, then he was laughing over it with us. This can't be that different."

"I don't know," I muttered, flushing under Chaz's sudden, intense scrutiny. "Maybe you're right. I'm probably reading too much into it."

"That's the spirit!"

I mustered up a smile and climbed into the Jeep as Chaz tossed my bag in the back and slid into the driver's side. Sara cheerfully waved us off as we pulled into traffic.

"Have a great trip! Don't get into trouble, 'cause I'm not driving out into the boondocks to get you."

Laughing, Chaz and I shared a look. The day was full of promise. We'd hit traffic until we got well past the Jersey Turnpike, but after that it should be smooth sailing. We'd taken road trips a handful of times before, but we'd never had so much time together without worry or responsibility. True, his pack would be hanging around, but I was thinking more about the time we'd be spending together—just the two of us.

He shot me a glance. I thought I detected a shadow of doubt in his eyes, but before I could ask about it he spoke. "Have you been looking forward to this as much as I have?"

"You bet. I couldn't think about anything else all day."

His expression eased into a wide smile. "I'm glad to hear it. I was a little worried you might get cold feet. Not everyone would be willing to hang around a bunch of Weres when we're shifted."

I gave his hand a reassuring squeeze. "Don't worry about it. I've come a long way since the first time we met."

There was an understatement if ever I'd made one. I still felt a twinge when I recalled some of the unthinking things I'd said in front of Chaz before I found out he was a Were. He'd been persistent in sticking by my side through some tough times, and his loyalty and bravery had shown me that I'd been plenty stupid for breaking up with him after he revealed his true nature. We got back together after I figured out that not all Others are unthinking, violent monsters, and that I had unnecessarily given up a good thing. He had stood by my side and protected me while I fought some pretty scary crap over the last year; that, too, showed he was a keeper.

It had taken me a long time to set aside my misgivings and come to the decision to commit. Signing the contract meant, legally, I could be turned into a werewolf. Though Chaz knew me well enough to know I'd never forgive him if he did such a thing, my life would be in his hands. Putting that kind of trust in him would hopefully close the rift that had come between us when Royce bound me by blood.

On the bright side, after we signed that contract, we could do a lot more than hold hands. That might ease some of the tension—in more than one sense—that had been building between us over the last month or so. Considering I hadn't let things get intimate since I found out he was a werewolf—had it really been almost a year ago?—it was a wonder he wasn't pushing me harder to jump in the sack, contract or no. The man had the patience and fortitude of a saint. I wasn't about to risk letting him slip through my fingers again. Once everything was sorted out between us, I could figure out the other, harder issues raised by signing the contract.

Like telling my parents about him. That could wait, for sure. Maybe I'd put off that little surprise until sometime around Christmas. My mom really liked him, but she thought he was human. Considering she'd only just come around to speaking to me after several weeks of being incommunicado, there was no telling how she'd react once I told her Chaz's little secret.

My mom and dad had listened to my explanation of why I'd been spending time around Weres, magi, and vampires with horror and incredulity once I'd discovered there was no way of hiding it from them. What with reporters and cops following me all over the place, and all the new bumps, bruises, stitches, and scars, hiding what was going on in my life wasn't an option anymore. The only details I hadn't mentioned were that Chaz was a Were and Sara's boyfriend Arnold was a mage. Fortunately, whenever they were around my parents or brothers, Arnold and Chaz minded their manners and kept any hints of their nature as Others carefully hidden. So far, none of my family seemed to have guessed. However, I suspected that my dad knew more than he was telling and was biding his time before confronting me about my "alternative lifestyle."

"What's the name of this place we're going to, again?"

Chaz pulled his hand out of mine to open the glove compartment and pass me a colorful trifold brochure.

"It's called the Pine Cone Lodge. The owner's name is Bruce Cassidy. He's been out there for years. He uses the place as a retreat and hideaway for Weres in the off-season. Dillon says he's run the place since Columbus spotted land."

"Yeesh, he's that ancient? Are you sure he's a Were, not a vamp?"

He laughed. "No, no. Nothing like that. It's just a joke. He is a Were, just an old one. From what I was told, he's in his early seventies."

"You haven't been there before?" I asked, perusing the brochure. It had scenic pictures of the forest, snowcapped mountains in the background, and some close-ups of tiny, rustic log and stone cabins nestled into the trees. Oh, they all had fireplaces! That had romantic evenings written all over it. At least until moonrise tomorrow night, when Chaz would have no choice but to shift and hunt with the rest of his pack.

"Not me personally, no. Dillon met him when he was part of the Firepaw pack. I've talked to Moonwalker, Ravenwood, and Timber Falls werewolves, and a few of the independent Were-cats," he said. "All of them reassured me the place is the best Were-friendly deal you can get on a budget without driving across the country."

My brows arched in surprise as I reached up to tie my unruly curls out of my face. "Were-cats? I didn't know we had any in the U.S. I thought they were all over in Africa and South America."

"Nah. There are a few natives here." He paused, navigating around some jerk who cut him off before continuing. "They're much more low-key than Rohrik Donovan and the Moonwalker pack."

"You could say that of any Weres compared to them. I've never seen anyone but the Moonwalkers take their pack pride so far as to put bumper stickers of their symbol on their cars."

"They have good reason to be proud. They did some great things in their time. If not for Rohrik, I'd still be human to you."

That made me laugh. "Yeah, I guess you would."

"The Sunstrikers are proud of who they are, too. Almost everyone has the pack symbol tattoo by now."

I reached out to brush my fingers over the hint of his pack tattoo on the upper portion of his right bicep, partially hidden by the sleeve of his T-shirt. It was a simple drawing of the sun pierced by a spear, nothing terribly elaborate. All of the Sunstrikers had this symbol. The part hidden under the sleeve was something a little different from what the rest of the pack had: a pair of crossed spears above the sun, just big enough to tell anyone who might look for it that Chaz was the leader of his pack.

Though I'd seen the tattoo hundreds of times before, I hadn't understood that it was a pack symbol until Chaz spelled it out for me. It hadn't

struck me as out of the ordinary until then, especially since he had a couple of others, usually
hidden under his clothes. The warmth and coiled
steel muscles bunching under his skin were a fasci-
nating diversion for me, too.

I was distracting him from driving, and stopped
teasing him once he came within inches of cream-
ing someone's bumper. He gave me a mock scowl,
and I reddened, giving him an apologetic grin.

"So what should I know before meeting everybody? I don't want to make any dumb mistakes
and make an ass of myself in front of all your
friends."

Chaz gave me an amused glance out of the
corner of his eye. "You? Come on."

I socked him lightly on the arm, grinning. "Yes,
me. Seriously, what do I need to know? I'd like to
make nice with these guys."

He soberly considered my question. After a
long moment, he spoke.

"Mostly, just be yourself. Avoid staring them in
the eyes. That's considered a challenge, and at
this time of the month they may take it too personally to let it slide. Otherwise, they'll most likely
end up playing human for you as much as they
can. Until it becomes unavoidable, anyway."

"By unavoidable, you mean when they shift,
right?"

"Yeah."

"So you don't do any weird stuff in private?" I
teased. "Nothing you wouldn't want me to see?"

He chuckled. "That's a matter of personal pref-
erence. We're just like anybody else, you know.
We've all got our bad habits and dirty secrets, just

like any human might." I didn't totally get the significance of the look he gave me, but flushed uncomfortably anyway. His words brought to mind a desire I once had for another man, another time, for blood instead of sex.

Or maybe a bit of both. At the same time.

I quite suddenly had to roll down the window a crack to get some air.

Chaz continued in a lighter tone, apparently oblivious to my discomfort as he returned his attention to the road. "The main difference is that even if we're not necessarily related by blood, we are all family and rely on each other for survival."

"Does that mean I should be worried?"

"Nah. It's true we've never had someone along on one of these trips who wasn't immediate family or going to be turned into one of us. So they might be a little nervous, but they all know who you are, and I can pretty much guarantee the whole pack will be on their best behavior. Seth and a couple of his friends might give you a little trouble, but everyone else is easygoing once you get to know them. Just talk to them and treat them like you do anyone else, and everything should be just fine."

"Okay. Who's Seth?"

"Seth is Ricky and Armina's kid. He's a bit of a dick. Hits on anything in a skirt. If he touches you, I'll kill him."

I shot a look at him.

"That was a joke, Shia."

A blush lit up my cheeks. "Sorry. I can't always tell."

His smile widened, making me feel even sillier for jumping to conclusions. "It's okay. I know we've got a rep. That's part of why I want you to come out and see what we're like when we're not trying to hide ourselves from the public eye. I doubt we're anything like what you thought."

"Me too," I said, looking again at the brochure in my hands. Whatever else, the place was rustic, scenic, and out in the middle of nowhere. At least if I embarrassed myself, there wouldn't be a bunch of cops or reporters looking to catch it on camera or video this time.

Just a whole lot of werewolves to spread the word back to the Other community what a spaz I am.

Chapter 3

Hunter, New York, was one of the coolest ski resort towns I'd ever seen. Well, the only one I'd ever seen. It was full of tiny businesses and big houses sprawled over a handful of streets and cradled in the shadows of the Catskill Mountains. Many of the stores were closed, some shuttered up tight, waiting for ski season to start. There were few streetlights, mostly on the main street in town. A handful of people were out picking up groceries or chatting with friends despite the chill in the clear mountain air. There weren't many restaurants, but we made note of them in case we got a hankering for takeout later.

We were staying somewhere deeper in the mountains, a few miles outside the town proper. We pulled off the main road and followed a side street for a little while and then turned onto a tiny, rutted dirt track. I hadn't spotted it until we were right on top of it. The path was wide enough that it was unmistakably a road, but one that didn't seem well traveled or maintained. The

hardy little Jeep bounced over the numerous
potholes, shocks squealing in protest, with the occasional low-hanging branch grazing the car.

Chaz made an offhand remark about a car
behind us that had followed us all the way up
here. Despite the dark, the driver was using dim
fog lights to get through the trees. Possibly whoever it was did not want us to know they were tailing us, but it could also have been another Were
with good night vision. I didn't pay it too much
mind; more of my attention was on the creepy,
dark road ahead of us.

Those grasping branches in the dark gave me
the willies. The tree limbs were so thickly inter-
twined overhead that the moonlight peeping
through didn't help much in illuminating our
way. Chaz had to let go of my hand to wrangle the
steering wheel and keep us on track. Beyond the
windows, I saw nothing but pitch-black, the only
light coming from the headlights swaying and
shivering over the heavy growth of trees and
brush. He reassured me a couple of times that he
could see perfectly well and that we were going
the right way. I trusted his eyes better than my
own, but I still clung to my seat hoping it would
be over soon.

After what felt like an eternity of jostling and
low scraping sounds, we pulled into a clearing so
well-lit that it momentarily blinded me. I squinted
against the glare, lifting my hand up to shade my
eyes as I surveyed the open ground.

We'd pulled into a parking lot in front of a
large timber lodge. Like the track, the lot was
nothing but packed dirt. Someone had taken the

time to lay treated lumber to define the edges and give some clue as to where to park. Forty or so other cars were scattered across the lot; Chaz and I must have been straggling behind the rest of the pack. We got out, and I shivered in the biting cold wind that rustled the trees around us. Pulling my light track jacket closed did nothing to ease the chill.

The lodge itself was impressive; a huge double-door entrance was lit with flickering gas lamps on either side, giving dim illumination to well-tended hedges that lined the front of the building and the carved wooden sign that read: WELCOME TO PINE CONE LODGE. The shutters had been folded back from the expansive windows, lights blazing and people moving around behind most of them. Wood smoke was heavy in the air, mixing with the clean scents of freshly turned earth, birch sap, and pine. An owl hooted somewhere off in the distance. The mountains thrust up around us, the place held in the cusp of a thickly wooded valley.

"It's beautiful," I said, hefting my purse up on my shoulder and helping Chaz pull luggage out of the trunk. "I haven't been up in the mountains for a while. This is great!"

"Yeah, I just wish the track led up to the actual cabins. It's going to be a pain to lug this stuff out there."

A glance over my shoulder didn't show anyone pulling into the lot behind us. Whoever had followed us down the track must have turned off onto some other path. Or didn't want us to know we'd been followed.

Shrugging off my lingering paranoia, I took Chaz's duffel while he hefted my suitcase off the ground. A few people were hanging around outside, some of them smoking and chatting, others rummaging in their cars. I looked around when a couple of them started clapping, trying to figure out what they were applauding. There weren't many doing it; some had wandered off looking disgusted. It took me a moment to figure out that they were clapping for *me*.

"What the hell are they doing?" I hissed the question under my breath, leaning in close to Chaz so that any Others in the crowd, with their supersensitive hearing, wouldn't overhear me.

Chaz gave them a grin and a wave, speaking to me out of the corner of his mouth. "They're glad you're here. A bunch of them didn't think you'd come. Just smile back at them or something, be polite."

Feeling inordinately cheesy, I did, and the people gave a few last hoots and hollers before running ahead into the lodge, presumably to spread the news that we'd arrived. One of them, a guy with an alarming array of piercings and tattoos, stayed behind to hold the door for us.

We hurried inside, taking in the expansive interior. Aside from the stone fireplace, blazing cheerful warmth from a roaring fire, everything was done in wood accents. The furniture all looked to be hand-carved. There were rugs and cushions in earthy tones, browns and greens. The windows on either side of the fireplace across the room overlooked the valley spotted with lights from smaller cabins outside.

There were a few people sitting around the fire, chatting over beers and glancing up with friendly waves as we walked in. I forced a smile when two of them saluted me with their drinks, and focused my attention on the ancient looking geezer who levered himself to his feet, shuffling over with a wide grin creasing his tanned, leathery face. Despite his age, solid muscle pulled his shirt taut over his shoulders and arms, and thick tufts of hair were visible above the collar and cuffs of his shirt.

The coiled energy of Were radiated off him in a way that had the hairs on the back of my neck standing at attention. Chaz didn't seem to be affected. He returned the guy's smile, setting the bags down to accept the offered handshake.

"Welcome, welcome! Are you part of the Sunstriker party?"

"Yes, sir. I'm Chaz Hallbrook, and this is Shia. You're Mr. Cassidy, right?"

"Just call me Bruce." He shook Chaz's hand in a hearty shake then turned to me, inclining his head. "Young lady, you look like you and your boy here could use a hot meal and a stiff drink. Let me get George to show you out to your cabin so you can freshen up. Dinner was already served, but we've still got plenty of food, so just come right on back up here when you're ready."

I smiled, shaking his hand when he offered it. His palm was as rough and calloused as sandpaper. "That sounds wonderful. Thank you."

"Oh, anytime," he said, turning away to shout toward a hallway to our left. "George!"

We waited a minute, the silence broken by the

snaps and crackles coming from the fireplace, and the low murmur of conversation.

"GEORGE!"

I jumped at the thunderous shout.

"WHAT?! I'm busy!" came back.

"Guests, George!"

I heard what sounded suspiciously like a muf-fled curse in reply. A large, barrel-chested man soon came into view. He was wearing a pair of loose jeans and little else. His skin was stained with what looked like soot and grease; a large wrench was slung over one shoulder. Though I didn't mean to stare, I wasn't quite able to stop myself. George's voice was deep and ponderous, tinged with minor irritation.

"Pops, I told you I was working on the backup generator. Can't Daisy do it?"

"She's serving at the bar. Just show them down to number twelve, would you?"

George shook his head, sweat-stringy locks sway-ing around his thick jaw, a cryptic smile curving his lips as he looked us over. He dwarfed Chaz by a few inches and maybe a hundred pounds, most of which looked to be muscle. "Ah, sure. Do you need help with the bags?"

"Nah, we got it," Chaz said, sliding his arm around my waist.

George grabbed a key from behind the recep-tion desk. He moved with a lumbering kind of grace that put me in mind of a large predator, one that was deceptively slow until provoked.

"Come on, I'll show you guys back."

Chaz's grip tightened on me as we followed

George's lead. He led us across the lobby and through a hall, past a dining area with an enormous bar, where a bunch of guys on stools watched football on the big screen TV with rapt attention. Other people were scattered at round tables throughout the room, relaxing and talking or brooding over cold beers. A couple of girls gave me, then Chaz, an odd look I couldn't read, before starting up a chattering storm of whispers. The disparity in attitudes between various Sunstrikers toward me was getting to be a bit much, and I was grateful once the people in that room were out of sight.

We walked through a set of double doors as large as the ones at the entrance that led into a little meadow in the back of the building. The strong scent of herbs—rosemary, basil, peppermint, and lemongrass—clued me in that at least part of this area was a garden. I could also hear the faint rush of running water from somewhere up ahead of us. After the warmth of the lodge, it was freezing out here.

"Watch your step. We had rain a couple days ago, and the path to the bridge is still a bit muddy."

I was glad I'd remembered to wear hiking boots instead of my usual sneakers, but even with the extra traction I was slipping and sliding a little in the mud. Chaz tried to help me, but he wasn't faring much better. By the time we reached the small wooden bridge that arched over a creek separating the cabins from the lodge, we were laughing and leaning on each other to get safely to the other side. A hand-carved sign on the other side of the creek, leaning at an angle in the mud, showed which fork to take for which cabin numbers.

The cabins were far enough apart for privacy, with heavy pines and cedars, thick with concealing foliage, separating the buildings. It was hard to tell by the landscaping if the trees had been planted or grew that way naturally since the log cabins faded into the foliage like a natural part of the scenery. The solar-powered lanterns in the ground helped light the path without being intrusive or detracting from the raw beauty of the place. The soft glow only made it more inviting and romantic.

George unlocked the cabin with the number twelve etched into the wooden door. He flicked the light on and handed the key over to Chaz, gesturing back toward the lodge. "If you need anything, just give us a ring up there. You'll find extra blankets in the closet and a few dry goods and coffee in the kitchen. Breakfast is served in the dining hall six-thirty through ten-thirty; lunch is at noon; and dinner is served from five-thirty until my mom decides to kick you out and close the kitchen. She'll be up late tonight since so many of you came in, but I wouldn't trust her to hang around for more than another hour."

"Great! Thanks, George," I said, giving him a warm smile.

"Anytime, pretty lady." He winked. "Just call if you need anything."

Chaz rolled his eyes and carried everything

inside. I followed him in, George closing the door behind me.

The place was cozy, just as inviting on the inside as it appeared from the outside. The furniture here matched the furniture in the lodge; the frames were all done in wood and the cushions and blankets in earth tones. The fireplace had soot stains but had been cleared of old ashes. New wood was laid out and a box of matches set on the mantel. The breakfast nook had a couple of modern amenities like a refrigerator and a coffeemaker. A round table was set next to the window with bleached white birch chairs around it, and a large bed with a mound of pillows and thick quilts was tucked in the corner across from the hearth.

It was perfect.

I started putting our things away in the drawers and closet while Chaz got a fire going in the hearth. Before long, light and warmth spilled into the tiny, open space, and the two of us met in front of it, wrapping our arms around each other. I breathed in the scent of musk and sweat that clung to him, closing my eyes and relaxing against his chest.

"So what do you think?"

"Hmm?"

"About this place? Like it?"

"Yes," I said. "Very much."

"Good."

With that, he tilted my chin up and bent down to kiss me. I met his lips hungrily, tightening my grip around his waist.

It was perfectly romantic and, rather inevitably, the moment was lost as a series of jeering hoots and hollers came from outside the window.

"Score one for the pack leader!"

"Hey, hot stuff, save some for me!"

"Don't stop on our account, chica! Let's see it all!"

I flushed in embarrassment, Chaz pulling away angrily, whirling to face the window. There were four teenagers leering in at us, laughing and making rude, suggestive gestures. Chaz stalked over to the door, the kids rapidly backpedalling and rushing to get out of the way. I hurried over to the window and pulled the curtains down, though I held one aside long enough to watch them rush off into the dark.

"Seth, if I catch your skinny ass over here again, I am going to kick it right back to the city! You hear me?"

Nothing but taunting laughter came out of the trees to answer him.

Shaking his head, Chaz slammed and locked the door, running a hand over his face. He was reddening under his tan. "Shia, I'm sorry. Those little shits didn't ruin everything, did they?"

I backed away from the window, frowning, but thoughtful. "No, I wouldn't say that. They're just being overly hormonal teenage boys. They remind me of my brothers at that age."

He snorted laughter at that. "Damien, sure. But Mikey, the big-shot lawyer, acting like that? Sorry, I can't picture it."

I flashed a wry smile. "You'd be surprised. Come

on, they're just jerking your chain. Don't get worked up over it. They're probably just jealous."

"Yeah, I suppose," he said, moodily eyeing the door. "I guess we can head back up and grab some dinner or something."

Arm in arm, we strolled back to the lodge, mindful of the muddy spots. There were still people hanging around in the front, but the dining hall was empty save for a couple of tired men at the bar drinking longnecks and watching the big screen. The blue-haired lady behind the counter—George's mom, we presumed—clucked and fussed over how tired Chaz and I looked, taking pity and giving us to-go boxes for our food.

Once back at the cabin, we changed into comfy sweats and chowed down in front of the fire, talking about what we'd do while we were here. Chaz wanted to take me on a scenic hike up in the hills. I wanted to check out the garden I'd spied beside the lodge. We could even sneak away to a waterfall Dillon had told Chaz about and see about catching a few fish.

We didn't talk about what would happen when Chaz had to leave me alone to go hunt with his pack after moonrise.

Before long, Chaz was speculatively eyeing the bed.

"Tired?"

"Yeah. Long drive," he said, though the look in his eyes made it clear he would be very *un*tired if I did anything to reciprocate his "come hither" look.

With no small measure of regret, I dismissed any thought of dropping the contract tucked away in my bag on him tonight. It was too early to talk about it. Still, I was tempted to pull off my clothes and drag him under the covers with me, contract or no. We'd broken those laws already, though it was before I'd known what he was. I wasn't worried about any danger other than what might happen to him if someone reported him for failure to adhere to the laws governing intimate physical contact between humans and Others.

It was dangerous to have sex with Weres mostly because they could lose control over their shape-shifting in the throes of passion. As an alpha, Chaz had better control over his ability to shift than most, meaning the usual risks weren't an issue. Sleeping with him might even make him more amenable to signing the papers.

On the other hand, he might look at it as some form of blackmail by forcing the issue on him later.

Instead of giving in to my urges, when we settled under the covers and his hand wandered to the hem of my shirt, I took hold of his wrist and pulled it to my stomach, twining my fingers with his. Chaz sighed but didn't say anything, pulling me against him until our bodies melded into a warm, comforting cocoon of limbs and blankets.

It was a very long, very frustrating night.

Chapter 4

The next morning, I woke up before Chaz. I lay there for a bit, curled up against his side and listening to the soft sounds of his breathing and heartbeat. His body was radiating warmth like a furnace. As the fire he'd started last night had burned down to only a few hotly glowing embers, it was welcome.

Rain fell in a soft, muted pattering on the roof. The little sunlight trickling through the gap in the curtains was dim and subdued. It was difficult to even consider moving, but hunger eventually goaded me into getting up.

Chaz mumbled something and rolled over, pulling a pillow over his head when I turned on the light. I chuckled and put the covers aside to tug on some heavy wool socks. It didn't do much against the chill in the air. Next I tossed a couple of pieces of wood onto the embers in the fireplace. It took a bit, and I had to throw on another match, but soon they caught and started blazing cheerily away.

Coffee, being an essential staple of my diet, was obviously next. Once it started brewing, I turned to Chaz. "You want me to make you a cup?"

He mumbled something unintelligible from under the pillow.

I grinned and walked over, rubbing his shoulder. "Come on, sleepyhead. Don't tell me you're thinking about missing breakfast?"

A little "eep" of surprise was startled out of me when he twisted around lightning fast to grab me around the waist and pull me onto the bed. My heart was doing a tap dance in my throat, his low laughter rumbling in my ear as I squirmed to escape.

"You do make it hard to get any sleep. Why don't you just stay right here with me? It's not like we've got somewhere to be today."

I gave him a gentle poke in the side, mock frowning at him. "Says you, mister. I'd like to start meeting the rest of your pack today."

"What's the rush?" He started doing things to my neck and collarbone that had me squirming and laughing before long. "We've got the whole weekend ahead of us. They can wait a little longer."

"Mm, I just wanted to get an early start. I'm curious; I don't really know anything about them."

"If you insist." He sighed dramatically, urging me to get up before swinging his legs around and standing with a yawn and a stretch. "I'll take some coffee, but I'm going to grab a quick shower before we head up there."

I headed to the kitchen, and poured myself a

cup. Normally I'd want cream in it, but since all they provided was the powdered crap in the little basket of goodies on the tiny counter, I'd take it black. "Okay, hurry up then. I'll hop in after you."

He nodded and headed into the bathroom, leaving the door open a crack. Cradling the hot mug, I walked over to the front door and tugged it open, intending to get a breath of the fresh mountain air and see what the rest of the place looked like.

Heavy mist swirled through the trees, clinging low to the ground. A bird was warbling off in the distance, muted by the rain. The creek was rushing along somewhere out of sight, and I couldn't see much more than hints of the cabins on either side through the trees and fog. I stood in the doorway, safe from the rain under the eaves, seeing what I could of the mountains out in the distance. Their shapes were indistinct, for the most part hidden by clouds and mist, but I could see them outlined against the meager sunlight filtering through in patches here and there.

A flutter caught my eye, and I glanced at the door. There was a piece of graph paper with torn, ragged edges folded in half and pinned to the door with a small pocket knife. Frowning, I tugged the knife out of the door and took the damp piece of paper inside, shutting the door as I opened it. The writing at the top done in thick, black marker had started to bleed down the page from the humidity.

*ATTN: THE KNUCKLE-DRAGGING MOUTH-
BREATHER IN CABIN 12
GO BACK TO THE CITY YOU ASSHOLE!*

Below that was another line written in jagged
pencil, the writing more hurried and smaller
than the carefully plain block letters of the first.

GTFO!

"The hell?" I muttered. "'GTFO'?"

With a shrug, I folded the paper back up and
put it and the knife down on the table, putting it
down to more of Seth's shenanigans. Chaz would
probably be pissed, but I doubted he'd do much
more than growl and huff over it.

I enjoyed the rest of my coffee in bed while I
waited for Chaz to finish up. When he walked out
of the shower in nothing but a towel around his
waist, I got up to give him a kiss and a few words
of warning. "Don't get mad, but it looks like Seth
and his buddies left a little love letter on the
door."

"Christ, I wish they'd been taken in by another
pack."

I shrugged, finishing off my coffee and setting
the mug aside. "Like I said last night, I wouldn't
worry about it too much. They're just being
rowdy, disrespectful teenagers."

He walked over to the table and picked up the
note, puzzling over it like I had. At least he
seemed more confused than angry over it. "What
the hell is 'GTFO' supposed to mean?"

"Don't know, don't care. I'm going to take that shower, then let's grab some food."

"Sounds like a plan."

I didn't take too long to get ready, and soon we were walking arm in arm through the light drizzle up to the lodge. When we got inside, we followed our noses to the dining hall, more than happy to find that we weren't too late for breakfast. There were only a handful of people in the dining hall: a trio of geeky looking guys who watched us groggily over cups of coffee from the corner furthest from the windows; one or two lone diners; and a bunch of Chaz's pack gathered by the big picture windows, laughing and chatting. Thankfully, Seth and his buddies were nowhere in sight.

A stout older woman with blue-gray hair and an apron was laughing along with what someone at one of the tables was saying. She smiled and waved us over with her notepad, gesturing for us to take a seat at a round table with four other Sunstrikers. I sat down next to a slender woman with a ponytail and a tan, Chaz next to a guy with a number of gold piercings and a couple of tattoos visible where he'd rolled up the sleeves of his sweatshirt. The scent of Were was heavy in the room, not unpleasant, but bordering on overpowering mixed with all the food.

The older woman who had waved us over—Mr. Cassidy's wife—beamed at us. "Good morning! Can I get you two started with some orange juice? Maybe some coffee or tea?"

"Coffee would be great," I said, returning her warm smile as I settled back into the seat Chaz had pulled out for me.

"Shiarra, right?" asked one of the guys at the table as Mrs. Cassidy hurried off to get the drinks. "I'm Sean. This is Nick, Paula, and Kimberly."

We all shook hands, me leaning over the table to reach across to Sean and Paula. Everyone seemed pleased enough to meet me, if a little bleary-eyed. Nick, the one with the tattoos and piercings, looked to be nursing a bit of a hangover. I was willing to bet he'd stayed up late to watch the game with some of the other guys at the bar. They all seemed younger than Chaz and me, perhaps in their early twenties, and were all wearing loose jeans or sweatpants and warm sweatshirts. The girls' stuff was not nearly as ratty as the guys' clothes, but they were still the kinds of things you wouldn't necessarily mind shifting in.

"Thank you for coming," Paula said, her cheeks dimpling with an impish smile. "Maybe having you here will keep these yahoos in line."

"Hey! We're not *that* much of a pain in the ass," Nick protested.

"No more than Seth, anyway," Kimberly said.

"Have you seen him and his cohorts?" Sean added. "They came in here this morning and were complaining so loudly about the food that Mr. Cassidy came in and told them they'd better go find someplace else to eat, or he'd personally whup their asses from here to Jersey. They slunk out of here with their tails between their legs and took off for town. It was great!"

"I'm not surprised," I replied, rolling my eyes. "He and his buddies seem like nothing but trouble."

"Don't you get started, too. It's bad enough I have to justify keeping them in the pack to the rest of the Sunstrikers."

I leaned over to kiss Chaz's cheek, ruffling his damp hair. "Don't be grouchy. You're the leader, right? I'm sure everyone else will listen if you put your foot down."

Kimberly laughed, her warm brown eyes sparkling with humor. "It's not quite like that, hon. If there's too much dissension in the ranks, someone could challenge him to take his place. It doesn't happen often, but if Seth gets enough people behind him, he might try to oust Chaz."

"'Oust' him? Why would he do that?"

"Not everyone is happy with having Chaz lead us. He's not made many friends by calling us in to help the Moonwalkers before, especially since we never really got anything in return. And working with that leech, Royce? Not a popular move either. Seth's young, so he can get away with some open opposition, but there's grumbling in the rest of the ranks. Not everyone agrees with having you here, either. Just the way it is." She laughed again, Paula snickering along with her. "At least, until he cracks some heads together. Then it might settle things down again. For a little while anyway."

I frowned at her, not finding the idea particularly funny. "Is that true, Chaz?"

He was giving Kimberly a pointed look that she was just as pointedly ignoring, sipping her OJ.

"Sort of. The ones who disagree are in the minority. Seth won't get too many people willing to back him up against me. I'm still the alpha, and he knows it."

The laughter and knowing looks faded under the bit of emphasis Chaz put to that last statement. Sean cleared his throat to break the silence, and then smiled encouragingly at me. "Don't worry. We won't let anything happen to you. Just be careful once everyone shifts, and stick close to the cabins and lodge at night."

"Yeah, don't wander off into the woods alone. I heard there are a couple other shifters in town. Don't want to tempt them," Nick said.

I made a face. "No worries of that. I wasn't planning on going anywhere without Chaz."

He slid his arm around my shoulders and pulled me close enough to brush a kiss over my temple, some of the tension in his frame filtering away. "I'm going to have to do some work with the pack while we're here, but it shouldn't keep me away too much. If I'm not around, any of these guys can help keep an eye on you and show you the ropes. Right?"

There was hurried agreement from everyone else, and we all quieted down a bit as Mrs. Cassidy returned with our drinks. As I sipped my coffee, I took a look around at the others, thoughtful. Paula's pixie cut made her look innocent and cute, but her laughter at Kimberly's mocking comments about Chaz's enemies made me wonder if those two were among those not happy to have me here. Kimberly seemed nice enough, if a bit brazen. She offered me the cream for my coffee when she saw me searching for it, reaching over to give me a light squeeze on the shoulder.

"Don't worry, we'll protect you. Whether it's Seth or someone else, we're behind Chaz all the way."

I smiled thinly at her. "I think I'll be okay."

Mrs. Cassidy chimed in, leaning over to give Nick a refill on his coffee. "Oh, are you a norm? Sorry, my dears, couldn't help but overhear."

I shrugged uncomfortably, flushing at the amused looks the others were sharing amongst themselves. "Yeah, I'm here with the Sunstrikers, but I'm not a Were."

"Oh, lovely, lovely. So good to have you here. If you run into any trouble with *any* of our guests, you just tell me or Bruce, and we'll set it to rights."

I was starting to feel like I was surrounded by overprotective parents. I already had two; I didn't need any more. "Thanks, Mrs. Cassidy. I'll keep that in mind."

We ordered breakfast and got to know each other. Sean was a waiter at some diner and was taking college classes through the Internet to get a business degree. Paula was an interior designer with aspirations to get a regular part on one of those home makeover shows. Nick was a tattoo artist, and Kimberly a massage therapist whose office was next to the gym where Chaz and I worked out. She had met him when she signed up for one of his cardio classes. I couldn't recall having seen her around, but she wasn't particularly surprised.

"I keep odd hours," she explained. "Especially since I got infected with lycanthropy. It changed everything."

Amen to that.

Chapter 5

Nick and Sean offered to take me out hiking tomorrow once the rain cleared up. Chaz was going to be busy dealing with some pack politics and helping their newest member cope with some of the pre-change weirdness his body was going through. Ethan had accidentally gotten caught up in a scuffle between two Weres that became too heated. One of them nicked him with its teeth when he tried to rush off, and he'd been too afraid to go to the hospital to get the vaccine.

This was not altogether surprising. Most of the big hospitals report lycanthropy infections to a database that's only supposed to be accessed by government and law enforcement agencies. Theoretically, the database would help lead to the culprits of any unauthorized Other attacks, since a good ninety-five percent or so were by newly turned vampires and Weres who hadn't mastered their hungers yet.

However, the number of Others who had disappeared over the last couple of years—even accounting for violence by groups like the White Hats and the Anti-Other Alliance—had caused enough comment and speculation that few Others were willing to risk going to hospitals. There was even some paranoia about going to private practitioners, since some of them reported their findings as well. The problem was that the major hospitals were the best source of the vaccine that could, if administered quickly enough, halt the spread of lycanthropy infection. It didn't work every time, but if it meant the difference between staying human or becoming part of a Were pack, most people would damn the consequences and take the medicine.

Ethan had been infected and had waited too long to treat the virus. A couple days ago, one of the other pack members had found the poor guy freaking out in the parking lot outside a doctor's office. Someone inside had just delivered the news that he was beyond treatment. The Sunstrikers had taken him in, made him part of the group, and would help him through his first change.

This was as much for their protection as his. Without a mentor, Ethan could have gone rogue and ended up injuring himself or, worse, some innocent human, in the process of the change. No Were or vampire likes to hear the news that innocent bystanders got hurt by one of their own. It was bad publicity, made it harder for them to bolster their ranks, so the majority of the time they'd take in the strays. Plus, the rash of panic and angry hunters that inevitably followed in the wake of a newly turned Other with no experienced mentor to guide them or rein them in made life hard on all the rest.

I'd heard stories about what some of the vamps did to their own after unsanctioned kills. It was the stuff of nightmares. The only time I'd ever witnessed it happen, it had turned into a blood-bath. Max Carlyle had negotiated his way out, but I'm reasonably certain the only reason he wasn't toast was because Royce would not have been able to kill him without too much cost to himself.

Weres were more understanding, but no more tolerant. They were as likely as vampires to hunt and put down one of their own who made an un-sanctioned kill, though perhaps they did it a little more cleanly.

Ethan was currently holed up in one of the cabins with a couple of other pack members. Chaz had promised to check in on him frequently and had cautioned me to stay away from him until after the height of the lunar cycle was over. They weren't so concerned he would accidentally Were. The problem lay in his becoming attuned to my scent and trying to hunt me down the first time or two he was shifted. Curious as I was about him, that was deterrent enough to keep me away.

Through the rest of the day, I met a lot of Sun-strikers whose names I did my best to keep straight. As Chaz had mentioned, they were people, too. Every one of them came from a dif-ferent background and walk of life. Some of them were as friendly and cordial as I'd been promised. Others did not seem so happy to meet me and, I was sure, only shook my hand because Chaz was standing next to me.

Later in the afternoon, just before dinner, we were hanging out in the game room playing pool with a bunch of Chaz's buddies. Seth and his cronies swaggered in, trying to look tough in their piercings and leather jackets. Mostly they looked like teenagers trying too hard to be cool. We ignored them, getting on with our game, chatting amiably as we took turns at the two pool tables. The foosball game across the room was free, and the four troublemakers headed over there, not bothering the rest of us—probably because there were three times as many of us as there were of them. A few too many for them to pull anything obnoxious.

I sat on the edge of one of the chairs lining the room while I waited for my turn, talking quietly with Paula and Kimberly. They were a lot nicer and more willing to chat than I'd thought they would be. Turns out they were both fascinated with my job, about as much as I was fascinated with the fact they were Weres, and we were having a great time swapping stories between turns.

"How long have you been doing the P.I. thing?" Kimberly asked, sipping her beer. Chaz kept glancing over, clearly listening in, but I wasn't quite sure what he was so concerned about. Aside from the comments earlier, she and Paula seemed nice enough.

"Since a few months after I graduated from NYU—about six years ago. My friend Sara put up most of the collateral, and together we started H&W Investigations."

"Wow, that long? I'm surprised Chaz has let you keep doing something so dangerous for so long."

I frowned at her, not liking that turn of phrase at all. "'Let me' do it? It's not his choice; it's mine. Besides, I'd been at this since long before I met him, and the type of investigative work I do isn't as dangerous as the books and movies make it out to be."

"Oh," she said, her brows furrowing in confusion. "What sort of investigations do you do, then? I thought I heard something about divorce cases and cheating spouses—"

"You're up, Shia," Chaz cut in, stepping aside and leaning casually on his pool cue.

"We'll chat more later," I promised, excusing myself. I rose, studied the layout for a moment, and bent over to line up and take a shot. "Five solid, corner pocket."

"You'll scratch if you take that shot."

I threw an annoyed glance over my shoulder, not liking Seth's amused smirk as he eyed my backside. "Who asked you?"

"Nobody. I'm just saying."

"Fuck off," I muttered, ignoring him again and concentrating on my shot.

"You'll mi-iss," he singsonged.

"Shut up," somebody muttered from the other table. Chaz growled softly, low in his throat, eyes narrowed in anger. Seth raised his hands and took a step back, still smirking.

I gritted my teeth and took the shot, pleased when the cue ball hit and the five slid smoothly into the corner pocket. Stepping back, I gave Seth my own smart-ass smirk, though I didn't keep it up for long. Taunting Weres is never a good thing, even when you've got a bigger, badder Were there to protect you.

"Nice shot," he acknowledged, turning away. I fought back the urge to stick out my tongue at him, and just returned my attention to the game.

We continued for another set, and by the time we were done, the smell of dinner drew us out toward the dining hall again. It was early but, as everyone would be furry tonight, it wasn't a bad idea for us to eat while the sun was still up.

Seth stayed behind, but it was unnerving how he and his buddies watched us go, mostly keeping an eye on me or Chaz. Nobody else seemed concerned, but I had to wonder what was up his sleeve. When he saw me staring, he blew me a little kiss. I curled my lip in distaste and pressed closer to Chaz, doing my best to take no notice of him as the others were doing.

Mrs. Cassidy had made a few dishes in bulk to feed the Sunstriker pack. Everyone had turned out for this little get-together, and the few members of the pack who hadn't been present to fight against Alec Royce and the Moonwalker Weres had come along for the ride this time. Some of those I hadn't met were too young or too old to fight. Others were just new to the pack, strays like Ethan who had been taken in and one or two who had left other packs to join this one. There were just shy of fifty members, and all of them except for Seth and the three yahoos shadowing him, as well as Ethan and his two babysitters, were here for dinner.

"Hey, good to see you," one of the Weres seated near the door said, smiling warmly at me as he leaned back in his chair to brush his fingers over my hand. As the others took note of our entrance, the hum of conversation died into a low murmur of welcome, some of them lifting their hands in cheerful waves, others rising to greet us. A handful moved to the back, out of the way, but their dark looks were easily lost in the crowd of well-wishers.

"It's her, look. . . ."

"Remember me? Hi!"

"I can't believe she came!"

I suddenly found myself surrounded by warm, friendly hands, brushing over my hair, shoulders, arms, crushing my hands as they shook them. One of the guys who'd grabbed my hand shouldered his way a little closer, grinning at me happily. "I know I look different without the fur, but I hope you remember me. Thank you so much!"

I turned wide eyes on Chaz, who had stepped to one side and was simply grinning with amused tolerance. "What the hell is going on?"

"You saved them from getting overtaken by the *Dominari* Focus, remember? They're just happy you're here."

"You're a hero," another said, pounding me enthusiastically on the back. "Better, you're one of us, not one of those pansy Moonwalkers. It's an honor to have you here."

The nods and words of agreement that flowed around me were so embarrassing, I thought strongly of retreating to our cabin and forgoing this weird dinner. Sadly, I was surrounded. Though I had wanted to get to know Chaz's pack, I certainly didn't want to be fawned over like this. The Focus had been designed to give a dangerous amount of power to its holder, and I'd destroyed it mostly out of fear of what Royce or Chaz or even Sara's boyfriend, Arnold, might have done with it. That it meant assured freedom for these guys was just an added bonus.

"Um, thanks, guys. Really, it was nothing."

An older guy threw his arm around my shoulders, guiding me to one of the tables right in the middle of the mess of seated Weres. His gruff voice was husky from years of cigarette smoking and carried a touch of some European accent I couldn't place. "Facing that mage and his spelled minions by yourself—especially without the pack there to back you up—takes a kind of bravery and courage most of us had never seen before. Let us have this moment to thank you in our own way. We never had the chance to before."

I warily nodded agreement, doing my best to relax my stiff posture. It was a little nerve-wracking to know I was one of few humans in a room full of predators who could tear me apart or even eat me if they were so inclined. Having a bunch of them putting their hands on me made me jittery. They meant well, but it was still freaky.

Chaz had never said anything, so I hadn't realized that the pack felt so strongly about what I had done. The only Weres I'd seen after the big fight above *La Petite Boisson* were Rohrik Donovan, who came to thank me in person at the hospital, a few of Chaz's friends who'd been around for movies or dinner, and that cab driver whose name I'd never learned. Maybe since I was human, they were afraid to approach me themselves and had just been waiting for a moment like this to thank me.

"Relax, you smell afraid. Don't offend your fans," Chaz whispered into my ear as he leaned down to seat himself next to me. I gave him a withering look. He portrayed nothing but bland innocence.

Eventually, the casual chatter returned, many of the Weres drifting back to their seats. The clink of silverware and chiming of laughter from a table across the room sounded so normal, so *human,* that it would be easy to forget what they really were. Blending in this way was as much survival instinct as it was sheer habit. Some of the people in this room had been born Were. Most started out as fullbloods, like me, and then contracted the infection later. They wouldn't do something so crass as to act uncivilized until their furry side came out. Once shifted, they'd still be doing their best to stay as far out of humanity's sight as possible.

Except for me. I'd get to see them as they really were.

"Hey, Shiarra?" A voice I didn't recognize piped up from across the table, mangling my name. I twisted in my seat to see a young kid, maybe five or six years old, seated between a couple I took to be his mom and dad and waving to get my attention. "My dad says you're an investigator. Do you fight bad guys like that scum-sucking leech Alec Royce all the time?"

"Hush, Billy, she doesn't want to talk about that kind of thing right now," the guy seated next to the kid said, giving me an embarrassed, apologetic look. He probably hadn't realized he'd been overheard or hadn't expected to have his kid parrot off his description of the elder vampire.

"No, it's okay," I said, amused with the way the kid was squirming with delight that I was paying some attention to him and his not too far off the mark description of Royce. "I try not to fight bad guys if I can avoid it. My job isn't to fight them, just to find out stuff about them. Most of the time, I'm hiding somewhere they can't see me, taking video or pictures."

"But Dad said you killed some bad guys!" He was now giving his mortified father an accusing look. "He said you fought a mage and a vampire and the Moonwalker leader."

It was my turn to feel embarrassed, especially as an intent, interested hush fell across the room. Everyone else was listening in for my answer. Peachy. "I did fight them once, but they're stronger and faster and a heck of a lot scarier than I am. I almost died."

His eyes widened; he was suitably impressed. "Wow! Did you get hurt? Do you have scars?"

"Yes, I have some."

He promptly tugged up his shirt, showing me a purplish line just under his ribcage. "I got my 'pendix taken out. Does it look like this? Can I see?"

"Billy," the woman next to him hissed this time, "put your shirt back down!"

I couldn't help but laugh. "Yes, it's like that. Don't worry, ma'am, it's okay. I'll tell you what,

Billy, I'll show you later." Somewhere not in front of fifty pairs of prying Were eyes.

His parents both looked extremely gratified that I wasn't upset, though Billy's mom was still mortified. Billy looked like he'd just won the biggest prize at the carnival. Chaz was grinning at me, leaning in to whisper in my ear. "Much better."

I gave him a wry grin of my own, and a suggestive waggle of my brows. "Practice."

"For what?"

"When we've got one of our own."

His shock slowly faded into a pleased, possessive look, and he leaned in for a kiss. I didn't care that everyone was watching—no, not just watching, cheering—since it was exactly the response I'd hoped to get out of him.

Chapter 6

Over dessert, a few of the other Weres came over and introduced themselves, switching out seats with ones at our table every few minutes so everyone got a chance to talk to me or Chaz. Some of the Weres who hadn't been too cordial with me earlier warmed up over this reception.

After dessert, some left, headed for their cabins or the gaming room. Daisy the bartender put a hockey game on the big screen, pouring drinks for the guys who exchanged their tables for bar stools. The evening was winding down.

Paula, Kimberly, Sean, Nick, and two other Weres I knew, Simon and Dillon, joined us for a round of beers at the table. Everyone was pleasant except Paula, who seemed a bit surly and quiet since returning from a short trip to her cabin. I didn't pay her much mind, as everyone else was making up for her silence.

Simon and Dillon had been present for the fight I had miraculously survived in the basement of Royce's daytime resting place about a month ago. The same one during which I'd drunk some of Royce's blood so Max Carlyle couldn't call me to his side. Seeing them again made it difficult to forget, as I'd tried so hard to do. It must have been hard for them to see me, too; they'd lost their friend, Vincent, in that fight.

Neither one mentioned a thing about what had happened, keeping the conversation limited to sports and movies, and it helped put me at ease.

"There's a special midnight showing of *Rocky Horror* downtown on Friday the thirteenth. You guys want to come?" Dillon asked, looking far too excited at the prospect. Most of us groaned. "You know it's going to be wild!"

"You've got to be kidding."

"Oh, come on! It's a classic."

Kimberly shook her head, smoothing dyed blond locks out of her face. "I don't know. Seeing Tim Curry running around in fishnets and heels is a little too disturbing for my tastes."

"Yeah, I know what you mean," Sean said, making a face.

"Reminds me a little too much of a vamp. Wonder if he is one?"

Speculation quieted the rest of us for a minute, as we thought over the possibilities.

"I heard you got bound by a vamp." Paula turned to me suddenly, cutting the easy conversation to bits. Her tone was icy, oddly so considering how nice she'd been earlier. "The news said you signed papers, that you were a willing thrall. That true?"

I was shocked by the directness and malice behind the question. Chaz's anger was enough to make her turn her brown eyes away from mine, putting up her hands in surrender.

"That's enough, Paula. If she wants to talk about it, she will."

She hissed out, venom thick in her voice, even as she shrank back in her chair. "I think we have a right to know if our pack leader brought a leech's pet to the table."

A low, collective gasp escaped a few throats, including mine. The looks I was getting from the others now were nothing short of horrified. The only ones who didn't react were Dillon and Simon; they seemed more surprised at Paula's hostility than by her announcement, and I'm sure that was only because they already knew I'd been bound.

Chaz inched up to standing, towering over the smaller woman. Slowly, deliberately, he reached out until he had her sweatshirt balled up in his fist, dragging her closer so he could growl right into her face. Her eyes went wide in surprise, but she didn't fight his grip. "I said that's enough. Don't bring it up again."

I rose a little shakily, not meeting the curious, furtive looks any of the others were giving me. "I'm going back to the cabin. I'll see you guys tomorrow."

"Shia, wait. . . ." Chaz's disappointment was palpable, his grip loosening on Paula's shirt enough that she gracelessly dropped back into her chair. Everyone's eyes were on me, the mixture of unspoken disbelief and revulsion too much for me to deal with. I shook my head and hurried away from the table, taking my beer with me.

Once outside, I took a few deep breaths, trying not to give in to the sting of tears. The sun had almost set, leaving deep shadows between the trees.

After this afternoon, I hadn't thought Paula would be so mean to me. We'd played pool, exchanged beauty secrets and workout tips. We'd talked about movies and music, nothing to do with the pack or my past. She hadn't given any hint of the malice I'd seen in her eyes tonight. She'd been rather quiet over the beers until that moment, then she seized the turn of the conversation to make sure her words would cut to the bone.

It was common knowledge that Weres and vampires don't get along. I had ties to both, but I tried not to think too much about having been bound to Royce and to Max by blood. I hadn't willingly been their plaything, but based on Paula's reaction, it was clear not everyone saw it that way.

While that part of my past was not exactly a secret, I had to wonder why it had come up now. I sipped at the drink in my hand, wishing I had something stronger, ignoring the chill that raced through me from more than the cold wind sighing through the trees. She had said she'd "heard" I'd been bound. The only people here who had any knowledge about the binding were Chaz, Simon, and Dillon. The group had separated for a couple hours after dinner. Had something happened after we split up? Had one of them told her? I couldn't understand why they would, particularly now. Why not say something before this stupid trip started? Why wait until we were all stuck here with moonrise coming in another hour or two?

It didn't make any sense. There might be others who had picked it up through the grapevine, or maybe just clung to the speculations reported in the news at the time. Was someone here trying to make life difficult for me by whispering in the ears of Chaz's pack?

Who the hell could it be? And why?

"Out here all alone? Not wise."

I cringed as Seth's voice broke into my reverie. I couldn't see much in the shadows. He was hiding somewhere in the tree line, keeping out of sight. I was willing to bet his friends were out here somewhere too. "What do you want?"

"Nothing. Just wondering why you're out here by yourself, no big, bad pack leader to protect you."

"I can protect myself," I shot back, edging toward the doors that led back inside the lodge. Back to safety.

"Not from us." The laughter that came from the trees had me searching, looking for signs of where the others were. I spotted two by the slight luminescence reflecting off their eyes, glowing cat-like in the dark. Seth and the other one remained hidden from my view. Too far to rush me before I could get inside, I thought. "Not that you have anything to worry about. You're not my problem."

"What the hell is that supposed to mean?"

He'd gone quiet. The two Weres I'd seen walked

out into the light, followed soon by Seth and the remaining Were. Their movements were completely silent, not a snapping twig or crunch of dead leaves to give away their whereabouts. All of them were smirking in amusement, watching me with hungry, predatory eyes. It wasn't Seth, but one of the others who answered me.

"It means we don't give a shit whether you live or die. Just stay out of our way."

The four of them filed inside, one of them turning to give me a grim smile as he went. Shivering, I turned away, unable to meet his eyes as I hurried off in the dark toward the sound of rushing water and the cabins beyond.

I didn't meet anyone else in my haste to get as far away from the lodge as I could. My thoughts raced as I tried not to slip in the mud, anger and fear warring for dominance in my mind. Coming out here had been a mistake. It had only been one day, and already I was sorely regretting my decision to come along on this crazy camping trip. If the night hadn't ended so badly, I might have even pulled out the contract to surprise Chaz with tonight after he came back from the hunt. As it was, I had the whole rest of the weekend to get through, and nobody had even shifted yet.

Would whoever set off Paula start whispering in the ears of the rest of the pack? Would the others start giving me venomous looks, or thinking those terrible things about me?

Were they thinking them already?

Rubbing at the tears gathering in my eyes, I thought about digging out my cell phone and calling Sara. Maybe she would know what to do.

I wouldn't have reception, but I could get the number out of my phone and use the land-line provided in the cabin.

Thoughts of home vanished when I saw the cabin. The door was open a crack. No lights shown through the gap.

Warily, I stepped a little closer, noting that the wood around the small lock had splintered. Something was burning, the scent strong enough to make me wrinkle my nose in disgust. I listened cautiously, trying to determine if anyone was still inside.

The only sounds I heard were some music drift-ing from one of the other cabins a few doors down and the faint drip of water pattering on the ground as the wind gusted today's earlier rain off the leaves.

Pushing the door the rest of the way open, I im-mediately flicked on the light and stepped aside in case someone was planning to rush me. There wasn't anybody inside, but what I found was worse. Far worse.

"Shit!" I cried, slamming a closed fist against the door, making it bounce against the wall.

Some of the furniture had been upended, one chair smashed to bits. All of our stuff had been yanked out of the drawers and tossed across the floor. It looked like my bras and panties were all missing. A bunch of Chaz's stuff had been tossed in the fireplace, only a few charred scraps of his clothes and the vague remnants of a sneaker remaining. That's where the bad smell came from, the lingering odor much stronger now that I was inside. I lifted my arm to use my shirt as a filter over my nose and mouth. It didn't help much. My cell phone was in pieces, bits of pink plastic littering the small counter in the kitchen. Chaz's phone was ground into shards on the table.

The slim laptop I'd borrowed from Arnold so I could check my e-mail had been turned upside down. The battery was missing, and I didn't see the carrying case with the power hookup and extra cables anywhere. At least it wasn't busted like the rest of the stuff in the room. There were coffee grounds spilled all over the floor, the coffeemaker smashed up against, and stuck partway into, the wall. Miraculously, the pot itself had survived, the last dregs of this morning's brew congealed at the bottom of the glass container.

Moving in a daze, I picked a few shreds of torn clothing and a mangled paperback off the floor. Whoever had done this hadn't gone through the closet, so our bags were untouched, the few things that hadn't been unpacked left alone. Chaz was not going to be happy that the only clothes left that hadn't been torn to bits in the break-in were the ones that would likely get torn to bits when he shifted. Unless he wanted to parade around naked until moonrise.

Interesting thought, that.

Who might have done this? Who hated me or Chaz enough to do something this crappy? Considering moonrise was so close, as soon as he got here, Chaz would likely fly into a rage, shift, and tear off into the woods after whoever had destroyed our stuff. Though I wasn't sure why, maybe someone was trying to piss him off on purpose so he'd lose it. To make him angry enough to hurt me? Unlikely, but a possibility I couldn't dismiss outright. Someone was pissed off enough to stir unrest in the ranks of Weres, but it was unclear whether this mess was the result of someone's trying to get to me, to Chaz, or to both of us.

When I got closer to the bed, I froze, shock stopping me in my tracks. I could see the sheets and blankets had been shredded in a couple of places. There were claw marks on the thin birch logs that made up the headboard, so deep they stopped just shy of cutting right through. It looked like something large and monstrous had jumped up on the bed, put its talons up on the headboard, and raked down it like some giant cat sharpening its claws on a scratching post.

Instantly, my haze of disbelief shifted into anger. I was willing to bet Seth and his band of merry misfits were responsible. It was a wonder they hadn't marked their territory, I thought savagely, grabbing up what clothes and things could be salvaged and putting them together on the ravaged bed.

I'd been right. It looked like all of my panties and bras were gone, maybe burned to ash with the rest of Chaz's clothes. Looked like I'd be spending the rest of the time I was here going commando, unless there was a clothing store somewhere in the mix of tiny shops we'd passed on the main boulevard on our way here. People lived here year-round, so there had to be a place where we could pick up some new clothes.

We wouldn't be able to stay in the cabin tonight,

but I wasn't about to turn tail and run back to the city. This was just a stupid threat; somebody was trying to drive me away. I'd find out who was responsible and find a way to make them pay.

Anger kept me warm as I hurriedly threw our remaining things together, wishing mightily for my silver stakes and guns. I wasn't usually bloody-minded without the sentient hunter's belt to urge me on, but for whoever did this, I would make an exception.

Chapter 7

By the time I'd finished repacking what remained of our salvageable stuff, my anger had cooled off enough that I didn't think it would be a bright idea to stick around. Whoever had done this was still out there somewhere, and he or she might come back when Chaz wasn't around. Without the belt to give me strength, speed, and stamina, I had no hope of surviving a Were attack. Not a very cheering thought to keep me company on the nice, long walk alone through a wooded path in the dark to get back to the lodge. Chaz was probably still there, drinking and feeling like a shit for letting one of his pack get uppity with me.

All in all, staying here was more dangerous than going back. I looked around the room to see if there was anything I could take with me and use as a weapon if I needed to. Eventually, I settled on a chair leg. Laughable as a defense, but better than nothing at all. There were a couple that looked heavy and solid enough to use like baseball bats. Maybe I could crack the thing's skull before it tore out my insides.

Right. And maybe the tooth fairy would swing by to play backup for me next.

I didn't take anything else with me, leaving the bags to one side of the door to come back for later. I put the laptop with them, too, grimacing at the thought of Arnold's reaction if whoever this was had damaged his coveted Fragware 5000. It was Sara who'd convinced him to part with it so I could keep in touch with the rest of the world while I was out here in the woods. Strange that it had been left for the most part untouched, just the battery and carrying case with all the accessories missing. Oh well. Better that than smashed to bits like the coffee machine.

Hefting the chair leg up to my shoulder, I stood on the doorstep, staring out into the night. Some of the windows of the cabins threw dim light on the trees and underbrush lining the buildings and the path, but the little lamps on the ground marking the way back up to the lodge didn't illuminate much more than the fronts of the buildings. I couldn't see if anything was hiding in the underbrush and couldn't hear anything moving out there. That didn't mean much. Even in human form, Weres are good—very good—at hiding themselves in this kind of landscape. If the Were was shifted, I wouldn't hear or see it coming until it was right on top of me.

There was a low, gravelly caw from somewhere over my head, a protesting sound from a raven or crow. The unexpected sound made me jump, but was a good sign. If there were a big predator around, the bird would've nested elsewhere or stayed quiet in the hopes of being overlooked. Kind of like me.

I crept along, shivering in the bitter cold. Surges of adrenaline from my terrified reaction as twigs snapped or branches rustled around me alternated with feeling like an absolute dork for scuttling around in the dark like I was playing at being a secret agent. Though there wasn't a lot of light, I could still see my breath fogging the air in front of me.

Hazy moonlight glinted off the shifting surface of the running water. As I got to the bridge, something moved against the wind in the trees above me. Tensing, I swung about so I could see whatever it was, my knuckles cracking as my grip tightened on the busted chair leg.

The stupid crow cackled at me again, watching me with beady eyes from a perch high up in the trees. The big, gangly bird hopped down another branch to move closer, and I made a shooing motion at it, annoyed.

"Um, maybe this is a stupid question, but what are you doing with that stick?"

A little cry escaped me, as I stumbled back to the raucous sound of something suspiciously like laughter from the bird. As it flew off, I raised a hand to my brow, letting the makeshift bat swing at my side.

"Kimberly, Jesus Christ. You almost gave me a heart attack."

"Sorry," she said, not sounding sorry at all. She looked me up and down, warily amused. "Seriously, what's going on? Are you okay?"

"No. Somebody tore the shit out of our cabin. There are claw marks all over the furniture, so I think it was a Were. I didn't want to wait there by myself in case it came back. Come on, let's get out of here."

Brown eyes wide with surprise, she nodded agreement, ushering me ahead of her as we rushed back toward the lodge. I left the chair leg by the creek since it was basically useless, and I figured Kimberly would be better able to deal with anything that attacked than I would. She was in amazing shape and, if something came at us, she could always shift into Were form to scare it off or fight, which I had to admit was a pretty useful quality in a girlfriend.

We hurried through the trees, me breathing hard, Kimberly barely showing any sign of effort. I vowed silently to hit the gym a little more once I got home. And, damn, it was cold, made colder still by the wind rushing against the fear-induced sweat that had broken out over my body.

The warmth inside the building was like a balm to my frazzled nerves. We followed the easy hum of conversation to the bar where Chaz was in heated discussion about something with a few of the guys. They looked up when we stopped in the doorway to the dining hall, surprise etching Chaz's face when he saw our expressions.

"Shia? What happened? Are you okay?"

Kimberly hesitantly touched my arm to indicate she wanted to speak. I nodded assent. She turned to address Daisy, who'd stopped rubbing down the bar mid-motion, and the Weres in the room. "Someone's gone rogue."

A long pause followed those words. I didn't like the dangerous light that came into the Weres' eyes. Clearing my throat, I spoke up, hating that my voice was so unsteady. "Our cabin was trashed. Some of the furniture was busted, and there are scratches on the furniture that look like they came from claws."

Chaz stood up, pacing over to join us with that easy, liquid grace that said he was pissed and on the verge of shifting. Great. "I'll bet it was Seth. That little shit finally went off the deep end."

"Excuse me, but before you start tearing up more of our property, you better go speak to my father-in-law," said Daisy from behind the bar. She drew herself up straight, looking almost as nervous as I felt when she met Chaz's eyes. "If what she said is true, someone better pay for the damage."

Chaz stared at her a long moment before giving a slow nod, though the anger didn't fade from his manner or expression. "I will talk to him. We'll make sure it's handled."

She nodded in return, still looking uneasy. I didn't blame her. At last, she bent back to the task of wiping down the bar, putting a little more elbow grease into it than was strictly necessary, making it a point to keep her eyes off his. Smart move on her part. Continuing to stare at him could've been construed as a challenge.

Chaz took my hand and led the way toward the back, looking for Mr. Cassidy. I had to admire the way the others simply fell into step behind him, following in silent support of their pack leader. I silently prayed that they'd all make it through the night without shifting in anger. Yes, I had come here to see them shift, but not when they were pissed off. That could lead to bites and scratches and, while your chances of contracting the lycanthropy infection from either one weren't astronomical, they weren't small either.

"Mr. Cassidy! Hello?" Chaz bellowed out as we reached the empty front desk.

The old man peered through the hallway opposite the dining hall, bushy brows arched high as he and George approached. "No need to shout, sonny, I'm right here. What's wrong?"

Chaz glanced down at me, frowning in a mix of worry and preoccupation. "Someone broke into our cabin and destroyed some of our things. It may have been one of mine, and if it was, I'll see he or she pays for any damages. Is there another cabin we can stay in for now?"

"Blazes and tarnation, boy! When did this happen?"

I noted with mild interest that everyone, including Chaz, fell into step behind Mr. Cassidy. He didn't move as swiftly and smoothly as the others, but there was determination in his pace, and irritation was strong on his features.

When we got back outside, I huddled against Chaz for warmth. He wrapped an arm around me, but didn't slow down. Nobody said anything until we got to the cabin. I waited outside and rubbed my arms while Mr. Cassidy, Chaz, and a couple of the guys stepped inside, taking note of the damage. The space was too small for many people to fit comfortably, and I'd already seen as much of the place as I wanted. I studied the trees, careful not to look at the other Weres standing around with me as they muttered quietly to each other. I overheard Paula, who had followed us out here for who knew what reason, and another one saying something about "vamp-bait" to each other—and had to grit my teeth to ignore it. Never a good idea to stare at a riled-up Were, even if they were acting like assholes. Chaz was cursing loudly enough that I could hear him from where I was standing. Even Mr. Cassidy gave voice to a few oaths that would make a dock foreman blush.

They came back out a minute or two later, shaking their heads. Chaz was holding the burnt up shoe in one hand. With a furious growl, he threw it as far as he could into the woods.

"They got the scents good and mixed in there, so no hope of figuring out who it was that way. All this rain would have washed away any lingering scent out here, covering their trail. Whoever did this planned it pretty well," Sean said, putting a hand on Chaz's shoulder as he seethed silently, fists clenching and unclenching at his sides as he scanned the trees lining the path. "It doesn't seem like Seth's handiwork. He's too much of a coward to pull something like this."

"I don't care who the hell it was," Mr. Cassidy said, wiping one of his hands off on a rag as he stepped out of the cabin. "Somebody's paying for that mess."

"We'll figure out who it was and make them pay for it," Nick put in, watching Chaz with concern.

I didn't think he'd shift, but it was so close to the full moon, and his temper was already shot, so there was a chance he might.

A few other people seemed to be having the same thought, watching him closely, lending a supportive hand or a calming word here and there. Even Paula and the guy she was talking with had quieted down, presumably because they'd figured out that the last thing Chaz needed was more stress and discord in his space. After a little while, he took a deep breath and relaxed somewhat, closing his eyes. It was good to see the tension visibly easing from his shoulders.

"All right. Mr. Cassidy," Chaz finally said, turning to the man, "I'm sorry for the mess. I don't know who is responsible, but we'll find them."

"Damned right, you will. George and I will help. In the meantime, you and the young lady can stay in cabin twenty-seven. It's the last one on the lot, and the only one that isn't occupied right now. Sorry, son, but I'll need a second deposit on it. You understand."

Chaz gritted his teeth, but nodded assent.

"Good. George, can you clean up this mess and see about fixing that door? The rest of you, go on inside. You two, come with me, and I'll get the paperwork and keys from up front."

Chaz and I followed Mr. Cassidy, listening to him harrumph and curse every now and again under his breath. The other Weres headed off to their own cabins or trailed along as we headed up to the lodge. Chaz's grip on my hand was a little tight, but I didn't think now would be a good time to start complaining.

Before we reached the doors, Mr. Cassidy gestured for us to halt, waiting for the others to go in before speaking. The only thing breaking the silence was the whisper of leaves and muted chirp of a cricket somewhere nearby.

"Look, I don't know what kind of trouble you kids brought with you from the city, but I don't want it. I'd be more understanding if it were an accident, someone shifting outside the lunar cycle and not making it outside in time. But if this happens again, I want the whole lot of you out of here. I don't let troublemakers into my range. You get me, son?"

Chaz nodded solemnly, looking drawn and troubled. "Yes, Mr. Cassidy, I understand."

"Good," he said. "I may not look like much, but I'm still alpha enough to kick somebody's ass, and it *will* be kicked as soon as I find out who did this."

That I could believe.

"As for you, missy—"

I started when he turned to me, giving him my wide-eyed attention.

"I don't want to see innocent blood spilled on my turf either. I'd appreciate it if you'd limit yourself to the lodge or your cabin after sunset while you're here."

I frowned, pulling my hand out of Chaz's so I could fold my arms. "I came out here to see the pack. I've been around when they've shifted before."

"That may be, but it's not just your safety on the line. I've got a reputation to uphold, and that isn't going to happen if things get rowdy and you end up getting bit or scratched in a scuffle."

"That's not fair! Chaz can protect me. He's done it before. Right?" I looked at him, pleading for assistance. He nodded a bit grudgingly, not meeting my eyes, just enough to show Mr. Cassidy I was telling the truth. "There, see?"

"I don't think you understand the danger you're in. Someone went Were outside the lunar cycle. Yes, it's close, but it takes some powerful emotions to force that out of a person. Judging by the state of that cabin, somebody's a mite pissed at you or your alpha here. I'm not risking my business just so you can appease your curiosity. You get me?"

Some of my anger deflated. "Yeah, I get you."

"So you'll stay inside, then?" he prodded, frowning at me.

I threw one last, pleading glance at Chaz. No help from that quarter. With a deeply resigned sigh, I nodded, thinking for the umpteenth time of throttling whoever had trashed that cabin.

"Good," Mr. Cassidy said, turning back to the doors and heading inside. "You made the right choice, m'girl. We'll keep you safe."

My mood as black as the shadowed forest surrounding this little valley, I trailed in the wake of Chaz and Mr. Cassidy. Somebody was really going to pay for ruining my vacation like this.

Soon.

Chapter 8

The next day, I woke up a little stiff and very cold. The fire had long since burned down to ashes. Chaz wasn't in bed with me. I didn't have my cell, so I had no idea what time it was, but I was guessing probably midmorning by the amount of sun peeking through the drab tan curtains of our new cabin.

I burrowed under the covers and groaned as I thought about facing the day. More unwanted mystery and avoiding unknown monsters out to make my life miserable did not sound like a good time. Neither did finding out how much further the "rumors" about my being a "leech's pet" had spread.

Soon enough, hunger and a desire to find out what the heck had happened to Chaz were enough of a goad to get me to leave the bed. I didn't bother to shower. Instead, I grabbed a T-shirt and jeans out of the lone bag to survive our little "visit" yesterday, the bag that held the scant remains of my wardrobe. I got dressed, slipped on my shoes and track jacket, and headed outside, shading my eyes with a hand as I scanned the surroundings.

The sun was well over the horizon, the sky a flawless blue, not a single cloud to hint at rain or fog. Birds chirped merrily in the underbrush, and the air smelled clean and fresh. It was warmer than yesterday, but the grass and dirt paths were still damp and a bit muddy. If I still went out for a walk in the woods with Nick and Sean, I'd have to wear my hiking boots instead of sneakers. Fortunately, they'd survived the rampage.

I took a deep breath, enjoying the crisp mountain air as I walked the longer trail up to the lodge. A couple sharing a cup of coffee on the step in front of their cabin waved and smiled as I passed. I could tell by the amount of hair visible on their arms and the backs of their hands, as well as the thick stubble on the guy's face, that they were Weres. Maybe word about my ties to Royce hadn't spread to the entire pack after all. I wasn't sure who else was staying here, but I had seen people who weren't part of the pack in the dining hall. It was good to know that some of the other people here didn't have a problem with the Sunstrikers, because that would've made the rest of this trip positively intolerable.

Feeling a little better, I continued with more of a spring in my step. There were some people making a ruckus in the game room, but the dining hall was practically deserted. Mrs. Cassidy was clearing away a few dishes from a table, but she gave me a friendly smile and a nod when she saw me take a seat by one of the windows.

I wondered where everybody was. There was a skinny, geeky-looking guy munching on some toast as he read a paperback off by himself in the corner. Not part of the Sunstrikers, though I'd seen him in here with a couple other guys yesterday. There was another stranger reading a newspaper at the far end of the room. George and Daisy the bartender were sitting together, heads close, and I could see the light touches to each other's hands and gentle smiles they were giving each other. They made an incongruous couple, what with his bulk and her diminutive stature, but they seemed happy. I couldn't tell if the girl was human, but I was sure George was Were of some flavor or another. Judging by his size and the ponderous way he moved, somehow I didn't think it was wolf. No, it was something else. Something bigger. Bear, maybe.

Mrs. Cassidy came by a few minutes later, a mug and coffee pot in hand. "Your young man has his hands full with that poor boy who's turning for the first time this month. He said you might come by looking for him."

I lifted a brow, cradling my hands around the mug for the warmth as she poured coffee for me. "Oh, is that where he is? All right."

"Mmhm. In the meantime, what can I get you? We've got some fresh-made blueberry pancakes."

"That sounds great, thanks."

"Okay, I'll have that out to you in a jiffy. Don't you worry about your boy, now. He'll be along once the new blood's settled down a bit."

I hadn't been particularly worried, but her repeated reassurance made me wonder if I should be. At my absent nod, she whisked off, deftly weaving between the tables to refill the coffee mugs for George and his girl, then for the geek in the corner. Everything was quiet except for the muted whispers of the lovers, and as I tasted the coffee, bitter from sitting on the burner too long, I pondered what to do about all the problems that had cropped up.

Someone was behind it all. Someone was whispering bad things in the ears of the pack, stirring them up, pissing them off. Somebody didn't want me here or was angry at Chaz, and was willing to do some bad things to drive us away. Why?

As convenient as it would be to blame Alec Royce, I didn't think my being bound by blood to him for a whopping twelve days was enough to piss off the Sunstrikers. They knew I had a connection to him after that deal with the *Dominari* Focus, and that I had saved the vamp as well as Were packs in New York City from enslavement by a crazy sorcerer. Shouldn't that be enough to balance out the ugliness of being bound for a few measly days?

Granted, I'd never fully work him out of my system after what had happened. You could say the same of Max Carlyle. If the guy was in close enough proximity, he could call me back to his side. I didn't think Royce would tolerate Max's coming back to New York for any reason, and if the police caught wind of his return, his butt would fry in the sun in no time. He'd tried to pin the mass murders he'd committed on Royce, and while it had been proven conclusively that Max was the one responsible, it had still tarnished Royce's relatively good name. There were questions of his involvement and, now and again, mine as well. Could it be that someone was upset about the murders and was trying to turn everyone against me?

No. No, the "flavor" of the pranks of the last few days seemed too personal. It wasn't just an attempt to turn Others against me for something as nebulous as my possible involvement in the massacres of a month ago. Actually, it probably wasn't even because I had some kind of connection to Royce. Whatever it might be, it had something to do with my relationship with Chaz.

You don't burn someone's clothes and shoes unless you've got a special beef. The rumors and handwritten notes didn't seem like the handiwork of the same person. You don't leap from weird, somewhat childish notes to violence on this scale without some serious provocation, and I wasn't sure that Chaz or I could've managed to piss somebody off this badly in so short a period. For that matter, was it me or Chaz they were targeting? Both? Did that mean that the same person was mad at us for different reasons, or that two different people were simultaneously taking out their frustrations on one or both of us?

I closed my eyes and leaned back in the chair, concentrating on piecing together what was going on with the clues I had. Sara would be laughing her ass off at me right now. Sitting around drinking coffee, hiding inside when I should be hunting down the root of the problem and confronting it. Whatever. I'd take care of the problem on my own time. Aside from which, I doubted whoever it was would be raising his or her hand and conveniently saying, "Oh yes, that was me!" when I started asking around to scare up some clues.

"Here you go, sweetie. You just call me over if you need anything else."

I cracked an eye open as Mrs. Cassidy set the plate down. Just looking at the mile-high stack of blueberry pancakes dripping with butter was enough to give me heart palpitations.

"Thank you," I said with a grateful smile, tugging the cloth napkin out from under my silverware and putting it across my lap. She settled a dish with extra butter and a trencher of warm syrup down in front of me, giving me a light, friendly pat on the shoulder. I dug in, giving a blissful moan of pleasure at the first bite. The soft, fluffy pancakes were fantastic, practically melting on my tongue.

I stuffed myself, taking some time about it after the first few hurried bites. After all, I didn't have anywhere to be today, and I wasn't going to go traipsing around in the woods by myself. If I was going to go hiking later, it would be with Nick and Sean, but I had the feeling they were most likely busy helping Chaz deal with Ethan if the new werewolf was having a rough time with the change.

I downed the last of my coffee and rose, stretching languorously as I considered what to do. Maybe the geek didn't have such a bad idea with that paperback. I thought I might have stuffed some cheesy romance novel in my remaining duffel before I left, just in case of emergencies—like now. Still, I didn't feel like reading; I wanted to do something. Hanging around the garden, or maybe catching some sun by the creek should be safe enough.

The man with the newspaper folded the pages down, revealing his features. His sharp hazel eyes were locked on me, watching my every move, and I inwardly cursed my lack of attentiveness.

Jim Pradiz was getting up to join me. I thought about making a run for it, but there wasn't anywhere for me to go unless I wanted to stay locked in my cabin for the rest of the trip.

He gave me a blindingly white smile, extending his hand as he approached. "Ms. Waynest, good to see you again."

I ignored the offered hand. He let it drop without comment, and without losing that ingratiating grin. "J.P. I assume you're the one who was following us the night before last?"

"Why, yes. I hope I didn't alarm you. Want to tell me what made you choose this establishment for your little outing?"

"That's none of your damn business," I snarled, though I toned it down and forced the tension out of my shoulders as everyone, including the kid with the paperback, dropped what he or she was doing to stare curiously at us. "I'm on vacation, okay? Aren't there rules about leaving people on vacation alone? Go crawl back to the city and find someone else to harass."

"I'm hardly harassing you, Ms. Waynest. Just

looking for a story. Funny that I always find one when I spend enough time following you."

"Jim, please don't do this to me. I'm trying to have a relaxing getaway—this isn't helping."

That smile of his never wavered. It bugged the hell out of me. "I'll be watching, but you won't see much of me. I'm not staying here, just swinging by to see what the Sunstriker pack is up to so far from the city. You're not the only story I followed up here. Don't worry, I'll keep it discreet. If you change your mind about giving a statement later, you know how to reach me."

He afforded me a nod, waving the paper at me in what might have been mockery or threat as he breezed by. No doubt he'd find someplace to hole up and watch us, taking photos of whatever he thought might sell to the tabloids. I wasn't happy about it, but it had become depressingly commonplace lately. Anything that connected me with Others was newsworthy these days; it was part of why I was on this vacation in the first place. Sara had been taking on more of the footwork that I normally did since too many people now recognized me on the street.

My good mood gone, I stalked out of the dining hall and headed outside, pausing on the trail to enjoy the cool breeze that rustled the grasses and herbs, letting the sensations wash over me and ease the edge off of my agitation. The heady scent of lemongrass was drowning out the more subtle smells. Someone had cut a swath through it recently, maybe for something Mrs. Cassidy was whipping up in the kitchen tonight.

Breathing in the sour-sweet smell, I turned off the main path and walked into the garden, following the less-packed dirt trail that led through the herbs and vegetables. There wasn't much still growing this late in the year, and much of what was left had been harvested already, but a few of the hardier plants were still going strong. I brushed my fingers through the rosemary and basil, liking how their dusky scents clung to my skin. There was peppermint out here, too. I could smell it, but they must have had it hidden in pots away from the rest of the plants to keep it from taking over the garden.

There were no benches or gardening tools that I could see, and I wasn't sure Mr. Cassidy would take too kindly to my digging around in his garden anyway. I used to love gardening growing up, but apartment living wasn't exactly conducive to growing my own produce. After sampling the amazing food they served here, I was starting to regret that a little.

Wanting to sit down, forget about Jim Pradiz, and just enjoy the sun for a while, I ambled my way out of the garden and toward the creek. After the rain, it was swollen with runoff from the peaks around us. I found a good-sized rock a little way off the path to sit on, dipping my fingers in the icy cold water and turning my face up to the sun. It was pleasant, doing nothing, just enjoying the sounds of birds calling to each other in the trees and a couple of kids running around nearby. Probably Billy and one or two of the other Weres' kids.

Out here relaxing in the sun and fresh air was

nice, but at this rate I knew I'd be bouncing off the cabin walls to go home by Sunday at the latest. I sorely hoped Ethan wouldn't keep everyone for too long, and that he hadn't hurt himself or anybody else. It bugged me that nobody was around, that it was so quiet, and that there wasn't much to do since I couldn't go walking or hiking by myself.

Actually, it was really quiet.

Now that my attention was on it, I opened my eyes and looked around. There were no people walking around. The kids had stopped yelling and carrying on. Even the birds singing in the trees had quieted.

Uneasy, I rose to my feet, wiping my wet hands off on my jeans. I took a look around but didn't see anyone hiding in the greenery. The woods grew thick near the bank of the creek not that far off the trail, and somebody could theoretically be hiding in the tree line. The sun was bright and high in the sky, but the bushes were dense and rife with deep shadows.

I carefully moved up the bank to the grass, rubbing some of the mud off my sneakers before taking the path over the creek and toward the cabins. I hoped I could find Kimberly, but I wasn't sure where she was staying, and there was the added worry that she and Paula seemed to be good friends. Kimberly hadn't been rude to me like Paula, but I wasn't sure how she felt about me after hearing the news I'd been Royce's little pet blood doll.

Chaz, followed closely by Simon and Dillon, was ambling up the path toward me. Whatever was in the brush hightailed it, making quite a lot of noise as it rushed off on their approach. Chaz frowned when he reached me, staring off into the bushes even as he gave me a quick hug.

"Hey, love. Hope you weren't too bored without me."

"Nah," I replied, getting up on tiptoe to kiss his cheek. "Heard the new guy was giving you trouble. Everything okay?"

Simon and Dillon exchanged a look I couldn't read. Chaz's brows arched in surprise, but his smile eased my worry I'd said something wrong.

"Ethan will be fine. He's having a rough transition. I left a couple of the guys with him. As for you"—I squealed when he picked me up, laughing as he spun around to face the woods and cabins before setting me back down on my feet; the other two Weres were rolling their eyes, but I didn't care—"I'm not letting anything get in the way of our afternoon together."

Chapter 9

At my pleading look, Chaz dismissed Simon and Dillon. The two breathed very obvious sighs of relief and rushed off, not giving Chaz a chance to change his mind. Though I could tell he was annoyed, he quickly lost track of his irritation once I slid my arm around his waist and pressed up against his side.

"So, what did you have in mind for this afternoon?" I asked.

He soon replaced the irritation with playfulness, grinning down at me while his fingers toyed with the bra strap peeking out of my shirt collar. "It's a surprise."

My eyebrows arched at that, as I worked my hand under his shirt to rub against the smooth plane of hard muscle on his back. My smile grew wider when he flexed, responding so readily to my touch. He urged me to move, and it was with a mixture of disappointment and curiosity that I noted he wasn't leading me to our cabin—we were headed somewhere into the woods.

"Where are we going?"

"No questions yet. You'll see," he said.

I kept my mouth shut, but both of us explored the bounds of our self-imposed chastity by letting our hands wander and pressing against each other as we walked. The trees were soon close around us, limbs lightly slapping against our arms and legs as we walked, giving us that much greater an excuse to hold each other close as we followed some half-formed path through the underbrush. I barely noticed. He laughed when I stumbled over a root in the mulch, tightening his grip on me in a way I didn't mind at all.

I'm not sure how long we walked. I was too distracted to notice where we were going until Chaz halted, and the sound of running water drew my attention to my surroundings.

It looked like something out of a fairy tale. The path led to a stream fed by a small waterfall trickling down over mossy rocks. Birds occasionally darted out to snap up a bug and bullfrogs sang their rough songs from the pool at the base of the falls. Someone had long ago dragged a stone bench out here and set it in a grassy clearing looking over the water; the wilds no doubt would have reclaimed it save that someone had cut back the worst of the brush, leaving the bench barely visible in the field of waving green stalks. The trail curved to follow the stream, and I could see where it picked up on the other side, just beyond some large stepping stones cutting a path through the water.

"Do you like it?"

"It's beautiful," I breathed, settling back against Chaz's chest as he wrapped his arms around me.

We stayed like that for a while, him holding me while I drank in the beauty of the place. The heavy scent of pine wasn't as thick here; instead, there was an odd smell, reminiscent of parsnips, which Chaz told me was the scent of the huge hemlock growing near the base of the waterfall.

Hand in hand, we waded through the thick grass to the edge of the water, avoiding the wavering hemlock clusters that would bloom with white or green flowers come springtime. I pulled a cattail that still had the brown, densely packed seeds on the top, using it to stir the water near the edge. We settled down in the grass, laughing and grabbing at each other for balance as the cold water soaked through our jeans.

He helped me take off my shoes and roll up my pants to my knees, then I set aside my cattail and did the same for him. We stuck our bare feet in the water, and he chuckled at my gasp of shock. We scooted closer on the shore, twining our legs together as we wiggled our toes against the chill. He held me against him, and we watched the frogs and salamanders and fish gradually build up the courage to return to this invaded slice of their haven.

"Shia?"

"Yes?"

"You've never talked to me about what happened while you were with Royce."

Startled, I withdrew. "Chaz—"

"No, Shia," he said, tightening his grip on me so I couldn't pull away. I glanced up, afraid of what emotions I'd see reflected in his eyes, but he was staring across the water instead of at me. A muscle in his jaw was twitching; not a good sign. "I think I have a right to know. I brought you out here for a few reasons. One of them was to see if we have a future together. If we're ever going to get past what happened, if we're ever going to be like we were, then you need to talk to me."

I didn't answer right away, shocked beyond speech that he would bring this up now. His grip on me was too tight to pull away from, and the intimacy of the moment was completely shattered by sudden memories of being at the vampire's beck and call. Panic at being imprisoned by Chaz's hold subsided as I reached for his other hand to grasp it in both of my own. He didn't return the squeeze of reassurance I gave him.

"I want a future with you, Chaz. I can't imagine being without you. You've saved my life, more than once, and stood by me during some of the toughest trials I've ever endured." I lifted a hand up to his cheek, making him look at me. The hurt so raw in his expression cut me deeper than I would have expected, made it hard to say my next words. "When I was bound to Royce, I loved him."

Chaz started to pull away, withdrawing his arm from around me. My hand fell to his shoulder, holding him there while I straddled his waist, preventing him from rising. He glared up at me, brows furrowed and teeth suddenly bared in an angry sneer.

"Don't," he growled. "You've said enough."

"Chaz, shut the fuck up and let me finish," I snarled back. Startled, he leaned back, anger still glinting in his icy blue eyes, but some of the tension trickling out of him as he settled down beneath me. "I loved him because I *had* to. I had no choice. Do you understand? It wasn't real. His blood made me want to be with him and do what he said. Hell, I couldn't have said no if he'd really pushed me to let him touch me or drink my blood. He never asked, but I wouldn't have been able to say no if he did. That's *nothing* like what we have. I'm with you because I have a choice, and because I care about you. I won't blindly do what you say—but if I did, is that how you'd want me?"

He stared up at me, anger and confusion and hurt warring with a sudden understanding. He knew now, knew what neither of us had had the courage to say since I ran on bloodied feet from the divided loyalties that waited for me in Royce's shadow.

When he answered, his voice was low, hardly a whisper.

"No."

Not satisfied, I bunched up his shirt in my fists, anger getting the better of me the more I thought about it. Chaz couldn't possibly understand what it had been like for me. How hard it had been to stay sane, stay *me,* and walk away when it was over. Worse, wrong or not, he still felt jealous of the vampire for having some part of me he'd never touched.

"I craved his blood, Chaz. He could have kept me there, given me more when I begged for it, and made me his. He didn't. He let me go. Don't blame him for doing what he thought he had to do to keep me safe."

"Why not, Shia?" Chaz grabbed me by the shoulders, startling me when he reversed our positions, his legs now on either side of my hips. Cold water from the pool bit at my toes and seeped into my shirt from the grass under my back. His weight on my legs was light, but I couldn't sit up. "Why shouldn't I blame him? Hell, we've slept together, but you two were more intimate than we've ever been. You're bound to him by blood and by contract. Do you want the leech instead? Should I let you go?"

If not for the tears in his eyes, I would've been offended. I hadn't realized the depth of his hurt until now. He was angry, so angry, but that anger was built upon something neither of us had any control over.

With a low growl, I answered him in the only way I could think of that wouldn't hurt him more. I threw my arms around his neck and pulled myself up to kiss him, not letting him draw away when he jerked back. Digging my nails into his shoulders, I poured every ounce of anger and frustration and need into that moment, hungrily slanting my mouth over his. Before long, his hands were crushing me to him, an equal passion driving him to devour my kiss like he was starving for the taste of me.

We tugged and pulled at each other's clothing, the wet grass sliding under my back and legs as my shirt and pants disappeared. One of the buttons on Chaz's shirt popped off and plunked into the water, forgotten as skin met skin, the heat generated between us making it easy to forget the cold and the mud. His teeth grazed my skin as he kissed and licked his way from my cheek, down my neck, and settled to a light suckling on my nipple through the thin material of my bra.

My breath caught as his fingers, rough and calloused, brushed along my stomach and down between my legs. We'd done far more than this without a contract, but that was before I knew what he was. We shouldn't have been doing this. He'd never hurt me—I knew he wouldn't—but there were so many things that could go wrong if we ignored the law.

Sensing my hesitation, Chaz paused, regarding me with a mixture of lust and anger so intense a shiver of fear trickled down my spine.

"Do you want me to stop?"

His question meant more than what he was asking. If he stopped now, it would be the end of everything between us.

I shook my head, wrapping my legs around his waist and reaching up to tug his mouth back down to my breast in answer. Pressed as tightly against him as I was, I felt the shudder of something—maybe relief?—roll through him.

A gasp escaped me as first one, and then another finger explored me. Chaz shifted to cover my mouth with his, swallowing my cries as he swiftly worked me into a frenzy of desire. My nails dug into his back and shoulders, the pressure between my legs growing unbearable. Too soon, not soon enough, a shudder wracked me as my pleasure reached its peak.

He pulled away long enough to hear me cry

out, both his hands sliding up to cup my cheeks, cradling my face as he pressed a few featherlight kisses on my brow. Chaz positioned himself even as the tremors leaving my thighs quaking tapered off, and I eagerly opened myself to him.

Suddenly, he stiffened—and not in the good way. He lifted his head, frowning as he levered himself up on his arms. Breathless, I stared at him, wondering why he had stopped.

A faint, strange sound echoed across the valley. Chaz hastily rose to his feet, slipping in the mud.

"Stay here. I'll be back soon."

"Wait! Chaz, what is it?" I struggled to sit up, shivering as the wind bit against my wet skin. The loss of warmth was doing more to kill my desire than Chaz's uneasiness and the abrupt halt to our "festivities." I wrapped my arms around myself while he threw his clothes on, not bothering to take the time to button his shirt or put on his shoes.

"Someone's hurt. I need to check it out." He glanced down at me as he (carefully) zipped up, a wry smile not easing the strain of worry or frustration at the interruption from his features. "Being the pack leader's a bitch sometimes."

"I'll go with you," I said, reaching for my shirt. He shook his head.

"No, wait here. It could be dangerous. Let me make sure everything is okay. I'll come back and get you when it's safe."

"Be careful," I said, heart lodged in my throat as I watched him race along the path back to the cabins.

Chapter 10

Coitus interruptus does not a happy camper make. I may have gotten my jollies, but I'd been expecting to do a lot more before Chaz and I were cut short. I sat in the meadow sulking for a few minutes, long enough to realize my back and legs were covered in mud and there was grass tangled in my hair.

Irritated beyond measure, I glanced around to make sure I was alone. Picking up my muddy clothes, I rose to rinse everything off, including myself, in the knee-deep water.

I don't know how the frogs and fish could stand the cold. The goose bumps were so bad, I couldn't tell right away if I'd gotten all the mud off my back when I reached to scrub. The cattail I'd picked earlier came in handy for that. Moments later, I screamed and rushed out of the water. A leech had latched onto my ankle, leaving me panting and cursing on the shore as I tore the little monster off.

Putting on my wet clothes was almost as bad as

rinsing off in the water. I shivered on the stone bench for a while, but the cold from that seeped into my butt, too, and soon drove me to get up and pace. My socks and shoes were dry. Thank goodness for small favors. I braved the bench long enough to put them on, then stomped back toward the cabins. I needed a hot shower, coffee, and dry clothes. Maybe to get the fireplace going, too. Chaz may have been worried about danger, but I was more concerned with getting a Band-Aid for my leg and warming up.

As I was trudging along the path, carefully avoiding some poison oak I hadn't noticed on the way earlier, something seemed different. It took a few minutes for me to put my finger on what was wrong.

The woods were unnaturally quiet again. Unnerved, I sped up my pace.

My heart jumped into my throat when I heard the bushes rustle behind me. Someone was there.

I broke into a run. The rustling at my back turned into a dull snapping of wet twigs, the quiet patter of feet rapidly catching up behind me on the path.

I didn't look back.

Breath catching, I rushed down the trail, praying that whoever it was would lose interest, would head off on a different part of the path. For one brief second, I held on to the hope that it was that stupid reporter trailing me. If not him, then maybe it was someone out for a mid-afternoon jog, someone who wasn't really after me. Stupid but, hey, a girl can dream. I tried to gauge how close my pursuer was by the even footfalls and snapping of twigs. With all the bends and twists to the trail, not to mention grasping branches that I was continually stepping over or dodging around, I didn't want to risk looking behind me.

A heavy hand fell on my shoulder, closing on my upper arm and hauling me off balance. I caught a glimpse of leather and light gleaming on silver studs before I spun to my knees, hair whipping into my face, momentarily blinding me.

"Don't make a fucking sound," came a harsh whisper as someone clamped his hand over my mouth and dragged me to my feet.

I squirmed as much as I could to break free. My left arm felt like it had just about been torn out of the socket, and the right was pinned to my side by whoever had grabbed me. I growled around the hand over my mouth, eyes narrowing when I saw one of Seth's idiot friends in the trees, gesturing at the guy holding me.

One thing to be said for the boy who'd grabbed me: he might have been stupid, but he was fast and strong. Even without his Were strength, he had the build of a guy who'd spent too much time at the gym, muscles straining against his T-shirt and tight jeans. I couldn't budge his grip on me, and we were moving into the underbrush faster and more quietly than I would've believed possible. Seth crept out of the shade from somewhere to our left, taking the lead. The other two idiots followed, dragging me along in spite of my efforts to dig my heels in.

We were quickly surrounded by thick under-brush and low-hanging boughs. Some of the ever-greens scratched my arms since the guy pulling me with him wasn't being too careful about following any kind of a path, only about keeping me from crying out or getting away.

We passed the bench and the waterfall, one of the boys making a crack that brought all the blood rushing to my face. They'd seen—or could smell—enough to know what Chaz and I had been doing. Seth growled something that made the others quiet their jeers and laughter, and we soon came to another clearing deeper in the woods. The fourth member of Seth's little group of misfits, a lanky teenager with a Day-Glo blue Mohawk and some fuzzy scruff that might have been an attempt at a goatee, was waiting for us with rope and duct tape. My heart sank at that. They'd planned this. Waiting for a moment when I'd be alone so they could snatch me up. Despite what Chaz had said, these guys must have been the ones who had burned up and destroyed our stuff. What a peachy keen development.

"Hold her hands out," the guy with the Mohawk said. "Do you want to tie her ankles up, too? Or just her wrists?"

"Nah," Seth replied, looking back the way we'd come. He scratched at a reddened patch on his neck where a silver necklace lay; dumb shit was trying to look tough, I suppose. "Just the wrists. She has legs, she can walk."

"Yeah, but she might run."

"Let her try."

I didn't like the dark amusement behind those words. Though I pulled against their grip, the boys were too strong. Between the guy who was holding me pinned against his chest and the one who held my wrists so the third could twine the rope around them, I didn't have a prayer of escape.

Quick, businesslike, as though they'd done this a thousand times before, the guy who'd waited for us tightly bound my wrists and pulled off a strip of duct tape. I twisted away to scream when the guy holding me moved his hand, but the other covered my mouth with the tape before I got out much more than a squeak. The big guy who was holding me shifted his grip to my upper left arm, tight enough to hurt. I glared into his dull brown eyes and kicked his shin, making him wince and shake me.

"Stop that, you stupid bitch!"

"Shut up, Gabe," Seth hissed out. "We're still too close. Someone might hear you. Let's go."

Once again, I found myself moving, though whenever I dug in my heels, the guy—Gabe— just dragged me along. I felt like a three-year-old having a fit about leaving the toy store, and my fighting was about as effective against his strength, but I did everything I could to slow our progress down.

Finally, I managed to hook one foot under a root, forcing him to stumble as I locked my leg and pulled him up short. Growling low obscenities under his breath, making the others chuckle, he stopped and hefted me over his shoulder. His shoulder was a little bony, but his grip was like iron, the heat radiating from under his creased leather jacket and the strong scent of musk marking him as close to shifting. Irritated, I hit his back with my bound hands as he started walking again. I jerked away when one of the others reached out to brush his fingers through my trailing hair.

"What a pain in the ass. Are you sure he'll come after her?"

"Yeah. Ethan will keep him busy for another hour or two with all the bane I put in that herbal shit they were feeding him. Once it wears off, it shouldn't take too long for someone to figure out she's missing."

Oh, that was just great. They were purposely making Ethan's transition harder on him to distract Chaz and take me? Clever. Far more clever a plan than I would've given the little shit credit for thinking up.

We continued in silence for a while, and I could tell we were going down the mountainside by the incline and how Gabe continually shifted his stance to balance and account for my weight. I picked at the tape over my mouth, but every time I reached for it, he jostled me until I stopped. The birds singing in the trees quieted as we passed, and small, unseen animals rushed off into the underbrush. The four guys turned their heads sometimes to follow things I couldn't see or sniff the air to take in scents too subtle for my poor human senses, but for the most part we kept to what I could now see was an old, mostly overgrown, deer run.

What felt like hours passed, though the sun was still well up in the sky when we came to a halt by a sheer granite cleft in the side of the mountain, overgrown with vines and eaten away by wind and water. Lichen crept up the stone and covered the trunks of nearby trees. Jagged pieces of stone were scattered along the ground or sticking out of the mulch where time and water had broken them off of the rock face. There were standing pools of runoff here and there, bugs idly buzzing over the still surfaces. It was a gloomy, spooky place, one nobody in his or her right mind would use to make camp.

Gabe set me down none too gently, and I ended up landing on my ass in the mud. I shuddered as cold and dirty water immediately soaked into my already wet jeans, glaring as the guys all laughed at my expense. Eyeing them in their shifting clothes—mostly cheap, faux leather biker jackets and stretchy sweatpants (which made them look more like the teenagers they were than the bad-asses they were trying to come off as)—I had a hard time seeing them as a threat instead of an annoyance.

Then Seth leaned down and grabbed under my arm, dragging me through the slick mulch until my back was up against the rock, the steely strength and rough handling reminding me that I wasn't dealing with pushovers. Even low on the supernatural totem pole as they were, the four of them presented a terrible danger to me without my weapons or Chaz here to protect me.

That didn't mean I'd sit back and take whatever they wanted to dish out, though. I used the rock to help lever to my feet, and he stepped back to watch me, not bothering to help or hold me down. I grabbed at the tape, pulling it off with a sharp jerk, grimacing at the pull against my skin. "What the hell do you nut jobs think you're doing? What the fuck do you want?"

Gabe leered. "What do you think we want?"

"Shut up, asshole," Mohawk said, giving Gabe a shove hard enough to make him stumble. "I'm not dying today. I don't care what the plan said. You touch her, you know he'll kill us all."

Before I could say anything, a chunk of wood thicker than my torso slammed into the two, sending them sprawling.

"You aren't fighting him. *I* am. *I* am going to win this," Seth snarled, muscles and bones bulging under his skin in sickening waves. "This is my fight, not yours."

The two kept their eyes down, heads bobbing like those of marionettes on strings in their haste to show their agreement. Seth's anger gradually abated, the shifting and grating of bone popping back into place making my stomach lurch. His eyes, when he turned to face me, held a subtle yellow glow that was terrifyingly familiar. Jesus, he was close to going Were. Something about what he was doing had him wound up near to the breaking point. There were no guarantees that he would be able to control his instincts to hunt and kill if he tipped over the edge.

After what felt like forever, Seth looked away and patted down his pockets, pulling out a battered pack of cigarettes. He didn't offer them to anyone else, just lit up and took a deep drag. Within a few puffs, the others had gotten to their feet and settled down cautiously on big rocks or tree stumps nearby. Seth chose a perch on an uneven slab of lichen-covered granite, his attention firmly fixed on the path we'd taken.

"How long do you think he'll take?" Gabe ventured to ask.

Seth didn't bother to look at him. "Fuck all if I know. We left an obvious trail. Shouldn't take too long."

I dared a question, meeting his eyes when he glanced at me. "If you want to fight Chaz so badly, why didn't you do it back at the cabins?"

He smirked at me, shaking his head and returning his attention back to the path. The others gave me furtive glances, but didn't dare speak.

Anger soon replaced my fear. Who the hell did he think he was? If not for him, Chaz and I could have been busy discussing the terms of the contract. Or busy doing other, far more pleasant, things.

"I see," I said, taking a few steps until I could assume an indolent lean against a nearby tree. I hoped my expression was as disdainful as I was going for. The trick would be to keep them worried about Chaz without pissing them off enough that they would hurt me. "You're planning to cheat, aren't you? You wanted to lure him out here so you could ambush him."

"No," Seth said, turning sharply to face me. "Shut up. You don't know anything about us."

"I know you won't win."

"I *will* win this," he snarled, fists clenching at his sides.

"Doesn't matter what you try. He'll still kick

your asses." I kept my voice as level as possible, hoping what I was saying was true. My faith in Chaz would undermine Seth's confidence if I played my cards right. Little enough, but it could turn the odds more in Chaz's favor once he came to save me. "He's the only Were to fight Rohrik Donovan and live."

"Give me a break," Seth said, his anger shifting abruptly into an amused smirk. "Rohrik didn't want him dead. Somewhere under the influence of the Focus, he had to have known what you were there for. Why don't you just sit down, get comfortable, and shut up. We're not going to hurt you unless you do something stupid, and he won't be here for a while."

Cursing softly under my breath, I took a look around, wondering how far I'd get if I bolted. They were alert now, watchful for escape attempts. It wouldn't do me much good, since I already knew they were faster and stronger than I was. They might tie up my ankles if I ran. Or possibly take a more violent turn. I wouldn't put it past them, though they hadn't actually hurt me—yet.

Irritated, I stalked over to a fallen log, sitting down on that instead of in the mud. Wrenching at the ropes around my wrists, I brought the knots up to my teeth to work myself free. Nobody made a move to stop me, and I guessed that they didn't consider me much of a threat with or without free hands. One of them even pulled out his cell phone and started fiddling with it, like he was playing a game or texting. Genius.

"Why this cavalier shit?" I asked again after the

rope loosened and I didn't need to tug at it with my teeth anymore.

Seth ran a hand lightly over the scruffy stubble on his jaw, not paying me much mind. "I want control of the pack. I won't get it unless I fight him for it. Too many back there would make it into a bloodbath instead of letting us work out right of ascension."

"Too many of the pack would try to stop you, you mean."

He glanced in my direction, giving me a wry grin. "That's what I said. I want a pack to lead, not a bunch of broken bodies and sore losers who would fight me for right of ascension as soon as Chaz is out of the way."

I curled my lip in a sneer, taking the rope up into a snarled tangle and throwing it as far from me as I could. "What makes you think you can beat him? He's bigger and stronger than you."

"Big and strong doesn't always equal faster or smarter. We've got you. He might just turn over leadership without a fuss if we press him right."

Meaning, if they threatened to do something to me, he might just give in and turn over leadership without a fight. I rubbed at my chafed wrists, staring down at my hands while I tried to think of how to get away.

"Why are you talking to her? She's just bait," Gabe asked, peeling the leaves one at a time off a branch he'd broken from a tree.

"You have anything better to do? I'm bored; she's listening."

"She might use it later."

"How?" The guy who had tied up my wrists

earlier asked, looking up from his cell phone. "She's not going anywhere."

"She fought Rohrik and that vampire, asshat. She's tougher or smarter than she looks. She's dangerous."

I rolled my eyes, stopping when I saw Seth doing the same thing. Making a little mulch pyramid with the toe of my sneaker, I propped my elbows on my knees and put my chin in my hands, staring at Gabe. He might be a danger to me later. Maybe I could use his wariness of me somehow. That in mind, I gave him a grim smile, narrowing my eyes.

"You afraid of little ole me? Big, scary Were like you? Jesus, Seth, you need friends with backbones."

Gabe straightened, dropping the branch and clenching thick fists at his sides. "Shut your mouth. Nobody asked you."

"Don't talk about me like I'm not here, then. Later, just you and me, we're going to have a little talk. I'll make sure you walk away with a lesson in manners you'll never forget, you dumb shit." Lord knew how I'd manage, but sometimes the threat was as good as the deed. Royce had taught me as much.

Gabe clenched his fists together so tightly, I could hear his knuckles cracking. He looked at Seth, silently asking permission for something. The other Were shook his head, a smile quirking his lips. "I see why Chaz likes you. You are one brass-balled bitch."

"Hey, I'm a New Yorker. What did you expect?"

"You should be afraid," Gabe said, his voice gone deeper, guttural with anger. Seth turned around, watching, but not saying anything. I think he was more curious how I'd handle a pissed off Were than worried something might happen to me or his friend. "You aren't one of us. Don't you know what we could do to you?"

"Try me, Fluffy. I've fought your kind before. You kids don't know who you're messing with."

Gabe snarled and started closer, but the other guy, the quiet one, reached out an arm to bar his way. "She's trying to rile you up. Don't fall for it. We'll need you later."

The angry Were stopped, staring back at me, his eyes taking on a subtle greenish luminescence. When he spoke, I took note of the hint of upper and lower fangs peeking between his lips. "You must have a death wish. Keep it up, and I'll oblige you later, once your boy toy is out of the way."

"Yeah, right. If there's anything left when Chaz is done with you, come talk to me."

I think the fact that I managed to pull off appearing bored, keeping the waver out of my voice, was part of what was making him so mad. That, and because I most likely had touched a sore point with him. He was worried that Seth wouldn't win, that Chaz would hurt him, and had no one to take it out on. His worry would become their worry. It would eat at them, make them doubt. It would give Chaz a better chance at coming out on top.

As the other two guys looked at each other, I

saw the unspoken hesitation there. Even Seth seemed nervous now, absently twining his fingers through a thick chain at his belt, something he hadn't been doing before.

It was enough to make me smile.

Chapter 11

God, I was bored. The guys had a pack of cards and were playing poker, but wouldn't let me in on the game. They kept a wary eye on me, staying close, but not bothering or talking to me. Gabe calmed down after a while. The other two, Richard of the near-silent disposition, and Curtis of the Day-Glo Mohawk, had talked him out of his upset, urging him into passing the time with the cards.

All of them had removed their jackets and shoes, prepped for a quick change in loose jeans or sweats and what looked like ratty secondhand T-shirts. None of them seemed to mind the cold on their bare arms or getting mud between their toes, whereas I was freezing my ass off in my damp clothes.

As the minutes, then hours, ticked by, I passed the time bored and annoyed, sitting on my butt staring off into the trees or watching them play. It was eerie how quiet the forest was. The only birdsong I could hear was distant, nowhere close to where we were sitting. No squirrels or rabbits or other small wildlife had come anywhere near us. Guess the wild animals were smart enough to stay away from Weres this close to the full moon, even if they still wore their human countenances.

I hoped Chaz wouldn't be too much longer. I was bored out of my skull and really had to pee. I wasn't about to ask the Goof Troop over there to let me hustle off into the bushes. Like it hadn't been embarrassing enough having been carted off like a sack of grain and then dealing with their snide comments about the scents on me.

I leaned back a little, staring up into the trees. There was one bird up there, a big, scrawny crow. Maybe the same one that had been in the trees the other night. It was staring down at us, watching the little gathering with one bright, beady eye, not making a sound. Probably waiting to see if we'd leave it some food or something.

Abruptly, the four guys lifted their heads in unison, staring back in the direction of the cabins. Chaz, Sean, Nick, Simon, and Dillon were standing in the dappled shadows filtering through the boughs, anger and irritation etched into their features. As soon as they knew they'd been spotted, they came closer, Seth and his men rising to meet them.

I surged up to my feet, intending to run to Chaz's side. Richard reached out and grabbed my arm before I'd taken two steps. "Not yet," he growled, his grip tight enough to make me wince.

"What the hell do you think you're doing, Seth?" Chaz demanded, looming over the shorter teenager.

"Right of ascension. Dragging you out here was the only way to do it without fighting everyone in the pack for a chance at you."

Chaz shook his head, his frown lessening and a sly, dark smile curving his lips. "If you wanted me to kick your ass, you didn't have to resort to trashing my cabin or hurting Shia to get it. I'll gladly take you on, anytime, anywhere."

Confusion briefly clouded Seth's features, soon replaced by anger. "I didn't touch your cabin."

"Whatever," Chaz snarled, his gaze shifting in my direction as he barked out a command at Richard. "You've done enough. Let her go. She doesn't have anything to do with this."

Richard's grip on me loosened marginally, but Seth twisted back and held up a staying hand. "No! You take your orders from me, not him."

Richard shifted uncomfortably, looking back and forth between Seth and his pack leader. Eventually, he lowered his head, pulling me closer in a silent affirmation of Seth's seniority. Chaz growled, the sound echoed by the other Weres at his side.

I simplified the problem by bringing my heel down sharply on Richard's instep, causing him to let go of me to clutch his injured foot. I followed up with an elbow into his face as he folded. Ducking the grasping hands of Gabe and Curtis, I rushed to Chaz's side, wrapping my arms around his waist as I slid to a stop. He squeezed my hand reassuringly, but pulled away, taking one threatening step closer to Seth.

Richard was on his knees, clutching his bleeding nose and cursing vehemently as he slumped in the mud. Curtis and Gabe didn't risk getting too close to Chaz's enforcers, who quickly stepped forward to shield me from them. Unlike the teenagers, these grown men were experienced fighters. Considering that their eyes were glittering with malice and the first signs of the change, daring them to keep coming, I didn't blame Seth's people for backing a few hasty steps away, leaving Seth to face Chaz alone.

"Good job, love," Chaz said, giving me a brief, fierce grin. I returned it in kind, proud of myself for the damage I'd done. I might not have had the belt with me, augmenting my strength, speed, and giving me tips and pointers on how to fight, but the self-defense classes I'd been taking helped keep me from being entirely useless in situations like this.

The bass rumbling in Seth's chest was unmistakably a threat, and I noted his eyes had shifted from a deep hazel into an amber color similar to my own. Sean and Dillon pulled me back to shield me from him, and I had to stand on tiptoe to see over their shoulders what happened next.

Between one blink and the next, Seth was shifting. He cried out a challenge before his human vocal cords were too changed by the shift to allow for speech, his last words trailing off into a long, drawn-out howl. "You're dead! You're all dead, unless you yield to me!"

I watched, fascinated, as Seth's chest deepened and his arms grew thick with muscle. The crack of bone and sinew adjusting and reforming was sickening, but fortunately didn't last very long since he'd forced a quick change. The fur that sprang out of his skin was a shade of deep brown a little darker than his hair, covering sleek muscles and a powerful frame that would rival Chaz for size if he had shifted, too. No wonder Seth thought he was badass. Still, size didn't necessarily mean one had smarts or skill or experience, things Chaz had in abundance.

Seth wasn't going full wolf either; he was assuming the half-and-half shape that he would be stuck in again tonight—just like the rest of the Weres—once the moon was full. If he survived, that is.

Doing this now was stupid. Despite the benefit of immense size and strength, he'd be weak for a few minutes from the pain of forcing a quick shift, more still as it wasn't yet nightfall. Chaz took advantage, stepping forward to clamp iron fingers around the wolfman's windpipe at the peak of his challenging howl, cutting off the sound with a high-pitched *"yark!"* With inhuman strength, Chaz slowly pulled the snarling, slavering jaws down until the wolf was eye-level, ignoring the claws that reached up and dug deep into his forearms.

"You made a big mistake, buddy. I've been waiting for this for a long time."

Dillon urged me to back up, and I noted Seth's boys were moving, too, giving the two men room to fight. Seth was scrabbling at Chaz's arms, fighting for air as his pack leader's grip tightened on his throat.

"See, this is why you'd never make pack leader. You're big and tough, sure. But you don't think things through."

Chaz shoved Seth back in a move that looked

casual, but had enough force behind it to partially uproot the tree he slammed the shifted Were into. The snap of roots was audible under the mud, and the tree listed dangerously to one side, swaying unsteadily as Seth used it to lever himself back up to his feet. Chaz didn't give him the opportunity to get his balance, one fist lashing out to punch Seth's jaw hard enough for blood and a few sharp teeth to go flying into the underbrush and mulch.

"Instead of leaning on low tricks and pranks, you could've fought your way up the ranks and gained some respect in the process."

He kicked Seth in the ribs, hard, as he tried to crawl away, whimpering in pain. Even I winced a little in sympathy at the thud of Chaz's hiking boot connecting with furred flesh, sure to leave a bruise deep enough that it would probably show even when Seth shifted back into his human form. Seth's buddies were all looking green around the gills, their gazes creeping up to the canopy above instead of watching their friend get the shit beaten out of him.

"Right now, you're just pathetic. You will continue to be pathetic until you realize that the pack structure is in place for a reason." It was painful to watch as Chaz tangled his fingers in the fur at the scruff of Seth's neck, yanking him up to grind the harsh words home, speaking right into one of those triangular, tufted ears. "You don't fuck with the structure unless you're ready to take a higher place in it. You. Are. Not. Ready. You won't be ready for a long time, not unless you learn some fucking respect. If you start showing me and your superiors that respect, maybe we'll teach you how to climb in the hierarchy without getting your ass handed to you."

With that, Chaz let Seth drop to sprawl gracelessly on the ground, tail tucked between his legs as he curled up on his side. Blood trickled down the side of the Were's jaw as he voiced low, pained whimpers. Throughout the entire fight, if you could call it that, Chaz hadn't broken a sweat and had barely ruffled his hair. The only signs he'd even taken part in it were the gouges in his forearms and the slightest spattering of mud around the hem of his jeans.

He brushed his hands off, staring down at the fallen Were for a long moment, and I soon realized he was waiting for something. Seth eventually managed to work himself up to a position where he could reach out and lick at one of Chaz's hands, keeping crouched low to the ground with his head down, looking like a dog that had just gotten a kick from its master. Chaz reached out and absently ran his hand over the silken fur between Seth's ears, at once a comforting and a warning gesture.

"Let's not do this again for a while, hmm?"

Without waiting for any sign of agreement, he turned away from Seth and walked over to me. Dillon and Sean moved aside so he could wrap an arm around my shoulders. Though I was grateful for the warmth and protection he afforded, the casual violence he'd just visited on Seth made it difficult to relax against him.

"Sorry you had to see that, love. They didn't hurt you, did they?"

"No, I'm okay," I said, glancing back over my

shoulder to see Curtis and Gabe moving over to Seth's side, helping him to stand. At Chaz's light nudge, I turned my attention back on him, and we started on the path back to the cabins. "What about you? And is Ethan okay? Seth said something about bane. . . ."

"Don't worry about Ethan."

The way he said it made me quiet for a moment, biting my lower lip. The silence stretched uncomfortably, punctuated by the crackling of twigs underfoot.

"That was really something," I ventured, hesitant. He didn't look terribly upset, but his eyes were still glowing with agitation. "I didn't know you could beat up a shifted Were like that."

"If he'd stayed human, or if I'd shifted too, it might have gotten ugly. He was vulnerable because of forcing the shift so fast, and I took advantage of it." Chaz shrugged, grimacing as he held up his free arm to look over the deep scratches. "I'm just glad he didn't hurt you. I might have had to do some real damage if he had."

Nick laughed, and some of the tension eased from Chaz's too-tight muscles. "You are such a show-off."

"Part of what makes him a good pack leader," Sean said, clapping Chaz lightly on the shoulder as he came up beside us. "You had me worried for a second. I wasn't sure what you were waiting for when Seth started to change."

"Timing is everything," Chaz said, rubbing his hand up and down my arm as I shivered and leaned into his warmth. It was dark between the trees, and I didn't like the idea of having a bunch of unfriendly werewolves behind us, possibly planning revenge. "I hope he learned enough of a lesson not to push his luck and try me again for a while."

"He didn't," Sean said flatly, ducking a low-hanging branch. "He'll lick his wounds for a bit, and then figure out some other way to try to get you out of the way. He won't accept that he lost so badly with grace."

Simon snorted. Dillon shook his head and rolled his eyes. Chaz remained thoughtful.

"I don't know. He barely scratched Chaz, and he's not stupid. He's got to know that means he's lost some face, and that no one will follow him now," I said, glancing at Sean.

"That's true. Curtis, Gabe, and Richard have to know they aren't going to be welcome back into the pack without making some amends for snubbing Chaz." Nick rubbed his jaw thoughtfully, looking back over his shoulder. "Not that they were very welcome to begin with, but they'll either take the fall back to the lowest of the low with Seth, or they'll try to save face by ignoring him now."

"There's nothing saving them from the fall they're about to take," Chaz said, fingers tightening briefly on my shoulder as I stiffened at the mix of anger and fierce satisfaction in his voice. "I was giving this some thought earlier. Alec Royce offered to pay a pretty hefty sum to have a couple of the pack work for him as bodyguards and to possibly act as the occasional donor. It'll help out the rest of the pack overall, improve relations with the leech, and teach them a lesson in one fell swoop."

My jaw dropped in shock. It took a second for me to realize I wasn't the only one shocked speechless. Relations between vamps and Weres just didn't account for something like this. It just wasn't done. Chaz would be making inroads to a place that didn't bode well for anybody; it would either make his pack respected and feared as much as the Moonwalkers, or backfire and result in the Sunstrikers being social pariahs to the other packs.

"That's pretty harsh," Dillon muttered, the first to find his voice.

"Yes, but it will be worth it. They'll be out of my hair, and learn a lesson in the process of doing the whole pack some good."

"I didn't take you for a player in politics," I said, hiding the tremor in my voice with bravado. The fact that he was talking to Royce without my knowledge worried me a great deal, even more so now that he was planning on farming out some of his wayward pack members to the vampires. I knew Chaz could be cold, but I hadn't thought he could be *this* ruthless. It bothered me more than I would've thought, especially considering what those boys had done. Yes, I wanted them to pay for it, but not necessarily like that. The rest of the pack would be scared shitless that the same might happen to them, I was sure. Not to mention that Royce often had other reasons behind why he did things, reasons you wouldn't find out about until it was too late and you were in too deep to pull yourself out again.

"Don't worry," Chaz said, eyes bright as he looked down to me. "Think of it this way. They'll never bother you again, and anybody else who might have thought to try something will have to think twice. If they even consider doing anything, they know it'll mean going back to the vamps. That should be enough to stop anyone in the pack from messing with either of us."

"Yeah," I said, not quite meeting his eyes. Yes, it would be an effective deterrent. But at what cost?

Chapter 12

When we got back, Chaz made me swear up and down that I wouldn't go anywhere without an escort—not even back and forth from our cabin to the lodge. Nobody thought Seth would try anything again so soon, particularly as he didn't know yet exactly how much trouble he was in, but Chaz wasn't willing to take any chances.

Considering what I'd just gone through, I didn't argue too much. While I wasn't sure a babysitter was necessary just to head up to the lodge, I did have to admit I was worried that Gabe or Richard might seek revenge on me. Despite my showing off back there, like Chaz, I'd used guile and the element of surprise to do what little damage I had done. If they had been shifted, my strength wouldn't have been enough to do much more than ruffle their hair. Not to mention the fact that I could've been at risk of being turned furry, too. While I didn't mind it happening to someone else, the idea of howling at the moon a few days out of the month myself was not a pleasant prospect.

The other guys hung around our cabin, ostensibly to stick with Chaz until moonrise. I was pretty sure they were really there to deter anyone else who might have been thinking about having a go at him. Since Seth had obviously been defeated, I didn't think any other Were would go after him now, but their caution and show of loyalty pleased me.

While they sat around the table and on the bed, making the tiny space incredibly cramped, I found fresh clothes to change into. I didn't pay much attention while they talked, though it was amusing that they were still hyped up and excited from the scuffle. They were so busy talking over each other, I don't think they noticed when I slipped into the bathroom to change.

When I stepped out of the bathroom to find that Kimberly and Paula had joined the impromptu party, I had to make an effort to clamp down on my irritation. Kimberly I didn't mind so much; she smiled and gave me a wave of greeting. Paula was another matter. The look on her face was one of thinly disguised dislike. God, you'd think I'd gone and kicked her favorite puppy or something.

Both of them were sitting on the bed and watching me as I headed to the kitchenette to prep hot water and towels to clean up Chaz's wounds. Since they'd been caused by the claws of another Were, they would heal slowly. For most Weres, that would mean days instead of weeks to heal up the damage. For Chaz, that meant hours instead of minutes, thanks to his status as an alpha. He wouldn't get an infection from the wounds, but I didn't like looking at the gouges or the idea of him forgetting and getting blood on more of his clothes or the bed or something.

Nick vacated a chair for me, and I scooted over to pull Chaz's arm into my lap. The girls didn't say anything while the guys talked and joked about Seth's getting his ass handed to him, and how much he was going to enjoy being the vampire's little pet plaything.

Sean was snickering at something Dillon had muttered that I really wasn't interested in hearing. "You beat him up pretty bad. He's going to have a hell of a time with the hunt missing those teeth."

"He deserved it," Simon said. "He's lucky he didn't get branded rogue and kicked out of the pack for all the trouble he's caused."

"It's a life lesson they've all got to learn sometime. I was almost as much of a disrespectful cur as he's being now," Chaz said, wincing as I scrubbed a bit harder than was strictly necessary at the dried blood on his arm. "You can't piss on the pack leader's parade and expect to get away with it. He's lucky he's Ricky and Armina's kid, or I might have done some permanent damage to teach him a lesson. I'm still ticked about my clothes. The bane in Ethan's tea, too; that was low, even for Seth."

"You will cause permanent damage once he figures out you're not kidding about sending him to Royce. Though, really," Dillon stopped himself and laughed, shaking his head before continuing,

"I have to say, I'd pay good money to see him playing cabana boy to a leech."

"I can't believe you, Chaz," Paula said, the disgust as thick in her voice as it was in her expression, deepening when she turned a hateful glare on me. "Are you doing this for her?"

Chaz's hand had been limp in my lap until Paula spoke; it abruptly turned into a tight fist, sending bright rivulets of blood spilling from the cuts. As he tensed in preparation to stand, I quickly wrapped a towel around his arm, then put a restraining hand on his shoulder as I stood instead.

"Let me handle this."

He glanced over at me, the low, ominous rumble in his throat dying into silence as curiosity won out over his anger. At his nod, I quietly moved over to where Paula sat on the bed. Kimberly slid away from us, leaving me to face Paula alone. I stopped a couple feet back from the bed, fists propped on my hips as I met the Were's baleful glare with a harsh stare of my own. She looked away first.

"I am tired of your shit, Paula. I didn't do anything to deserve the harsh words, the mean looks, or the petty name-calling. Was I in thrall to Royce at one point? Yes. Am I now? No. So," I said, taking another step forward, aggressive enough that she pulled away from me. "I don't know where this animosity is coming from, but how about you knock it the fuck off and try to treat me with a little respect, hmm?"

Her gaze darted to the others, her mouth opening in dismay at seeing that Kimberly had distanced herself from this argument. That was fine and dandy by me. The last thing I needed was more of the pack to turn on me.

"Fine," she muttered softly, so quiet I could barely hear it.

"If you have a beef with me, make it because of something I did to you, not over a rumor. Got it?"

"Yes," she said, a little louder now.

"Good," I said, though now that I'd won, I wasn't sure what to do. She just sat there, not looking at me, and everyone else was being awfully quiet. After a minute, I sighed and turned away, intending to fix up Chaz's other arm.

As soon as my back was turned, she was moving. The only reason I managed to duck out of the way in time was because I heard the squeak of bedsprings. Despite my quick reflexes, her nails raked down my arm, catching in the fabric of my sleeve. With her augmented strength, she might have broken the skin even with those blunt, French-manicured nails. Either way, I wasn't interested in finding out if she could, and I was pissed that she'd stooped to this tactic to deal with me. If I let this slide, the others would see me as a pushover. I'd never have anyone's respect in the pack, and she'd think she could get away with it time and again until I showed her I could stand up for myself.

She wanted to play hardball? I'd play it her way, then.

The others moved to hold Paula back, but before anyone could come between us, I spun around and decked her across the jaw. She staggered to the side, clutching at her bleeding mouth and staring at me in shock. Kimberly practically leapt off the bed and backed out of the way, giving us room.

Anger glinted in Paula's eyes, and she bared bloodstained teeth as she lashed out to return the favor. I was prepared for it this time. Despite her incredible speed and reflexes, I managed to avoid the worst of it and was only struck a glancing blow on the shoulder, stumbling back a step or two.

The pain was bad, but I ignored it and aimed a kick at her solar plexus, intending to put her off balance and knock the wind out of her. Thanks to my anger it was a sloppy move, and I had to hop back to regain my balance.

She doubled over, the air going out of her with a pained sound, so I helped her along to the floor by hooking my foot behind hers and sweeping her off her feet. Breath knocked out of her, she stayed down when I put my sock-covered toes on her throat with just enough pressure to constrict her air.

She clearly hadn't expected me to be trained to fight back and probably hadn't thought I could hurt her too badly with my measly human strength. Or that superior—in her case, supernatural—strength didn't always win out in a fight. To keep her from getting any ideas, I put enough pressure on her windpipe to cut her breaths down to wheezing whimpers.

One of the guys reached out to urge me to ease up, but I shrugged the grasping hand from my shoulder and kept my gaze locked on Paula's. Her fingers scrabbled at my sweats, seeking purchase to pull my leg off her. I leaned down harder and leveled a finger at her face, making sure she knew I wasn't kidding around.

"Listen up, Paula, and listen good. I may not have your strength or speed. Hell, I may not even be that good a hunter—but I've fought bigger, badder Others than you and come out on top before. Don't test me again. You'll lose."

She nodded vehemently, as best she could around my foot crushing her throat. Since she looked more concerned about getting air than getting revenge, I backed up, watching her warily. I about jumped out of my skin when I felt another hand on my uninjured shoulder, but it was just Chaz coming to stand behind me to show support. The others had gotten up and were doing the same, even Kimberly moving gracefully from behind the bed to stand at my back. It was odd, really odd, particularly as they had to cram themselves into a small space in order to be at my back, but exhilarating, too. They supported me, and that was what mattered.

Paula slowly rolled onto her hands and knees, creeping over to take my hand. I withdrew quickly when it looked like she was about to do the same thing Seth had done with Chaz, licking his hand and looking like a kicked dog begging forgiveness from its master.

"Don't. If you're sorry, just say so."

A brief flash of anger burned in her eyes as she glanced up at me before she nodded, sitting back on her heels. Once she found her voice, even through the rasping she sounded almost as petulant as I did whenever I had to apologize to Royce. "I'm sorry. I won't do it again."

Chaz nudged my arm. "She's acknowledging you as her superior. You could accept it with a little grace, you know."

I looked at him blankly. "What?"

"She's doing it because you bested her. This is how she publicly admits you're senior to her in the pack structure."

I made a face, gesturing at the others. Ouch, that pulled some muscles in my shoulder that really didn't want to be pulled. Note to self: no more fistfights with Weres. "I'm not part of the pack. You guys know that, right? I'm just the pack leader's girlfriend."

Chaz laughed faintly, though it sounded strained. "You became more than that when you saved us from the guy using the Focus. If not for you, there might not even be a Sunstriker pack anymore."

"I'd rather have you as part of the pack than not, even if you aren't a Were. You're strong enough to hold your own if you can best Paula with your bare hands. Or feet. Whatever," Simon said.

I rubbed a hand over my face, not happy with this. If they were going to look at me as a pack member, did that mean I had to act like one? Was I going to have to defend my stance as a dominant member every time somebody got peeved at me? Granted, it was satisfying knocking Paula on her butt, but I wasn't so sure I'd be able to do it again without the element of surprise on my side. It was a step up from being "the pack leader's girlfriend" in their eyes, but it was also dangerous, uncharted territory. It might give them ideas to pressure me into becoming a pack member for real before long. Particularly once they found out I'd brought a contract with me for Chaz to sign. It wouldn't be legal until filed with the courts, but they might consider it a gesture on my part to *really* join the pack.

Everyone eased back into his or her seat, acting like nothing had happened, like I hadn't just had a knock-down-drag-out fight with Paula. Even with the bruise purpling her jaw and the raspy breaths, she was looking more normal and relaxed than I'd seen her since she started going off on me about Royce. Apparently kicking her butt was just the right thing to make her respect me. Who would've thought?

Still, the speculative looks the others were giving me now, even if tempered with more respect than before, had me worried. I could almost hear their thoughts, they were so obvious. They might have been hiding it behind shifting the talk to what they'd do for dinner tonight, maybe hitting the town for pizza, but I still caught the twinkle of interest and concern as each of the Weres snuck glances at me now and again.

Tonight definitely wasn't the night to show the contract to Chaz—but the day's events did raise some tough questions I wasn't in any frame of mind to answer.

Would I consider becoming one of them and taking a place in the pack structure for real?

Chapter 13

We went to town for dinner. And by we, I mean the entire freaking pack. We all piled into about twenty cars and converged in a mob on one of the few restaurants scattered along the main street cutting through the town, taking up all the parking spaces for two or three blocks. The few people out and about tonight watched the strange, eclectic mix of people mingling together, a couple of young kids dashing between the adults, discussing whether to get pizza or check out the diner down the street.

Most of the votes swung for pizza, so that's where we went. There weren't nearly enough seats inside for so many of us, but we cheerfully harassed the poor kid behind the counter with enough orders to make his head spin. When he asked Dillon to repeat his order for the third time, Billy's mom got fed up and wrote everything down on a piece of paper for him. The teen was grateful, though when someone mentioned separate tabs he turned an interesting shade of white under the fading summer tan. Obviously they didn't get this many walk-ins very often or orders this big outside the tourist season. Maybe not even then.

It was even funnier when the kid realized we weren't having some kind of wacky family re-union. He gaped when he spotted a pack tattoo and recognized it for what it was, eyes dilating and his pallor swiftly shifting into a flush of fear and embarrassment as he stammered out that it would take them a couple hours to get this many pizzas ready on such short notice. That would cut it close to sunset, but we'd manage. His relief at the lack of disappointed growls and sudden shapeshifts was so obvious, it was comical.

I was surprised the kid was so nervous consider-ing the Cassidy family lived out here. Then again, maybe the Cassidys were more private with their business than the Sunstrikers. After all, we were visitors from the big city, and the tolerance for things with fur and fangs was generally a lot higher there than out in the boondocks. Not to mention the Sunstrikers currently outnumbered the townsfolk on the street.

They weren't making an effort to hide what they were either. Many of them were in short sleeves, not bothering with jackets, showing off their pack tats on their upper arms. Some of the women had halter tops, and the few who hadn't put their pack tattoo on their arms made sure they were visible on their shoulder blades. If the tattoos didn't do it, the scruffiness and lack of warm clothing to combat the bitter October chill would have given them away.

With this many of them together in public, I doubted anyone would try anything more than jacking up prices or whispering empty threats when they thought the Weres were out of earshot. Still, it worried me a little when the kid rushed off into the kitchen area as soon as he got the last payment, hiding back there with the two cooks. A handful of Sunstrikers lingered outside having a smoke or talking on cell phones while the rest of us were crammed inside.

A couple of the girls casually mentioned they were going to window-shop while they waited for the pizza. As I was rubbing my sore shoulder, Kimberly lightly brushed my arm to get my attention. "Do you want to come with us?"

I hesitated before answering, taking stock of who was going. Paula was sulking, off in one of the booths by herself. The other girls were smiling and waving me over, hoping I would come with them. Oh, what the hell. I needed new underwear anyway.

"Sure, why not," I said, hefting my purse up a little higher on my shoulder and giving Chaz's hand a reassuring squeeze before letting go and joining the group of women gathering at the door.

It was surprisingly enjoyable walking up and down the tiny boulevard, talking with these women, finding out who they were and exclaiming over some of the hiking and ski equipment in the windows of some of the shops. Though it was cold for me, none of them seemed bothered by it. The exertion of walking around kept my blood circulating, keeping the worst of the cold at bay. And it was nice to be accepted into the fold. Either they weren't aware of, or didn't care about, the drama-fest that had taken place with Paula or the fact that I'd once been bound to vampires.

I did pick up a couple of new T-shirts and pairs of jeans while we were out. Sadly, the only shop in this part of town that carried underclothes wasn't open and looked like it was closed for the season. Looked like I'd be going commando for the rest of the trip. Lucky me.

At one point, I pulled Kimberly aside to ask her about Paula. Since they were friends, I hoped that she might be able to shed some light on why Paula had such a beef with me. After some hedging on her part, I finally asked her directly if she knew what the problem was.

"Look," she said, with a tone of finality, "it's nothing you can do anything about. She's got issues with vampires and anyone connected with them. A lot of us do. Ignore it if you can, because she's not going to let it go, and I don't think there's anything you can do to change it."

With that lovely piece of advice, things stayed strained between us until I pointed out a fur-lined ski jacket on display in a picture window that we agreed would look adorable on her. She smiled and relaxed, oohing and aahing over it with the other girls.

Dropping the subject did seem the safest bet— for now. I'd dig into the problem later, when I had some of the bigger issues surrounding this trip sorted out.

After a bit, one of the guys hanging around outside the pizza parlor waved us over, and we all returned to our respective cars as the pizza boxes were piled into trunks or backseats or held on the laps of eager, hungry Weres. No doubt, there would be pizza crusts under seats and grease on door handles before we made it back to the lodge.

The rutted dirt road was far less frightening in daylight. Music was blaring out of somebody's radio as we all gathered in the parking lot, snagging slices of pizza, laughing and chatting and generally having a good time. Somebody went inside and got Mrs. Cassidy and George's girlfriend to bring out glasses and pitchers of beer and soda, and before I knew it, we had some of the other guests and the rest of the Cassidy clan joining our impromptu party in their parking lot.

We swapped stories and jokes. Kimberly goaded me into trying the Hawaiian style (which was totally gross—pineapple chunks and tomato sauce were never meant to meet). Billy even got me to show him my scars. He, his small friend, and the half dozen other Weres watching me, were all suitably impressed at the neat surgical incisions the doctors had made to repair my ribcage and halt some gnarly internal damage caused by being beaten to shit by Rohrik Donovan over a year ago. The Moonwalker pack leader hadn't wanted to kill me, so he'd bucked the command of the holder of the Focus by hurting me really, really badly instead. Afterward, he and his pack had helped pay a majority of the ungodly expensive medical bills.

Some secret benefactor had paid the rest. I still didn't know who was responsible, and was afraid of finding out whether it had been Alec Royce or The Circle. If it was Royce, he'd find a way to make me pay for it later. If it was The Circle, that meant the mage coven still wanted something out of me. Whoever it was wouldn't let it stay a secret forever, but I was perfectly willing to turn a blind eye until they reared their ugly heads and demanded some form of recompense.

Once a few of the guys got some alcohol in their systems, prompted by the stories I was regaling Billy with, they started showing off their scars and boasting about the fights they'd had. Mr. Cassidy was one of the first, proudly pulling up his shirt to show tanned, leathery skin puckered with an incredible number of scars, enough to show that life hadn't been easy for the friendly old fart. Chaz surprised me by pointing out a few of his own. Guess they were playing a game of "who's got the biggest cojones" for the sake of the few girls hanging around; we were giggling and whispering over what was revealed aside from a few imperfections on the men's skin.

I have to admit, it was a little disturbing when some of them got around to showing off the bites or claw marks that had led to their lycanthropy infection.

As the sun drifted closer to the horizon, people started drifting off to their cabins to get ready for the shift. Feeling a little worn out, I sidled over to Chaz to find out what he was up to. If I was lucky, he'd come spend a little time with me back in the privacy of our cabin before he had to leave and join the rest of the pack in the hunt.

He was deep in discussion with Dillon and Nick on what to do when Ethan shifted, and who was going to be responsible for keeping him from breaking off from the pack to hunt two-legged prey. Peachy.

"Hey, you've got to get ready for tonight, right?" I said, dearly hoping he'd catch the hint. "You ready to go?"

No such luck. "Not just yet. I've still got a little work to do. Dillon, can you take her?"

I sighed as the other Were nodded and got to his feet, giving me a brief, tight smile. He hid his irritation well, but I knew he didn't like babysitting me. He was the same Were who had fallen asleep when he should have been watching me while I was coming off the blood bond at Royce's downtown apartment building. I'd snuck right out of the building and gone tearing off into nearby Central Park to find the missing pieces of myself and put some semblance of my sanity back together. It had been an incredibly stressful time, what with being bound to two vampires simultaneously, having killed a bunch of people, and having watched others get murdered right before my eyes.

Yeah, that had worked out real well.

Chaz had never told me if he'd said or done anything to Dillon for slacking off, and Dillon had always been friendly enough when we went on group outings. The tightness of his mouth and faintest narrowing of his eyes was enough of a warning that he was still ticked at me for leaving him holding the bag at Royce's last month. I'd never thought about how awkward that must have been for him, having to explain, not just to Chaz but also to the vampire, how I'd escaped their protection. Catching a few zees wasn't a good excuse when your pack leader's girlfriend might potentially be called to the side of a murderous, psychotic vamp but, hey, I was myself again. I wasn't complaining.

It might not have helped much, but I gave him a weak, apologetic smile, doing what I could to muster up the courage to ask for forgiveness. His look of irritation faded, and he rose with the smooth grace that said his wolf instincts were urging him to shift and hunt. He came to a halt by my side.

"Be back in a few," he said to the others, who all nodded and turned back to their discussion. Chaz gave my hand a parting squeeze of reassurance before turning to answer a question from Simon.

We stayed quiet, walking side by side on the way back to the lodge. I thought about how I wanted to word my apology to him, since he deserved more than my ignoring the fact that, even if he'd slacked, he *had* helped me out. Judging by what Paula thought of me, I was sure it had taken some convincing on Chaz's part to get him to watch my sorry butt.

Just as we reached the doors leading inside, a howl of pain cut the air. Both of us stopped in our tracks, looking back the way we'd come. Dillon didn't hesitate long, shoving me behind him none too gently while he scanned the area for the source of the sound. People were shouting and shuffling around, either looking for cover or trying to locate the source of the cries.

"Go inside," he ordered, not waiting to see if I complied. He ran off among the cars, back the way we'd come.

I clung to the door handle for a second, hesitating. What the hell was going on?

Another voice sent slivers of ice threading through my veins, goading me into a run. "It's silver! They shot him with silver!"

I hadn't heard a gunshot, but it was enough to frighten me into action. Chaz had once been shot with silver. He had survived it, but a wound inflicted with the pure metal guaranteed it would heal close to human-slow if it wasn't removed immediately. Certainly it would scar. Who had been hurt, I wondered. Though, honestly, my worry was more about *where* the Were had been injured. If the damage was to something vital, he could bleed out or worse. I didn't like thinking that way, and until I saw it I was going to do my best not to think the worst. I'd pulled bullets out of Chaz; I could do it for someone else if I needed to.

A bunch of guys were going Were, luminescence glimmering in their eyes and fangs peeking out between their lips as they snarled in fury. About a dozen of them trotted off toward the tree line, I assumed to search for the culprit. To attack now, when the pack was together at the peak of their strength, took a depth of bravery or stupidity like nothing I'd ever seen. Whoever it was must be suicidal.

Mr. and Mrs. Cassidy were hovering where I'd

seen Chaz and his buddies sitting earlier. There
were too many crowding around to see who'd
been hurt. As soon as Nick spotted me trying to
see what was going on, he shoved a few people out
of the way and took my arm, yanking me closer.

I gave a high-pitched yelp at the rough treatment, giving him a mixed sheepish and rebellious
look as he growled at me. "Get down! Whoever it
is hasn't been caught yet; they might make a go
for you, too. Why didn't you go inside?"

"I thought I could help whoever was hurt," I
said, pulling out of his grip. Disgruntled at being
dragged around and then hovered over by the
concerned Weres, I gave him a belligerent poke
in the shoulder. "I'm not a child. Don't treat me
like one. Who's hurt?"

Looking as mad as I felt, he pointed at the
slumped figure on the ground, and I immediately
understood why they were all so concerned.

Chaz lay still on the ground, breath hissing out
between his teeth and eyes scrunched shut as he
clutched at his shoulder. An arrow shaft pro-
truded from between his fingers, and the skin visible between the blood and tears in his shirt was
raw and red from silver-reaction. The arrow
hadn't hit anything vital, but the silver could
spread like infection through his bloodstream if
it stayed there too long. As the blood drained
from my face, I elbowed past the others clustered
close to him to touch his cheek, a thread of fear
twisting my gut as he opened pain-glazed eyes to
look at me.

Damn it all to hell, whoever was doing this was
really going to pay.

Chapter 14

"Go inside, love; we'll take care of this," Chaz grated out, forcing the words. Someone had broken off the fletched end of the arrow, but the point was still deeply embedded in the muscle of his shoulder, and no one seemed to know what to do. It was obviously hurting him badly, because he was having a tough time speaking around the pain.

Someone had once told me that the touch of silver to a werewolf was like putting your hand against a frying pan with the flame turned up full. The longer you kept it there, the deeper the wound and the more flesh it burned. Keeping it against your skin would almost guarantee permanent damage. By itself, it wasn't a life-threatening wound, but if the arrow had come closer to his heart or some other vital organ, it could've been. The longer that little arrowhead stayed in there, the higher the chances the muscles around the wound would be too injured to heal properly, meaning he'd lose mobility in that shoulder or arm. A lesser Were might have bled out or had the silver taint their blood too much to recover, but as long as this was handled quickly, Chaz would be okay. He'd have nothing more than a scar to show for it.

We didn't have any doctors in the pack, and God alone knew where the nearest hospital was. If I could pry a bullet out of him, I could do this, too. I hoped.

"Back up, please. Give me some room, guys."

"No, Shia! Get inside. Whoever did this is still out there," Chaz said.

"I'll get inside as soon as I take that thing out. Guys, hold him down, please?" I turned to Nick and Dillon, gesturing for them to keep him still. They looked helplessly between me and Chaz, obviously not wanting to upset their pack leader, but also wanting to give me the chance to help him. None of them seemed interested in touching the wooden shaft of the arrow, as though that part of it would magically turn into silver and start hurting them too. "Come on, we don't have all night."

Reluctantly, the two guys gripped Chaz's upper arms, holding him down against the log we'd been sitting on earlier, muttering apologies as they did. Simon leaned on his legs without being asked, and I was grateful for the help. Growling soft epithets under his breath, Chaz shut his eyes and waited for the inevitable, his expression and the tension in his muscled frame telling me that he was steeling himself the way that someone else might for getting a shot at the doctor's office. This wasn't going to be pleasant.

I took a deep breath to steady myself and put

one hand around the shaft of the arrow. I didn't know whether it was barbed or not. Yanking it out might do more damage than leaving it in there. Using the edge of Chaz's ruined shirt, I gently brushed some of the blood out of the way and peered at the wound, trying to catch a glimpse of the silver head through the swelling, irritated flesh. Gross. Only the memories of having seen far, far worse from Max Carlyle's handiwork kept me from being too squeamish to do this.

The head of the thing didn't look barbed, but I wasn't sure. I had to move hair out of my face so I could see. The shifting shadows, as people behind me moved in and out of the light, also trying to catch a glimpse, didn't help either.

The arrow had lodged fairly deep and, though the silver was keeping the wound from closing, it was hard to see around the swelling the best way to drag it back out. Setting my free hand against his chest a little below where the arrow had pierced his skin, I used my other hand to pull it out as gently as I could.

There were a couple of times in the process of removing the stupid thing that I could feel it catch on muscle or tendon, making his breath hitch. I made every effort not to do any more damage on the way out than it had caused on the way in. Difficult to tell around the blood, but I was pretty sure I was pulling it out straight.

It took a few intense minutes, during which sudden muscle spasms or jerks made me grateful that some of the guys had agreed to hold Chaz down, but eventually the arrow was freed. I grimaced as I looked over the blood-coated shaft, noting that silver lined about half an inch of it above the arrowhead itself, guaranteeing the wound would be more irritated and slower to close. To a low-ranking Were, or a new shifter like Ethan, it would have been fatal.

Chaz lay there for a long moment, taking deep, shuddering breaths as the others stepped back, giving him room to recover. With a great deal of grumbling and groaning, he levered to his feet, waving off any efforts by the others to help. Keeping a hand pressed to the still-bleeding wound, he started off toward the woods, followed closely by the Weres who had stayed behind.

Despite the pain lacing his tone, there was anger and hard command in Chaz's voice. The promise of retaliation was almost enough to make me pity whoever had done this. Almost. "Do you know if the hunter has been found yet?"

"No," someone spoke up from behind us. "No one's come back from the forest yet. They're still looking."

Dillon touched my arm lightly as I moved to follow, giving me pause. "You should go inside now. Let us handle this."

"She can hold her own," Chaz said, looking back over his shoulder. "We might need her help if there's more silver involved. Just keep her safe."

Dillon looked back and forth between us before shrugging and taking up a protective stance at my side, lingering a little too close for my comfort. I wasn't used to having a bodyguard, but he looked ready and determined to take a bullet or arrow for me if necessary. Weird. On the bright side, Chaz had confidence in me, if not necessarily for the reasons I would've wanted. That much was comforting.

Several of the shifted Weres were sniffing around the edges of the parking lot, moving through the trees in the general direction they thought the arrow had come from. Chaz called out when we got closer, though it was probably more for my sake than theirs.

"Find anything?"

"No," someone replied, puzzled. "There's no spoor. Not a hint of anyone's having been out here except for the kids earlier."

"The hell?" Nick muttered. "There must be something."

Frowning, Dillon looked up in the trees. "Did anyone check for any sign up there?"

"No. Why?"

Dillon pointed upward, and though I looked, I couldn't see anything. The others around me muttered curses and exclaimed softly as they saw something I couldn't make out in the shadowed limbs above our heads.

"What is it?" I asked, momentarily annoyed at being handicapped by my paltry human senses.

Nick stomped over to a particular tree, and one of the shifted Weres came too and stared upward, holding out a clawed hand to catch Nick if he slipped as he started climbing. It was strange, but somehow right. I knew the wild-looking beast in front of me would never hurt one of his own. I was a different story. The way those feral golden eyes watched me when I came closer was just plain creepy.

"There's some equipment or something tucked

into the branches up there. Hold on a second,"
Nick called down, probably more for my sake than
anybody else's.

The others gathered around the base of the
tree. Chaz was looking better, and he slid his
good arm around my shoulders, head tilted up
like the rest of us to watch Nick climb.

A few moments later he shimmied back down,
landing in a crouch much more like a feral beast
than a man. He had a grim look on his face as he
showed a scrap of torn cloth and an arrow he'd
tied it around, along with a thick branch he'd obviously broken off. There were claw marks embedded in the wood, big and deep enough to
show they weren't from any ordinary bird or tree-
dwelling animal. No bear or other forest creature
large enough to make such marks would venture
so far up, practically to the top of the tree, where
the limbs would be too thin to carry its weight.
That was why Nick had climbed up there instead
of one of the shifted Weres.

"I don't recognize the scent on the cloth or the
branch. What about you, Armina?"

Armina? That meant the big black and gray
Were beside us was Seth's mom. I sorely hoped
she was more trustworthy than her son, though
I wasn't exactly holding my breath.

The great shaggy Were leaned forward, nostrils
flaring as it took in the scent of the cloth, arrow,
and tree branch. Shaking its—no, *her*—head, she
settled back on her haunches and spread her
clawed hands in a remarkably human gesture of
puzzlement. She didn't know who or what it was
from either. It was difficult to tell her thoughts

on the matter considering she couldn't talk in her current form, and the rapid shift would prevent her from turning back for a while. Most likely she wouldn't be able to talk about it until tomorrow, after the full moon had set and she'd gotten some sleep.

Did she not find anything because she was covering for her son? No, I didn't think so. There were other shifted Weres out here too, and they'd pick up what she missed—or covered up.

Some of the others came forward, pressing their faces close to the cloth or tree branch that Nick held out before him. Even Chaz took a cursory sniff, though none of them seemed to know what the scent was. Their inability to recognize it pissed Chaz off even more. I was alarmed to note his eyes were reflecting the last dying rays of sunlight filtering through the trees, cat-like in these shadows.

"This is un-fucking-believable. What the hell is out here? It's not one of us. It's not a Were-cat. What the hell is it?"

"I don't know," Nick said, fists clenched tightly around the items in his hands. "If I knew, I would tell you. It's Were-something, I just don't know what."

"Can I give it a whiff?" Mr. Cassidy asked, startling me. I hadn't seen him among the others earlier. Too busy getting blood on my hands and yanking arrows out of my boyfriend, I suppose. Mrs. Cassidy and George were also there, a little apart from the others. It struck me as an unspoken show of their being different from, but supportive of, the Sunstrikers.

"Sure, be my guest," Chaz muttered sourly. The luminescence in his eyes seemed to be fading now that he was more irritated than outright angry.

Mr. Cassidy came forward, extending his hand for the cloth and the arrow. Nick handed them over, careful not to let the silver arrowhead brush against any exposed skin. The old man lifted it up, closing his eyes and inhaling deeply through his nose. His eyes flashed open, and he looked down in surprise, then anger. "I know this scent. This was a guest, a recent one."

"Who was it?" Chaz demanded.

"He goes by Hawk. I have a hard time believing he's the one who did this, though. I'd like to speak with him myself, but he checked out earlier today. So did the other two boys he was here with."

Crap. "Did you get their contact information when they arrived? Like an address attached to a credit card, a cell phone number, anything like that?" I asked.

He shook his head, frowning. "Maybe. I'd have to check my records."

"Check them, and let us know what you find," Chaz said.

"I can't just give out his information. Really, let me try to contact him first; then I'll let you know what comes of it."

"Hey, I'm a P.I.," I said. "I can call my partner back in the city and have her run a trace on the guy if you can give me any information about him."

Mr. Cassidy gave me a thoroughly disapproving look, handing the stuff back to Nick while he spoke to me. "Young lady, I'm not in the business of telling the secrets of my patrons. If he really was responsible for this, I can guarantee you I won't let him get away with it, but I'm not going to start a witch hunt based on a scent. There's a chance I'm wrong, that it was somebody else, and I'd like to make sure before you all go jumping to conclusions and do something we'll all regret later."

Chaz growled softly, though I knew he was struggling mightily to keep his temper in check. He liked the Cassidy family and this retreat, so I doubted he wanted to do something to get himself banned from returning. "Look, we just want to ask him a few questions, too. We're not going to kill him unless he tries something like this again."

"Sonny, you listen up, and you listen good. This is my territory. You're here by my invitation, and I *will* revoke it if you abuse my hospitality and good will. Give me the opportunity to find out what's going on in my own damned territory before you start horning in, got it?"

I'd never seen Chaz look so sullenly submissive as he did right at that moment. "Yes, sir."

"Good." Mr. Cassidy relaxed a little, some of the tension filtering out of his brawny frame. "I'll find the boy and let you know what he says as soon as I hear from him."

Chapter 15

Chaz was in a terrible mood after dealing with Mr. Cassidy. He didn't want to go back to the cabin. He didn't want to be hovered over. He didn't want to hang around the lodge. He didn't want to let any of the rest of the pack wander around alone. Basically, he was being an uptight pain in the ass.

After a little while, between the efforts of Simon, Nick, Dillon, Sean, and myself, we convinced Chaz to come back to the cabin and rest up so he wouldn't be completely strung out when he was forced to shift at moonrise. It took some effort but, once the guys left, he finally agreed to lie down. He sprawled on his stomach on the bed while I rubbed some of the tension out of his shoulders. He seemed to enjoy the fact I was straddling him more than the back rub.

"I don't understand it, Shia," he said, grunting a little as I dug into a knot in his lower back. "Why is that old fart protecting the guy who did this? You'd think he'd want it taken care of."

"He does. You heard him. He wants to handle it himself."

"I know. I just don't get why. It's not like he was the one who got shot."

"No," I said, "but he's got more to lose than you do if the guy gets away. No one will think this place is safe anymore if he doesn't do something about it personally. Give him a chance to deal with it."

"I guess," he grumbled, quieting as I leaned forward to ruffle his hair and place a kiss on his un-injured shoulder. A sigh escaped him as I rolled over to one side to lie back on the bed, folding my hands over my stomach as I looked at him.

"Honey, nothing else is going to happen on it tonight. Can you just try to relax and get some sleep? I promise I'll use some handy-dandy detecting skills tomorrow to track the guy down for you."

He stayed quiet for a moment, mulling it over before giving reluctant agreement. "Okay. Promise me you won't search for this guy alone? I don't want you to get hurt."

"Sure," I said, inwardly cringing. As soon as he left to hunt in the woods, I was going to sneak up to the lodge to see what I could find out about Mr. Cassidy's mysterious guests.

Chaz stayed as he was, hands tucked under his cheek as he lay still and quiet on his stomach. I reached out to run my fingers through his short blond hair. It was a little stiff from being gelled up into spikes. Gradually, his eyes closed, and I could see the tension trickling out of his muscles little by little as he tried to relax.

I kept up with the soothing stroking of my fingertips over his scalp until the alarm on the table buzzed a ten minute warning. Chaz groaned and rolled to his feet, rubbing his hand across his face.

"Will you be gone all night?"

He glanced at me over his shoulder before heading to the door, expression troubled. "I'll be back before dawn. Stay inside. I don't want Ethan to have any reason to be lured back to the cabins. You can watch from the window while we shift if you want, but don't set foot outside until daybreak."

Fur was already sprouting on his back. He paused at the door as I called his name.

"Be careful. Please, for me?"

"You got it, love," he replied, giving me a grin that bared a few too many sharp teeth before he sprinted out into the night, the door swinging shut behind him. I got off the bed and hurried to the window just in time to catch a glimpse of him being swallowed up by the shadows in the trees.

Since I'd fallen asleep last night and missed it, I was hoping to see the pack shift tonight. Watching Seth quick-shift didn't hold the same majesty as watching the entire pack be taken by whatever it is in the phases of the moon that makes them all change at the same time. I'd seen the entire pack go through the process of turning into their half-man, half-wolf forms once before, but that had been in a dark alley when I was more afraid of being eaten or killed than interested in watching them change.

Though I watched for them, gaze darting over every shifting shadow between the cabins and the trees, I was disappointed when I heard a lone wolf howl grow into two, three, then dozens joining in chorus—somewhere deep in the woods. The pack had shifted far beyond my line of sight and moved well away from the cabins already. Probably for the best; I wasn't the only one who could potentially be hurt by Ethan if he broke from the ranks and came charging back this way. With a guilty start, I recalled Billy and his playmate. If they carried the gene, they wouldn't shift until puberty, so were at risk of being attacked. No doubt there must have been a few other humans who had come along to watch over the kids, though I hadn't taken note of who they were in all the whirlwind introductions.

I waited by the window for a while, listening carefully for calls that would give me any hints as to the whereabouts of the pack. Since I couldn't hear much of anything out there, I figured I'd brew a cup of coffee. By the time I was done with it, the caffeine infusion should keep me alert during my search, and the pack should be long gone, deep into the wilds.

Neither Chaz nor I had bothered to check the kitchen when we came in. There was a note on the counter just like the one that had been pinned to the door of our cabin yesterday morning. The thick scrawl was becoming annoyingly familiar, despite the odd spelling and weird words or acronyms they were using.

*ATTN: THE THICK-SKULLED ASSHOLE IN
CABIN 27
WE TOLD U TO GTFO! GO BACK TO THE CITY!*

Well, this was a peachy development. I swept the paper aside and made my java, considering the implications of this latest note. I couldn't recall seeing it when we came back from the woods, so someone had put it in the cabin between the time we left to pick up the pizza and when Chaz got shot with the arrow. Whoever this was either had access to the cabins or was among the group that had joined us after Chaz fought Seth, possibly leaving it on the counter on his or her way out. Could it be we had two separate threats to deal with—in addition to Seth and his lackeys? It was possible that one person or group was writing the childish, hostile notes, and another was resorting to violence using the silver-tipped arrow.

By the time I finished my coffee, put on a jacket, and crept outside, only one other cabin nearby still had lights on. I waited a few feet from the door, listening carefully for any large predator, or fifty, rustling through the underbrush, but there was nothing out of the ordinary I could detect other than the tentative chirp of a few late season crickets.

The lodge was a dark blur against the reflected lights from the parking lot on the other side, and I kept to the trail as I worked my way toward it. The tiny solar-powered lights that rimmed the trail didn't do a lot to steady my nerves. The lights and moonlight flashing through the clouds above kept me from tripping on roots or walking into trees in the dark, but they made for deep, ominous shadows in which any beast of legend might crouch unseen in the underbrush.

I knew I really shouldn't be doing this. I could get hurt by Ethan. I could get hurt by that Hawk guy. Hell, I could get hurt by falling and breaking my ass in the mud. However, I was worried about Chaz, and would do anything in my power to prevent anything else bad from happening to him. To accomplish that, we needed to find Hawk, track him down, and confront whatever his issue was so he'd leave us the hell alone.

So I crept out into the night, feeling like I was playing "secret agent man" all over again. I prayed this time I wouldn't stumble into one of the pack, that I'd go unnoticed. So far, so good. There was nothing but the low burble of the creek and the smell of herbs and wood smoke on the chill night air. The boards of the bridge groaned a little under my weight, but otherwise I was pretty proud of my stealth.

When I tugged the lodge door, it opened easily. All of the lights in the lodge had been dimmed. Everyone but the shifters in the family must have gone to bed. There was enough light to make my way by, and I crept along as quietly as I could, straining to detect signs of anyone awake and moving around. Nothing.

When I reached the end of the hall, the dining area to my left was empty and dark. I peered very, very slowly and quietly around the edge of the doorway to my right, checking for anyone at the front desk. That room was also empty, only one light glowing by the front door. Somebody could've been hiding in the shadows, I suppose, but unless they were practicing their Navy SEAL moves, I'm pretty sure I was the only one creeping around like a dork in the dark.

There was a sign set up on the desk that directed RING BELL FOR ASSISTANCE, THANKS!—THE MANAGEMENT. No, thank you, I'll just help myself.

I straightened and moved over to the desk, pleased to see that there was no computer, only a registry book under some papers. Thank God for technophobes. I opened it up and skimmed through the most recent entries. Mr. Cassidy must have put Chaz's name down at some point after we'd first showed up, as I found his name neatly scrawled as the last guest to arrive. I was grateful to see the Cassidys meticulously filled in the name of one guest per cabin, probably the one paying the bill, followed by how many people were sharing the room, the date of arrival, and the date of departure. I skimmed over the list, noting the ones marked as having checked out.

After scanning over the columns, I came across the only one noted as having left the lodge yesterday. The writing was neat and concise, unmistakable. Howard Thomas + 2 guests, Cabin 3. Great. So our culprit was Howard Thomas or one of his guests. The registry didn't make note of any addresses or phone numbers, and the records for whatever payment was accepted must have been kept somewhere else.

I put the book back and pulled open the desk drawers to see if they kept receipts or anything else up here. The only things I could find in the

drawers were a lot of pens, Post-it Notes, manila
folders with inventories and order forms for stuff
in the dining hall and cabins, and lots of dust.
Yuck. Nothing useful, nothing that gave me any
more clues how to track down Howard Thomas.

Damn. It had been a long shot—most people
aren't trusting enough to leave anything related
to business finances out in the open—but I'd
really been hoping to find something up here.
The full name was better than nothing. I'd call
Sara in the morning and ask her to run a trace.

Just as I had carefully tidied up so nothing
would look disturbed when the Cassidys came out
in the morning, George's voice drifted from the
hallway opposite the dining area. As quietly as I
could, I ducked back down, squeezing under the
desk in hopes of going overlooked.

". . . and they don't know who you are. No, Pops
kept quiet; he's just really concerned you're
going to pull that cowboy shit again. Stay away
until they're gone, okay?"

What the hell was this?

"No, genius, they already suspect he's covering
for you. Stay out of sight until they've gone back
to the city, okay?"

He listened to whatever the response was on
the other end of the line and walked off somewhere, the sound of his voice fading and leaving
me sitting on pins and needles waiting to see if
he had stopped somewhere that he might spot
me when I came out of hiding. He'd gone quiet,
listening to the other end of the conversation, so
I wasn't sure exactly where he was.

Just as I was edging my way out from under

the desk, I had to stifle a scream as something slammed down on the counter right above my head. George was right behind me, on the other side of the counter.

"What the hell do you think we've been doing? Look, that girl he's dating—she said she was a P.I. Pops didn't give your real name, but it's only a matter of time before she starts nosing around and figures it out. Enough with this high school shit. Either stop dicking around and kill him or go back to the city until they're gone."

My heart was pounding so hard, I was positive George must be able to hear it echoing through the cavernous room. He laughed at whatever the response was, and the wood above me creaked as he put his weight on it, maybe leaning against it.

"Nah, I don't want to go out there with that new blood they dragged with them. I'm going to bed in a few minutes. You coming over for the game next weekend?"

The rest of the conversation couldn't have taken more than ten minutes but felt a lot longer, and had nothing to do with me, the Sunstrikers, or anything to do with the lodge. My heart gradually eased in my chest as they discussed mundane matters like the upcoming World Series. My money was on the Yankees, of course.

They talked long enough for cramps to settle into the arches of my feet and my lower back from staying crammed under the desk so long. Fear of discovery was enough to keep me absolutely still. After an age, George finally said good-bye and tossed the cordless phone on the counter. I had to stifle a gasp as it thunked across the wood over my head. He yawned and wandered off, his footsteps echoing in the quiet dark.

I waited longer than was probably necessary to make sure George wasn't coming back. Staying low, I crept out from behind the desk, scanning the dimly lit room and hallways for any sign of company. Without taking the time to stretch out my cramped muscles, I rushed to the doors and ran out into the night, fleeing to my cabin.

Chapter 16

On my way back to the cabin, shortly after I crossed the bridge, something growled at me from the bushes.

The tendons in my neck creaked as I caught movement, and twisted to see what it was. My blood turned to ice water as what I'd taken to be a tree trunk shifted—against the wind. It was too dark to really see the shape of the thing, other than that it was big. *Very* big. Bigger than Chaz when he was Were. It was growling at me, a lone human in the dark with no weapon and no hope of outrunning a predator this big.

My knees trembled as I backed away, slowly so as not to invite it—whatever it was—to charge. The thing growled again, deeper this time, and I froze in panic.

My gaze shifted upward to focus on the source of the low rumbling. Large yellow eyes gleamed out of the shadows briefly before that great, huge *something* moved. At first, I thought it was coming after me, and rapidly backpedalled, slipping in the mud. The thing wasn't after me, though; it pulled away, disappearing between the trees.

Knees weak with relief, I stumbled along until I reached my cabin. My hands shook as I worked the lock, dropping the key in my haste to get inside. Cursing, I scattered dirt and wood chips as I searched for it by feel. Once I found the damned thing, it took longer than it should have for me to get inside, as I kept twisting around and flattening against the door at every rustling bush or crackling of a tree branch behind me.

Once I wrestled the lock open, I slammed and locked the door behind me.

Coffee and paranoia were my companions for the rest of the evening. I dead-bolted the cabin door and stuck a chair under the knob. It wouldn't do much to stop a determined, rampaging Were, but it should give me enough time and warning to slip out a window or grab a makeshift weapon. I found myself wishing for a power cable or something to get the laptop up and running; this place was horribly claustrophobic without a phone or computer to connect to the outside world. If you needed to make a call, they had a bank of antiquated pay phones in the lobby of the lodge. Being cut off from technology was supposed to be part of the charm of the place. With my luck, I should've known better.

The caffeine infusions I took to stay alert helped, but also made me jittery and didn't make it any easier to concentrate on the notes I was scribbling down of what I knew about our enemies thus far.

The Cassidy family was involved somehow. I

wouldn't approach them without the Sunstrikers at my back. Mr. Cassidy was a Were of some kind; some of the others in his household could be Were, too. Despite the location of his home, he might belong to a pack, which meant other shifters could be hiding somewhere in the town or elsewhere on the property. If they were in on whatever was planned to hurt Chaz, they could have made an attempt on his life before now—if they had the numbers to stand up against the rest of the pack. I was guessing they didn't, or they would've been more open about their attacks. Whatever had growled at me out there hadn't been part of the Sunstriker pack, lending credence to my suspicions that while there might be other shifters on the property backing the Cassidys and whoever George had been talking to, there weren't enough of them to make a concerted effort against the Sunstrikers.

That, or they only wanted Chaz.

Everything Mr. Cassidy had said now came into question. It was possible he was covering for whoever had trashed our first cabin, and shot Chaz, and that he was deliberately covering for whoever this Howard Thomas person was. Keeping track of all the possible connections and consequences (or maybe the caffeine overdose) was making my head hurt.

I watched through a gap in the curtains as the first rays of the sun crested over the mountaintops, chasing away some of the mist creeping along the path between the cabins and heralding the coming of Sunday morning. I also had to stifle a scream as the door shook in the frame.

"Shia? What the hell! Open up!" Chaz sounded grumpier than he had been before he left last night.

Embarrassed by my reaction, I blotted up the few drops of coffee I'd spilled on my notes and rushed to the door, shoving the chair out of the way and yanking it open.

Chaz was clearly exhausted. There were dark circles under his eyes, which were bloodshot and hooded. He hadn't buttoned his jeans, and there was a bit of mud spattered on his arms. He slid past me, dropping some clothing on the chair and collapsing facedown on the bed. A few of the other Sunstrikers were sluggishly wandering from the tree line, some with jeans or sweatpants on, but most with clothes tucked under their arms. I slammed and bolted the door shut, returning the chair to its place under the knob.

Chaz regarded my antics with one eye, his voice gravelly and exhausted. "What are you doing?"

Rubbing my arms for warmth, I skittered over to the fireplace and poked at the log I'd tossed on there earlier, willing the flames to chase away the bone-deep chill I was feeling. "We've got a real problem here. I know you didn't want me to leave the cabin, but—"

"Jesus, Shia, you could have been killed! What did you do?"

"I'm sorry!" I crept over to the bed, easing down onto the edge as he twisted to face me. I kept my eyes averted, not wanting to meet his tired, angry glare. "Look, I knew you'd be worried if I told you I was going out. I went up to the lodge while you were out so I could get some information on that guy Mr. Cassidy mentioned."

"Hawk?"

"Yeah. I think his real name is Howard Thomas. I know what cabin he was staying in and that there were two other people with him. That's not the interesting part, though."

Chaz rubbed at his eyes, levering himself to sit up and wrapping his arms around me when he saw my expression. I gratefully leaned into his warmth, though I was worried what he'd have to say by the time I was done telling my tale.

"George Cassidy was up there, and I overheard him talking to somebody about us. I think the Cassidy family is in on what's been happening around here: the cabin, the arrow, the weird notes. . . ."

He made a disbelieving sound, and I poked him in the side. "Let me finish! Chaz, he was talking about killing you. We've got to get out of here. These people are crazy. I think they might have some other Weres out here, too. I ran into one on my way back to the cabin."

He stiffened, grip tightening painfully around me. "What? What happened? Is that why you barricaded the door?"

I squirmed until he eased up, nodding. "Yeah. It growled at me and ran off. I barely saw it in the dark, would've walked right past it if it hadn't made some noise to let me know it was there."

Chaz huffed, a low growl of his own rumbling in his throat. "Jesus, Mary, and Joseph—did it ever occur to you that you could have died out there? I don't want to lose you, Shia. Please do what I say next time."

I nodded again, squirming and twisting until

I could wrap my arms around his waist and bury my head against his chest. "I'm sorry," I mumbled against him, not sorry at all. If I hadn't done my reconnaissance mission, we might not have known until it was too late that the Cassidys were in on the plot to kill Chaz.

"It's okay," he said, sighing as he pressed his cheek against my hair. He ran his fingers through the red strands, tangling them in the curls. "I know you only wanted to help. It's good you found out what you did—but next time, don't investigate a Were's territory alone."

"All right."

"Listen, love, whoever you ran into last night is going to be as wiped out as I am. I need to sleep, but we should be okay for the next few hours. Let's get some rest. As soon as I wake up, I'll go check out that Howard guy's cabin."

"Okay," I agreed, nestling against his chest as he lay back down. He curled his arms around me, keeping me close, and I was grateful for the warmth and protection he afforded. It must have taken a heroic effort for him to be as lucid in conversation as he'd been; he dropped off into sleep in no time, snoring quietly.

Despite my caffeine jitters, it didn't take long for me to join him.

Chapter 17

I woke before Chaz. He'd shifted to his back in his sleep, the movement jarring me when he tugged me along. At my nudging, he eased up his grip on me, and I slid further up his body to peer down at him. The planes of his face were hard, angular, drawn with strain. Icy blue eyes fogged with sleep gazed up at me half-lidded, questioning. I pressed a hand to his cheek, a soothing stroke that soon had him closing his eyes again. He reached up to gently cradle my face, pulling me down to meet him. His lips found mine, and we tasted each other for a time, a simple, loving gesture that spoke more of comfort than desire.

We lay sprawled together like that for quite a while. He needed the rest, and I didn't protest when he ended the kiss and settled to a slow, lazy caress of my back.

Just as my eyes were drifting shut again, the sudden realization of what the slant of the sun against the curtains meant alarmed me into wakefulness.

We'd lost a number of hours of daylight. We wouldn't have much time to investigate and hunt down the people who were after Chaz before the moon would force the shift on the Sunstrikers— and possibly Chaz's enemies—again. My eyes fell on a scrap of white; another note had been slid under the door, the thick black ink visible from across the room.

Chaz stirred as I pulled away, padding over to the door and picking up the folded sheet of paper. Despite the block letters, the handwriting was a little different. The message was essentially the same.

ATTN: THE WINDOW-LICKING JOHN MADDEN THROWBACK IN CABIN 27 LAST CHANCE FOR U + UR GIRLFRIEND! GTFO BEFORE NIGHTFALL OR THE NIGHTSTRIKERS WILL PWN U!

I tossed it on the table along with the paperwork I'd been working on last night. I jumped when Chaz's hand reached past me, picking up the note so he could stare at it. He'd been so quiet, I hadn't heard him come up behind me.

His grumpy expression shifted to anger, and the paper was soon crumpled in his fist. He dropped it and stalked across the room, dug through the drawers until he had some fresh clothes, and yanked them on with quick, savage movements.

"Get dressed. We're going to find whoever is writing these notes and put a stop to this— right now."

I hurried to comply, grabbing some jeans and a bulky sweatshirt to combat the chill in the air. Chaz didn't wait for me to tug on my sneakers before he was out the door, stalking purposefully down the path and calling out for the Sunstrikers to assemble.

Sleepy people stumbled out of the cabins, some of them tugging on shirts or shoes as they hurried to join us. Simon hadn't bothered with a shirt; his abs were crisscrossed with long scars, marring otherwise flawless pale brown skin. His dark, slanted eyes narrowed when they lit on me, but he returned my nod of greeting. Dillon barely glanced at me as he took his place next to Chaz. Everyone looked tired but wary, and all but a handful were giving both me and Chaz questioning looks.

Once most of the Sunstrikers had gathered by our cabin, Chaz turned to me. He kept his voice low and level, but it did nothing to disguise his irritation. "Shia, which cabin were those people staying in?"

"Number three."

The others glanced between themselves, shrugging and muttering questions, but Chaz offered no explanation. We followed him as he stalked in the direction of cabin number three, a disorderly mass halting behind him at the door. He didn't bother to knock. Instead, he kicked the door in, splintering the lock, and stalked inside. A few of us, including myself, Simon, and Dillon, followed him in.

The place was a mess. There were empty soda cans and chip bags everywhere. Junk crunched underfoot. Some kind of gaming console was hooked up to a TV in the corner, and there were dirty clothes and comic books scattered all over the floor. Unwashed dishes were stacked in the sink and on the counter. The place reeked like old cheese mixed with Were musk, a combination that had the Weres around me covering their noses and making gagging noises.

Aside from the biohazardous mold farm accruing on the upside-down pizza slice on the table, the place was empty of occupants.

"Christ, what died in there?" someone behind me complained.

Disgust plain, Chaz poked at some of the clothes until he found a shirt that wasn't too offensively dirty, picking it up gingerly between two fingers. He took it outside to get a whiff without the god-awful stench of the rest of the room interfering. I didn't follow. Instead, I glanced around the place for any clues.

This was clearly a hangout for some nerds who were far less tidy than Arnold, the only geek I knew. The place was too lived in to be a temporary vacation spot. The addition of the TV and gaming equipment, as well as the state of the place, meant that whoever Howard Thomas was, he and his friends spent a lot of time here.

All the dresser drawers were open. There was no clothing left inside, so they must have known we were coming and left in a hurry. With all the other stuff here, no doubt they were planning to come back.

While scanning the wreckage, my eyes lit upon something that made me shout a curse. Chaz, along with a couple other Weres, rushed back inside, tense and ready to face any threat.

"Damn it!" I stalked over to the tall dresser. I hadn't noticed at first with all the other stuff on top of it, but the missing battery to Arnold's laptop was sitting in a puddle of spilled soda. A few drops got on my shirt when I picked it up and shook it off. Resignedly, I wiped the rest of it off on the shirt, praying that it wasn't damaged. Arnold would kill me if it was. Or make me pay for a new one, at any rate.

Chaz shook his head and relaxed, giving me a faux-angry look for scaring him. I was too pissed to muster up more than a weak, sheepish grin. Some of the other Weres eased up from their battle-ready stances, fists unclenching and luminescence dying out of their eyes.

After a few more moments taken to skim the contents of the room, finding nothing, we hustled outside—only to be faced by an angry Mr. Cassidy shouldering his way through the crowd. George wasn't far behind, hefting a heavy wrench to his shoulder as he followed Mr. Cassidy. They halted a few feet away from us, the old man's leathery skin reddening under his tan.

"What the hell are you doing?" he demanded. "You'll pay for that damage, sonny, or I'll—"

"You'll what? Explain to the cops how you're involved in an attempted murder plot?" Chaz snarled, stalking forward. George's eyes widened, but Mr. Cassidy didn't bat a lash, holding his ground as Chaz advanced. "We know you have something to do with what's been happening around here."

"Even if I did, there isn't a cop within a hundred miles who would care about it. You're in my town, boy, and you play by my rules while you're here."

Chaz flexed his fingers. I was alarmed to notice they were now tipped with claws; I'd never seen him do a partial shift like that before. It was usually all or nothing.

His voice rumbled deep in his chest, but he turned away from the old man, pulling me close as he stalked off back in the direction of our cabin. The other Sunstrikers followed, leaving plenty of room between themselves and the two men. "If I find any proof you're hiding whoever shot that arrow, the Sunstrikers will raze this place to the ground."

"I haven't broken the laws of homestead, boy, and you'd best remember that. You make the first move, you'll be hard hunted by more than my clan."

Chaz didn't bother to reply, instead leaning in to brush his cheek against my own, whispering a few quiet words. "He's going to try something. I need to find these people before sundown. Stay with Dillon and Nick; they'll protect you."

"What about you? What law was he talking about?" I whispered back, both furious and relieved that he would leave me out of this hunt.

"Don't worry. I'll have the rest of the pack to back me up. Simon isn't my enforcer for nothing."

"And the law," I persisted, too agitated to let it go. "What about that?"

"It's nothing. The laws of homestead are something the Others in New York and a few other states stick to so we can avoid any big confrontations that might draw human attention. We don't trespass without invitation, and when an invitation is extended, neither party can cause any harm to the other. Anyone who breaks his word gets hunted down by the rest of the Others in the area. Keeps us all in line."

I stared at him. He rolled his eyes.

"I haven't broken the laws, Shia. He attempted harm on me first. We're allowed to fight back if we need to."

I didn't argue. Instead, I slid an arm around his waist and clung to him as tightly as I dared, not looking back. No doubt Mr. Cassidy wasn't happy and would contact whoever those crazies were as soon as we were out of sight.

He might not have broken the laws directly but, indirectly, he was responsible for some of the damage that had been caused. Laws or no laws, I'd do whatever it took to keep Chaz—and the rest of the Sunstrikers—safe.

Chapter 18

Chaz directed his pack to split up into groups and do a thorough search inside and around the cabins. Dillon and Nick weren't happy to be ordered to babysit me, but they obediently ushered me back into my cabin. Once inside, they settled at the table, frowning at me and each other, while I paced restlessly in front of the bed.

After a while, Dillon slumped in his chair and waved at me. "Do you mind? That's kind of distracting."

"Distracting from what? Nobody's going to bust in here," I said.

Nick was busy picking something out from under his thumbnail, not bothering to glance up as he answered. "It's the last day of the full moon, Shiarra. We're predators. You're hyped up, and your scent reeks of agitation. Try relaxing so we don't have to try so hard not to do something that might hurt you."

That sobered me. I halted my pacing and settled into an uneasy crouch on the edge of the bed, folding my arms across my stomach. That they were that affected by my actions wasn't at all obvious from their expressions or the way they held themselves. In fact, the way they draped themselves in their chairs seemed more like the languid lean of a lazy, well-fed cat. Dillon's chocolate brown eyes were focused intently on me, though, occasionally flashing the greenish-yellow that spoke of an internal battle not to act on his instincts. Now that I was looking for it, I saw Nick's normally hazel eyes had the faint golden luminescence of the shift burning in their depths.

Biting my lower lip, I turned my attention to the window, peering through the curtains. I couldn't see any of the other Sunstrikers outside, but the sun was edging closer and closer to the mountaintops. It probably hadn't been very long, but the wait felt interminable, particularly since neither of the men were being friendly at the moment. Their quiet intensity was downright scary, actually.

Never one to let a little awkward silence deter me, I gestured at the angle of the sun. "How long are we going to wait here? Maybe we should go check on everybody."

"No way," Dillon said, the hint of a growl turning his normally smooth voice into a rumble. "You're staying put. I'm not getting in trouble because of you again."

"Shit, I'm sorry," I said. "I never meant to—"

He cut me off. "Look, I don't like you. Never did." Nick shot him a look of surprise, pierced brows arching up in shock. "We're following

Chaz's orders. So sit tight, relax, and wait for him to come back. You're not going anywhere until he says you can."

At first, I was chagrined. He had gotten in a hot mess with the pack and with Royce when I'd run off right out from under his nose. He'd been assigned to watch over and protect me from the psychotic vampire Max Carlyle, who very well might have called me back to his side once I was beyond the reach of the Sunstrikers or Royce's people. However, Dillon had no right to treat me like a child, herding me around because Chaz said so. All those last words of his did was piss me off. I slowly got back to my feet, fists clenched tightly at my sides as I glared at him. Chaz had warned me that such a move was considered a direct challenge; right now, I didn't care.

"Dillon, I didn't do it intentionally. I'm sorry I got you in trouble, and I'm sorry you don't like me. But I'm not going to sit back and wait for Chaz to get hurt. What if he was shot with silver again? What if that's why he's taking so long to come back?"

"She's got a point, you know," Nick said, nudging Dillon's arm until he stopped returning my angry stare. "Maybe one of us should go check it out."

"We're both assigned to her. We can't abandon our post."

"Then let's go together and take a look. We'll stick close to the cabins. If they're searching out in the woods, well, we'll just come back here and wait like Chaz said to," I offered.

Dillon frowned severely at me, the smooth brown skin of his brow wrinkling into a scowl. I wasn't intimidated. He knew I was right; something could have happened, and if it involved silver again, it would take a human—like me—to do something about it.

"Fine," he snarled, shoving away from the table so hard it pressed into Nick's ribs, knocking the wind out of the other Were. "If he's not in the cabins we're coming straight back here."

"That's fine," I readily agreed, rushing to the door. His arm snaked out to stop me before I could bolt outside.

"Stay right by us. We can't protect you if you run off."

As much as I wanted to roll my eyes at him and say something sarcastic, I went for the civil approach instead. "All right. Lead the way."

Dillon glowered at me briefly before twisting around and heading outside, his smooth, swift gait requiring me to practically jog to keep up. Nick was chuckling at us, bringing up the rear.

We didn't get very far before a trio of the geekiest looking guys I'd ever seen rushed out of the shadows between two cabins to come to a jerky halt in front of us. They all had T-shirts with odd computer or gaming references that could've come straight out of Arnold's wardrobe. In fact, I could've sworn I'd seen a smaller, less faded version of the "/ATTACK GAZEBO" T-shirt that strained over the bulge of the bigger, hairier one's distended stomach on Arnold's skinny frame just last week. The two others had thick glasses that gave them owlish stares, distorting their narrowed eyes. The one in the lead was a couple inches shorter than me, wiry, and practically vibrating with excitement.

I might have laughed if they hadn't been wielding bows with silver-tipped arrows aimed with deadly precision at the Weres on either side of me.

"Come with us," the shortest one said, his voice pitched low and menacing. It might have been more frightening if he hadn't paused, lowering his weaponry to pull an inhaler from his jeans and take a deep pull. He coughed, cleared his throat, then resumed speaking in a normal tone. "You're ours now, newbs!"

"They're not newbs, dude," rumbled the over-weight one, rolling his eyes.

The third, tallest and skinniest, put in a few words. "Are you sure? I hear the girl ganked some fangs a few months ago. Wouldn't try to take her in a PVP round without major backup. Maybe we should've—"

"Doc, shut up." The first guy ran his hand over his face, then lifted his weapons again, gesturing for us to move. "Let's go."

Unwilling to risk injury from silver shot, the two men at my side hastily complied with the order. I, on the other hand, was too confused by their strange jargon and overblown entrance to do what the short one said right away.

"Uh, excuse me, but who the hell are you guys, and what the fuck do you think you're doing?"

"No questions right now. Move it!" he demanded, taking a step closer to me.

I did what he said this time, skittering back as he herded me closer to my bodyguards. They didn't take us far—we went straight back to the cabin I'd been sharing with Chaz.

Once inside, they did a fair job of tying up Dillon and Nick with some heavy chains one of them had been lugging along in a backpack. Though the pair's eyes gleamed with luminescence and both upper and lower fangs were visible when they lifted their lips in silent snarls, the threat those silver arrows presented was too much for them to risk defying those strange geeks right away. As soon as they were trussed up, the bigger guy pushed them into the cramped kitchenette and made them sit on the floor, back to back. He then hooked their chains together using what appeared to be carabiners—D-shaped rings with a spring catch, like the ones I'd seen my brother Damien pack with his mountain-climbing gear. Simple, but effective. Those two wouldn't be able to disengage themselves without help.

As soon as Nick and Dillon were out of the way, the trio turned their attention to me. I'd retreated to the back of the room, putting as much distance between us as possible. There was nothing close to hand that might serve as a weapon, and I wasn't too sure I'd be able to fight them off if it came down to it.

"You're Shiarra, right?" the short one asked, pulling out a chair. The other two followed his example, slumping into seats around the table, blocking any escape through the door.

"Yeah. You ready to tell me who you guys are?"

He smiled at me, and I flinched at the sight of elongated canines. It was daylight; vampires couldn't walk in daylight—

"We're the Nightstrikers," he said. The three of them sat a bit straighter, puffing with pride.

I stared blankly.

"Haven't you heard of us?"

"No, sorry. Should I have?"

He frowned, as did the other two. The tied-up Sunstrikers shook their heads in silent puzzlement as he turned a questioning gaze upon them. The taller, skinnier one addressed earlier as Doc started talking, drumming his fingers impatiently on the tabletop as he eyed me. "We're only the arch nemesis—nemesi? Nemesises? Whatever, the main enemies of the Sunstrikers. We've got the biggest following on the Other-net Web site."

"Never heard of you," said Dillon in a tone of dismissal that had all three of the geeks bristling with indignation.

"You've got to be kidding! We've been hunting Charles Hallbrook for the last twelve years."

"Thirteen, doofus," the bigger one said.

"Thirteen, yeah."

Dillon and Nick exchanged a look before shrugging in their chains. The geeks were not deterred, though they were a bit crestfallen.

"Shit. I can't believe you guys don't know who we are! Anyway, I'm Floyd, also known as Doc.

That"—the talkative one pointed to the big guy, who gave me a friendly wave—"is Howard. You can call him Spike; that's what we all do. And Hawk is our leader."

"You!" I shouted, finally putting two and two together. "You're the ones who trashed our cabin! And took all my underwear!"

Dillon and Nick very nearly choked on their laughter. Spike and Doc both reddened and looked away, clearly embarrassed, whereas Hawk was blasé about the matter.

"We would've given them back before you left. Besides—"

"I thought you said we were gonna keep them," Spike said, his face falling.

"Shut up," Doc hissed, while their leader rubbed a palm down his face. None of them seemed to care that I was seething.

"Anyway, that's not why we're here." Hawk, so short he barely came up to my chin, rose and paced with restless energy in front of the table. "We're not like the Sunstrikers. We've been biding our time long enough. We're an elite team—"

"Headshot! I call headshot."

Hawk gave Doc a withering glare for interrupting before returning his attention to me. "We're sick of your boyfriend's shit, basically. So you're going to play bait for us."

Under the circumstances, I think it was only fair to say I was confused. I edged around the bed so I could sit across from the three, collecting my thoughts before speaking. Whatever else was going on, these guys were nuts, so I didn't want to provoke them into doing something that might result in them hurting me, Nick, or Dillon.

"Okay, now, I get that you guys are upset about something. Clearly you have a beef with the Sunstrikers."

"No shit. We wouldn't be fragging your party if we didn't have a beef," said Spike.

"Right," I agreed. "Here's the thing, though. Don't take this the wrong way, but I have no idea what the heck you guys are mad about or why you've done all this. Were you the ones leaving the notes?"

"Yeah. Didn't you see our messages? You didn't listen."

"We thought it was some other people messing around. Plus we didn't know what half of the messages meant."

Hawk pressed his fingertips to his eyes, taking a few deep breaths. When he focused on me again, I was startled to see that there were no whites to his eyes any longer—they'd gone entirely pitch black.

"We were telling you to 'get the fuck out'—seems pretty clear to me."

"Sorry," I muttered, looking away so I wouldn't have to meet those freaky eyes. "Chaz thought it was some teenagers in the pack playing dominance games. We didn't know."

Hawk settled into a chair again, tapping his nails on the table. "Regardless, after tonight, I don't ever want to deal with that asshole again. Do you know where he is?"

"No. We were looking for him when you interrupted us."

"There's too many for us to go searching the cabins right now," Doc said, elbowing Hawk. "Maybe we should use them as bait to lure him into the woods? Don't see how we can pull this off without training the whole pack—and there's no zone line to shake 'em off, either."

"Dude, this is worse than trying to run Onyxia. We can't disconnect or call 50 DKP minus if someone pulls the crowd on the raid," complained Spike.

"Many whelps! Handle it!" crowed Doc, and the three men dissolved into sniggering laughter.

Nick, Dillon, and I shared a helpless look. None of us knew what the hell they were talking about.

I cut in, speaking over their laughter. "Hey, maybe I could talk to him for you. Get him to apologize. What are you so upset about, anyway?"

Hawk shook his head, his easy grin fading into an unhappy scowl. "Oh, no way. You'd just try to get away. He needs to pay for what he did."

"Which is?" I persisted.

"He was the popular kid. The school bully. He beat the shit out of us anytime he could corner us all through high school. Playing dominant alpha—setting the rest of the football team against us—"

"Yeah," grumbled Spike, clenching thick fists until his knuckles popped. "As soon as we heard he was here from my granddad—" Ah, so Mr. Cassidy was covering for Spike, not for Hawk. That's where the relation lay. "—we had to make him pay. The jockstrap headdresses and fake rubber breasts at prom were the last straw."

I had to fight to keep from cracking a disbelieving smile. These guys were obviously pissed, though if Chaz was being a dickish jock to them in high school, I could sort of understand. Why they'd carried a grudge this long was beyond me, though.

Nick and Dillon had no such qualms. They were snorting with laughter.

Doc glared behind the thick lenses of his glasses. "We want to make him pay, just like he did to us all those times."

"Plus, he stole my girlfriend," Hawk insisted, gesturing impatiently at me. "He's going to use you and leave you, too. Just like he did with her. You shouldn't be with a guy like that."

Right. I closed my eyes and took a deep breath to compose myself—a real task with Nick and Dillon still sputtering laughter from the kitchenette—then rose and approached the door.

"Guys, I'm sorry Chaz was mean to you in high school, but he's a very different person now. He's saved my life, more than once, and he's a very caring pack leader. Why don't we go look for him, and I'll help you talk it out together? Maybe you can make some kind of deal, and he can make it up to you. That way nobody has to get hurt."

Hawk regarded me dubiously, though he followed the others when Doc and Spike got to their feet and fell in beside me. The reek of Were musk, not of a breed I was familiar with, washed over me as they approached. "I don't know. I don't think it's possible for someone like that to change. I really want him to pay for what he did."

"We'll talk it out. He's not the same; you'll see."

They didn't argue, following me as I opened the door. Nick called out plaintively. "Hey, what about us?"

"We'll come back for you," I promised. Considering the Nightstrikers were hefting their weapons in readiness, Nick and Dillon's belittling laughter wouldn't help matters any if I was going to get them—or Chaz—to talk reason.

Chapter 19

We weren't sure where to start looking. After a bit of back and forth on it, Hawk snapped his fingers at the tall, skinny geek. Doc's tongue flickered out, tasting the air. He pointed and took off, the others hurrying after him, not waiting to see if I was following.

"What are you, exactly?" I asked once I caught up, trailing after the unexpectedly spry trio.

"Me? Were-python," replied Doc, his long strides eating up the ground.

That took me aback. I'd never heard of Were-reptiles. Hawk glanced at me and, at my look of shock, gave me a wry grin. "I'm a Were-crow. Howard's a Were-bear, like the rest of the Cassidy family. We all suffered the same problems in high school, so we stuck together and made our own pack—the Nightstrikers—once we got sick of facing Chaz and his cronies on our own."

"I see," I said, not entirely sure I did. Doc was ignoring us while intently tasting the air every few seconds, once in a while shifting directions, leading us on this strange chase. "How'd you guys meet?"

"Computer club," answered Spike.

That explained a lot.

We didn't say anything else for a while, following the invisible trail that Doc had picked up. Strangely, none of the Sunstrikers were around the cabins. Even the kids, usually heard if not seen, were nowhere in evidence. The whole place seemed deserted.

Doc paused and turned to focus on one of the cabins, then stopped in his tracks, furrows appearing between his brows. He scratched the back of his neck, his face reddening. The rest of us gave him questioning looks, but all he did was point vaguely at the entrance. The curtains were drawn, and it didn't look like anybody was there.

"What's wrong?" asked Hawk, brandishing his bow as his gaze darted over the shadows between the trees. Spike lifted his head, taking a whiff of whatever Doc had been scenting. His face also reddened, and he shot a look at Hawk.

"Eugene, I think we've got a situation here."

"What? What is it?" I demanded. Paused. "Eugene?"

"Yeah," said Hawk, grimacing. "That's my real name. Just call me Hawk, okay?"

I shook my head and turned back to Spike. "What's the problem?"

Spike didn't look at me, gesturing vaguely at the cabin as the Were-python had. Doc wasn't any help either; he'd backpedalled, scrubbing his mouth with the back of his hand. Hawk kept looking around for a threat, his bow drawn, clearly frustrated and unnerved at the lack of answers from his friends.

Figuring we weren't going to solve anything by waiting around, I rolled my eyes, threw my hands up, and stalked to the door. It opened easily under my touch.

At first, I wasn't sure exactly what I was looking at. There were clothes everywhere, strewn over furniture and the floor, some tangled in the bedding. On the bed, though, that's the thing that my brain didn't want to process right away.

The tangle of arms and legs wasn't the issue. Nor the obvious scents in the air, strong enough that my weak human senses could pick them up. Even the sound effects which, given the activity taking place, were not all that surprising.

It was the tattoo. The swirling tattoo of a Chinese dragon coiling down the bare right ass-cheek and across the hip of the man, clearly visible considering the position he'd taken over the woman sprawled beneath him on the bed.

Chaz's tattoo.

"What the blue flying *fuck*?!" I hollered, stalking forward.

The woman screamed, and Chaz twisted around, then promptly scrambled back on the bed, disengaging himself. He grabbed for the nearest pillow, hurriedly covering his groin. "Shia, I—"

"What the *fuck*?!" I cried again, stopping in my tracks as Kimberly drew herself up, yanking the covers over her breasts.

"Shia, please—"

"What the fuck is this? What in the fucking *hell* is this, Chaz?"

"What the hell do you think it is?" Kimberly screeched, throwing one of the pillows at me. "Get out!"

I turned on her, and she shrank back at the rage twisting my face into a hateful scowl. It didn't take me long to turn that bottomless hatred back on Chaz. He had the gall to gesture at me to calm down with one hand, even while he used the other to conceal his privates.

"Shia, please, let me explain—"

"You fucking bastard," I cried, the first prick of tears stinging their way in a hot trail down my cheeks. I sensed the Nightstrikers creeping up behind me, their frames shadowing the doorway. Chaz barely paid them a glance; his attention was focused entirely on me. "You cheating, lying son of a bitch. How could you do this to me?"

"What the hell did you expect?" Kimberly growled, scooting back against the headboard. "You don't put out; you leave him hanging—you didn't leave him with a lot of options."

"Shut up!" Chaz and I both shouted at her at once. She complied, folding her arms across her chest and sullenly glaring at me.

Chaz hastily filled the crackling silence. "Shia, I'm sorry. I know this looks bad, but it's not what you think! I still love you—"

"The hell you do!" I exploded, grabbing the nearest item to hand—a mug on the table—and hurling it at him, sending the coffee inside spilling over the sheets. He barely managed to deflect it, the porcelain shattering as it hit the floor. "You don't fuck around on the side when you love someone, you fucking asshole!"

I reached for the next closest throwable object, one of his sneakers, and this time managed to score his temple. "Stop!" he bellowed, batting at everything I threw at him in my haze of fury. "For God's sake, you don't understand! I can't function without a little relief now and then—"

My scream of fury had him cowering back. The laughter of the Nightstrikers only further spurred my rage into new heights of aggression. I was soon across the room, slapping him with all my might, leaving a reddened imprint across his perfectly sculpted cheek.

His eyes flashed yellow as he snarled, and I gasped when he reached out lightning quick to wrap his fingers around my wrists, halting my furious tirade.

"Shia, stop! Listen to me!"

I tugged to free myself, but he wouldn't loosen his hold. As soon as I figured out I wasn't going anywhere, I glared into his eyes, uncaring if the beast below the surface saw it as a challenge or not.

"Listen. Just listen! I can't go without sex or violence for too long, Shia. It's not the way I'm wired. I *have* to have an outlet. You have no idea how hard it is to fight those instincts. I managed for a little while, but when I saw you with Royce—"

"Don't you dare bring him into this, you—"

"Shut *up!*" he roared. "I never once complained. I didn't say a damned thing when you let that leech touch you. You have no right to judge me!"

I gasped in outrage, pulling at his grip again. This time he let me go, and I retreated several steps back toward the door. "Is that what you think of me? You think I *slept* with him?"

"Didn't you?" he snarled, withdrawing to put the pillow over himself again. "You were mooning over him for days. Hell, he might have ordered you to do it. I couldn't have stopped him if he did. I didn't hold it against you, and I know you didn't want to sign a contract with me, not after what happened with the leeches. I didn't press you because I didn't know how long it would take for you to get over it and come back to me. To come to your senses. To want to be part of the pack. Did you think I'd sit back and wait forever?"

At first, I didn't say anything. Couldn't.

Rage was too kind a word for what I felt in that instant.

Beyond caring, beyond speech, I turned around to face the Nightstrikers. Hawk had a look that could best be described as rapture plastered on his face as he watched our little drama play out. With no thought on the matter, I grabbed one of the arrows out of his hand and twisted around to hurl it at Chaz.

He jerked away, but it still hit one of his ribs and fell into his lap, and he awkwardly juggled it until it dropped to the floor. Everywhere the head and shaft of the arrow touched his bare skin they left behind the red streak of silver burn. He gave a howl of pain and shouted something I ignored as I brushed past Hawk, Doc, and Spike to rush out the door, my vision blurred with tears.

Even so, I couldn't miss the throng of Sunstrikers gathered outside. They were watching the spectacle from a safe distance, several yards from the cabin, all of them with wide eyes and open mouths. Paula was there. Her triumphant smirk and the glitter of success in her eyes weren't lost on me. Nor the shamed blushes and eyes cast aside rather than meeting mine when I spotted Sean and Simon. Their looks spoke of guilt—which meant they'd known about this. God, they'd all known and covered for Chaz, leaving me to think everything was just peachy while Chaz was screwing some other bitch on the side.

Paula stepped close enough to whisper a few soft words as I passed, and it was all I could do not to turn around and deck her for them. "See how much a leech's pet means in this pack? Stay away from us. You're not welcome here."

Enraged, I stalked along the path, brushing past the gathered Sunstrikers who hurriedly backed out of my way as I approached. None of them made any move to follow.

The shadows had lengthened, and night would fall soon. Chaz wouldn't be able to come after me to continue the argument; he'd be shifting soon enough, as would the rest of the pack. I thought about what to do while he was out of my hair for the next few hours. The Nightstrikers had gotten one thing right in their childish attempts at revenge—setting fire to what remained of Chaz's personal belongings would be an excellent place to start. I'd follow their example.

My planning was interrupted as Hawk, huffing a bit, caught up with me, settling into a slower pace to match my stride. I didn't bother to look at him.

"That was *awesome*," he said.

"Pretty impressive, lady," Spike rumbled from behind me, sending me stumbling when he patted my shoulder.

As soon as I caught my balance, I kept walking, silently seething. I wasn't sure what would come out of my mouth if I answered them just then.

"Hey, you just accomplished what we have been hoping to do for the last thirteen years. That was a hell of a way for him to lose face in front of his pack."

"Look," I growled, turning on a heel to shove an admonishing finger under Hawk's nose. He stopped in his tracks, surprised. "I didn't do any of that for you. I did that for me. Can you let me cool off before you try being chummy? Please?"

"Oh, sure," said Spike, tugging on Hawk's arm to pull him back. "No problem. We just wanted to let you know we're done now."

"Yeah," said Doc, his beaming smile revealing that wicked set of fangs again. Were his features narrower than before? "You helped us finish our quest."

"We won't bother you again," Hawk said.

I didn't reply, watching as the three gave me cheery waves and wandered off toward the lodge. My eyes weren't mistaken; inky black feathers were sprouting around the cuffs of Hawk's shirt, and Spike's hands were now shaped more like paws, tipped with huge curved claws. They joked and laughed as they wandered up the trail, past some trees, and beyond my line of sight.

A chill of foreboding ran through me. If they were shifting, the Sunstrikers must be close, too.

Chaz's temper would be fired up. The rest of the Sunstrikers had no reason to avoid me now that I was undoubtedly beyond the pack leader's protection. I had no weapons if they should come upon me in the dark.

I turned and ran.

Chapter 20

Nick and Dillon weren't happy to see me when I rushed back into the cabin. I'd forgotten about them.

They were straining at their bonds, teeth too prominent and hands sporting claws flexing as they twisted and fought against the chains. I very nearly turned around and left them there to take my chances in the woods.

"Get us out of here!" Dillon shouted.

They were still human enough to speak. Human enough to know better than to touch me. It didn't make it any easier to approach the struggling pair.

Dillon's eyes glowed green when I knelt in front of him, searching for all of the carabiners used to hook the chains together. He stilled when I put a hand to his shoulder, nostrils flared and breath hissing between his teeth.

Spike had used a few of the hefty clasps to secure the chains. My hands shook as I fumbled at the catch to the first one. The occasional ripples of shifting muscle as Dillon fought to keep still didn't help.

Soon, Dillon was freed, and he practically leapt to his feet as he shrugged out of the chains. I concentrated on freeing Nick, carefully not looking at Dillon as he tore off his clothes in preparation for the shift.

By the time Nick was free, Dillon was already sprouting fur, crouched low on the floor as his bones and muscles rearranged themselves. The sounds of popping tendons and creaking muscles made my stomach lurch. Worse, as I patted Nick's shoulder to let him know he was free, he twisted around to face me, his face distorting as his jaw extended into a muzzle baring teeth dripping with saliva.

I backpedaled, crab walking across the tile until I slammed my shoulders and the back of my skull against the cabinets behind me. Nick tilted his head back, a low, coughing growl escaping him as he shimmied his way out of the chains. Fabric tore and split as he fought his way free. Thick golden fur sprouted to cover his nakedness.

Dillon let loose with an ear-splitting howl, one that was soon answered by others in the pack outside. I tore my gaze off of Nick to see if Dillon had finished with his transformation.

To my horror, he had. He was the same black-coated Were with the cat-like green eyes that had once stalked me like prey, hunger glittering in his gaze as he approached me. He'd stopped in that stinking alley, leaving me alone only because Chaz had been there to protect me. He'd been there during the fight against Max Carlyle in

Royce's basement, too, though there had been too much going on at the time for him to be a danger to me. This time, there were no distractions, and Chaz wasn't here to stop him from attacking me.

My fingers practically split the wood of the cabinet as I grabbed the door to pull myself up off the floor.

Dillon watched me from his crouched position, lips pulled back on that dog-like muzzle to bare yellowish fangs. Triangular ears were pricked forward as he took a careful step closer, pausing as his claws dug furrows into the wooden floorboards.

Panting with terror, I reached for the closest thing to hand—the coffee pot—and held it out in front of me in warning. Comical, perhaps, but it was the only thing within reach that I could use to defend myself.

Nick voiced another low growl, and I had to stifle a scream as he reared up beside me. I arched back against the countertop as he bumped his head on the ceiling, grimacing and baring his teeth in a remarkably human expression of pain. Both clawed hands came up to cradle his skull, rubbing where he'd struck it.

Even in this form, he still had the piercings I remembered seeing on his brows, nose, and ears. When he tugged the tatters of his shirt off his chest, nipple piercings remained, too. I didn't dare peek lower to see if he had any others.

I flinched back when he leaned toward me, thrusting the coffee pot at him. He jerked back, then gave me a cursory sniff. Apparently satisfied, he turned away and lumbered toward the door, casting a glance at Dillon, who was still watching me with the intent hunger of a predator.

Dillon crept closer as Nick got out of the way, stalking forward on all fours. Panic at being trapped beat at my breast, and I frantically searched for some way—any way—out of this mess.

Nick growled, and Dillon froze. The pair looked at each other, ears flattening and lips lifting in threat, though now they made no sound.

Another howl split the air, this time much closer, from somewhere outside. As Nick turned to look, Dillon leapt at me.

I screamed, hurling the coffee pot at him in reflex. It struck a glancing blow on his snout before falling to the floor and shattering.

Just before Dillon reached me, though he was close enough for me to feel the fetid wash of his breath across my face, Nick knocked him off course and into the wall. Hot pain stung my arm, but all I knew was terror in that moment, and I skittered back as far as the tiny kitchenette allowed. The pair of wolves grappled, snapping and snarling at each other, claws soon wet with blood.

Unable to cope, I sank to my knees, clutching my arms around my chest as the two thrashed and fought. They crashed into the bed, shoving it into other furniture hard enough for wood to audibly crack. Nick thrust his jaws under Dillon's, closing on the black Were's windpipe as they rolled into the table, snapping one of the legs and sending the chairs tumbling to the floor. Nick soon had Dillon pinned on his back, his teeth digging tight into the fur and cutting off any hope of Dillon's gaining the breath to fight back.

Though Dillon's claws raked over his chest again and again, Nick didn't let go. I flinched as one of his nipple piercings rolled across the floor and struck my shoe, leaving behind a tiny spatter of blood. Eventually, Dillon subsided, stilling under the golden-furred Were.

Once he stopped fighting, Nick released him, backing up a few paces. Nick bared bloodied teeth, keeping his amber irises locked upon the gasping, choking Were before him.

Dillon remained on his back for a few minutes, furred chest heaving as he regained his breath. Soon he rolled onto all fours, keeping his body low to the ground and his tail between his legs as he crept closer to Nick. His lips and ears were drawn back, though he didn't show any teeth, and he only lifted his head long enough to lick Nick's muzzle with a few swipes of his tongue.

Nick's tail, which had been sticking straight out like an arrow, parallel to the ground, dropped, and he lowered his head, returning the fervent licks before glancing at me. I stayed where I was, unmoving, frozen with terror.

The pair didn't pay me any more attention, turning and rushing out the open door on all fours, Dillon following Nick's lead.

It was only after they were gone, as I was struggling up to my feet, that I realized my arm hurt and that I was bleeding.

Panic assailed me. I grabbed the closest chair with both hands, struggling to remain upright as my chest tightened, preventing me from pulling in enough air to fill my lungs.

Blood. My blood. Not Nick's, not Dillon's—mine. Dillon had cut me. With his claws.

Oh God.

Bile burned my throat as I stumbled to the counter, turning on the water and thrusting my arm under the stream, rubbing at the shallow cuts even though they now burned like fire. Panting with terror, I grabbed at the tiny bottle of anti-bacterial soap and dumped most of it on the wounds, scrubbing like it would make a difference.

Oh God.

I could be like them this time next month.

Oh *God.*

I couldn't hold it in. I threw up into the sink, crying even as I still frantically scrubbed at the cuts, knowing it wouldn't do any good. If I was infected, it was too late. Lycanthropy couldn't be washed out of the blood, no matter how good that soap was at cutting through grease and bacteria. The smallest nick of fangs or claws could carry enough of the virus to spread it to anyone unlucky enough to be attacked.

If it had made its way into my bloodstream, I was beyond fucked.

Chapter 21

It took a long, long time for the helpless tears to taper off. I remained limp and still against the counter, unable to bring myself to pull away from the running tap, though the water had long since ceased swirling in a pinkish streak down the drain.

After a while, it was the cold that brought me around. I was shivering so badly my teeth were chattering. The one lamp in the bedroom had miraculously survived the altercation between Nick and Dillon, illuminating the destruction and the first questing tendrils of night fog creeping in through the open door.

Wrapping a dish towel around the cuts, I slowly pulled away from the counter and trudged to the door. There were no visible signs of either Were pack outside save for a few tracks left behind by Nick and Dillon when they'd rushed off. Staring numbly into the white fog creeping between the trees, I listened for any hint of their whereabouts.

Not a sign.

Shutting the door, I stared around the room, taking in the wreckage in a detached way. The table was beyond repair, as was the dresser. Some clothes had spilled out when the lower drawers splintered. The floorboards were marred with claw marks.

Like the ones on my arm.

I covered my eyes with a hand, purposely holding my breath to keep from hyperventilating. The desire to gasp in air was powerful, but I couldn't afford to pass out. Not now.

When the worst of the involuntary trembles tapered off, I hobbled across the room on shaky legs, keeping my eyes averted from the furrows in the floor. I snatched a T-shirt from a drawer and tossed it over the marks, hiding them so I wouldn't have to see them every time I turned around.

Slowly, the rage that had fueled my actions earlier returned. None of this would have happened if I hadn't agreed to Chaz's suggestion to come here. If not for him, I wouldn't have been put in the position to be infected.

Even thinking the thought was enough to make my stomach churn uneasily again. Breath came short and sharp between my clenched teeth as I tore open the drawers and tugged out his things, throwing every last stitch of his clothing on the bed.

Next, I stalked over to the fireplace, gradually regaining my balance as purpose and anger took over. My hands shook from cold and fury as I reached for the matches. It took a few tries before I managed to light one. The tinder caught immediately, flaring up with warmth that matched my rage.

I fed the flames, watching them grow as they consumed every last article of clothing Chaz had left. There wasn't much after what the Nightstrikers had done to our first cabin. By the time I was done, the only set of clothes he'd have would be the ones he'd worn before he hopped into bed with that whore, Kimberly.

Fueled by reckless rage, that last thought gave me an excellent idea.

I rose, not bothering to look for a weapon to take with me as I exited the cabin. The fog could've hidden anything, from werewolves to Werebears, and I wouldn't have taken notice. All my anger and energy were focused on reaching Kimberly's cabin.

A big, rangy crow cackled at me from a nearby rooftop. I ignored it, but it followed me, fluttering from building to building as I wound my way along the muddy path.

Kimberly's door wasn't locked. I strolled right in and wasted no time in hunting down every last stitch of clothing and footwear I could find.

Once I had everything piled on the bed, I took an empty designer suitcase that had been tucked in the closet and tossed my findings inside. Intent on my mission, I lugged the full baggage outside. The crow had waited for me there, watching with bright, beady eyes, tilting its head this way and that as I struggled with the bag on the stairs.

The bird fluttered to the ground. Up close, it was much bigger than I'd thought; it was closer in size to an eagle than any other crow I'd ever seen. No wonder they called him "Hawk."

He squawked at me, and I paused, setting the bag down at my feet.

Apparently satisfied that I wasn't going anywhere, the oversized bird hopped in its gangly, awkward way behind a nearby bush. Familiar popping and stretching sounds, accompanied by a somewhat pained groan, were soon followed by Hawk's distinctive features—sans glasses, leaving his pitch black eyes clearly visible, even in the dark—peering at me from around the thick cover of leaves.

"Hey, look, I wanted to apologize. It didn't occur to me until later how upsetting that must've been for you."

I stayed where I was, swaying slightly on my feet as the absurdity of the situation and his statement hit me. Upsetting. Right.

"The Nightstrikers are around if you need us. Look us up on Other-net sometime, okay?"

"How are you—"

"Human?" He smiled. "Doc, Spike, and I aren't bound by the moon like the werewolves are. We're keeping an eye on things in case Chaz decides to pay you a visit tonight. Get out of town as early as possible tomorrow, okay? We'll stick around until we're sure he's not going to come back this way to take anything out on you."

"Thank you," I said, taking a few breaths to calm myself. "I don't think he'll be coming back until morning."

"Maybe. We'll be around for a couple of hours,

then we're heading back to the city. Until then, call for us if you need us."

I nodded, pressing a hand to my forehead and closing my eyes. When I opened them again, he was gone.

Too shaken by everything that had happened, I stayed where I was for a few minutes, shivering. Despite the blood loss and the cold, I felt energized. Vibrating with the need to destroy things. If I wasn't careful, I might end up doing more damage to myself in the rush of hate and fear-fueled adrenaline than Dillon had.

It took a while for me to get going again. Not because I didn't want to move, but because I knew that if I allowed myself to give in to the seething fury, I'd start screaming and never stop. I might do something irreparable, like hunting down every last Sunstriker until they cut me down, or until they were all dead.

Panting, I came to a halt before my cabin, tilting my head up and closing my eyes as I breathed in the night mist, forcing calm on my unraveled nerves. It took several long minutes before I felt composed enough to do what I intended.

With deliberate care, I unzipped the suitcase and sorted through the clothes until I found the shirt, pants, and underclothes Chaz had left behind in Kimberly's cabin. As I held up the pale blue silk boxers, the same color as his eyes, I dimly noted a few blood spots blooming on the slick cloth. I hadn't felt the sting of my nails biting into my palm, cutting even through the fabric.

With a sense of finality, I tossed all of his things into the muddiest spot I could find, the mulch still damp from the sprinkle of rain on our first night here. With a bit of stomping and grinding of my toe, I soon managed to cover every last inch of fabric with dirt and bits of leaf mold.

That task accomplished, I stepped over the suitcase and over the threshold, making a beeline for the closet. There, tucked away in the bottom of my duffel bag, lay the contract that sported my signature. My unspoken promise of devotion to Chaz and the rest of the Sunstrikers.

It took an effort not to toss it into the flames burning cheerily in the fireplace. Instead, I took it with me outside and promptly tore it into quarters, dropping the shredded fragments of paper onto the mound of muddy clothes. They stuck to the wet soil, soaking up the moisture, but the title and my unmistakable scrawl were still clear enough that Chaz wouldn't miss what he'd given up once he returned from the forest.

I spent the next hour or so feeding Kimberly's clothing, piece by piece, into the flames. She'd probably end up borrowing clothes from one of the other Sunstrikers, but doing this gave me a sense of deep, abiding satisfaction anyway.

After the last piece was eaten up by the fire, I sat on the edge of the bed for most of the night, watching the bloated moon creep toward the horizon and the stars fade into day.

In the predawn light, Chaz stalked out of the forest, pausing in the clearing before the cabin. Despite my haze of anger, he still looked magnificent, a golden god of the forest prowling in glorious, unabashed nakedness through the last tendrils of mist fading in the gentle rays of morning sun. I watched through the window, though I made no move to get up to confront him. Particularly when Kimberly leapt with the grace of a doe out into the sun, every bit the creature of the woods that Chaz was. A hot flare of jealousy beat in my breast as she pressed a hand to his bare back. The other hand swept her enviably straight blond hair back in a casual gesture that only served to set every hated, perfectly shaped asset she had to jiggling in ways that would have sparked envy if I hadn't been shaking with fury.

He wasn't paying her any mind, though. In the space of a few seconds, his expression shifted from wariness to surprise to anger to chagrin as he spotted the pile of ruined clothes and the torn shreds of the contract that would have bound me to him, body, mind, heart, and soul.

He slowly knelt down to pick up the damp pages, running his fingers over them. I watched as he clenched the fragments in his fists. He turned away before I could get a good look, but I thought I detected a glitter in his eyes that looked suspiciously like tears.

He was gone before long, taking the soggy mess of clothing with him. She followed, saying something I couldn't hear. The two were no doubt off to seek consolation from each other in privacy.

Some of the other Sunstrikers wandered by on their way to their cabins, looking tired and worn. Though I might have admired the lean bodies or been embarrassed by the nudity before this last hellish night, there was nothing left of me to be moved by the sight. Instead I sat dry-eyed, finger-tips of the opposite hand playing over the tiny ridges of scabs on my left bicep.

Dillon was among those to pass by my cabin. He flashed me a vicious grin when he spotted me in the window. I didn't give him the benefit of a reaction. His grin soon wavered as he found him-self unable to meet my unflinching gaze.

There would be a reckoning between us, I was sure. It would come as soon as I made up my mind whether I wanted to carry out that revenge myself or let the law do it for me; either way, he wouldn't survive it.

My unkind thoughts were disrupted by the sound of a woman's angry scream echoing across the valley. Kimberly discovering her things were missing, no doubt. I didn't bother to investigate, as some of the others outside were rushing off to do.

Some time later it dawned on me as I watched some of the Sunstrikers and their families wander past with bags and suitcases that I would need to figure out how to get home.

I had no cell phone to call Sara. Even after I cleaned the soda off the battery, Arnold's com-puter wouldn't boot up. The cost of a cab back to the city was far above and beyond my budget, and I hadn't seen any car rental places in the tiny town—even if I felt like walking the miles of wooded track to wander around the streets in hopes of finding one. Mr. Cassidy might let me use his phone, but I'm sure he was none too pleased with the Sunstriker party, and the rest of the Cassidy family were probably not feeling too charitable toward their guests just now.

After a sleepless night, still in my bloody clothes, I wasn't feeling brave enough to face the day. It stung when I remembered destroying the coffee pot in my efforts to stave off Dillon's attack; even that simple pleasure would be denied me this morning.

Fighting tears, I collected some clean clothes and shambled into the bathroom, losing myself in the warmth of a shower. It woke me up a little, swept the remnants of last night's fight from my skin, and gave me a chance to relax despite knowing I'd have to face the inevitable and speak to one of the Cassidys about finding a way home.

When I stepped out of the steaming bathroom wrapped in a towel, I very nearly screamed when I saw a hulking, menacing shadow hovering in the doorway.

Chaz stepped inside, holding up his hands. "Please, don't start that again. I came to talk to you."

He looked so earnest in the early morning light, dressed in someone else's clothes. They didn't quite fit him; the jeans hugged his hips and thighs too tightly, outlining the strong play of muscle beneath. In contrast, the shirt was too big; his fingertips dangled below the cuffs of the soft gray oxford sweater, a light sprinkle of chest hair peeking above the collar. His golden skin was perfectly smooth, his blue eyes radiating warmth and sincerity even as his lips turned in that babyish pout that I'd once found so very kissable and attractive.

It took every ounce of willpower I had not to retreat into the bathroom and slam the door in his face. Every moment he hesitated gave my anger time to reheat, the dying ashes flaring up with newfound life and purpose. It took a great deal of effort to stand there, dripping and cold, waiting for him to spit out whatever he wanted to say without screaming at him to get out and leave me the hell alone.

"Shia, I really don't want to fight with you this morning. I know you need to get home, so I wanted to offer you a ride. All I ask is that you promise to let me talk on the way. No interruptions, no fighting, just let me have my say. Agreed?"

"I'll find a ride with somebody else," I snarled, backing into the protection of the bathroom. Before I could shut the door, his voice cut through my angry haze, stopping me in my tracks.

"No one else will take you. I already asked. And unless you want to rent a moving truck, there are no car rentals for twenty miles. Do you really want to make Sara or Arnold drive all the way out here to come get you?"

I closed my eyes, baring my teeth as I fought the urge to shout something decidedly uncomplimentary back at him in response. He was right, of course. I knew Sara's schedule; even if I managed to reach her, she was supposed to be on a surveillance gig this afternoon until midnight. She would miss her mark, and a big paycheck, if she didn't stick to her agenda. There was little doubt that Chaz was right about no one else being willing to take me; he must have already investigated ways to get me home without causing a scene if he'd looked into car rentals.

"Fine," I said quietly, unclenching my fist when I

realized my nails were cutting into my palms again. "Give me a few minutes to get dressed and pack."

He inclined his head graciously, smiling like there was nothing wrong between us, like he hadn't destroyed every last salvageable facet of our relationship last night. "I'll get the car warmed up. Meet me in the parking lot."

The bathroom door slammed shut behind me.

Chapter 22

I didn't pay a lot of attention to what Chaz said on the way back. He talked nonstop for half an hour, explaining as I stared out the window at the passing trees and houses that being changed into a werewolf did something to your hormones, made you need sex and violence like drugs. All I'd walked in on was a quick, no-strings tryst. It was just an outlet, not a relationship. Not like what we had.

He knew how upsetting all this must be to me; he and Kimberly forgave me for my temper tantrum, though she'd like me to reimburse her for the clothing I'd destroyed. He, on the other hand, wouldn't hold my rash acts of the moment against me.

He talked about how understanding Kimberly had been, how very gracious she was about the whole thing. That she'd taken it all in stride when he explained to her that he might be sharing his body with her, but his heart lay with me.

It was all flowery and flattering and passionate—
and clearly horseshit. I didn't believe any of it
for a moment. His justifications were just that—
a means for him to make it okay to cheat on me.
The lengths to which he went to delude himself,
coupled with the tiny voice screaming in the back
of my mind about how I might have to seek him
out during the next full moon for help, edged a
spell of car sickness closer to a full-on bout of
vertigo-inducing nausea.

When he figured out I wasn't speaking to him,
he quieted, fingers tightening on the steering
wheel. I snuck a glance at him under my lashes;
he wore the tiniest frown, biting the inside of his
cheek as he sometimes did when stressed or uncertain what to say. It was a trait I'd once found remarkably endearing. Now the sight of him like
that further roiled my already upset stomach.

It took a couple of hours for us to get back to
the city. Thankfully, I didn't barf. We made one pit
stop on the way, otherwise shooting straight for
home, with little said between us other than an ac-
knowledgment of directions or curt remarks
about stopping for gas or food. When we reached
the heavy traffic on the New Jersey Turnpike that
preceded the George Washington Bridge, he
started talking again, this time with a touch of that
trademark anger that called so easily to my own.

"Why aren't you talking to me about this, Shia?
Why can't you accept what I am? I saw the contract—you very nearly did it. What's so hard about
letting me be who I really am? You know how perfect we are together. We can make this work."

I thought about all those lazy afternoons spent in his arms, the nights we shared before I found out what he was and kicked him out of my apartment over a year ago. He'd been deceitful then, and I hadn't given him an opportunity to explain himself or regain my good graces until my mom had intervened on his behalf at a badly timed moment. That led to his helping me fight the psychotic sorcerer planning to destroy or forcefully rule over all of the Others in New York, and me coming to realize that I'd been foolish to judge him for hiding his nature.

After all, my response to Chaz's revelation was typical—he'd decided a little wining and dining would make me more responsive to the truth. That he chose to shift in front of me right after we'd had sex had only served to underscore how shocked and appalled I'd been about being blind to all the signs.

Now that I'd had my nose rubbed in the fact that his entire fucking pack knew he was cheating on me while I'd been busy obliviously agonizing over whether or not to sign a contract, it stung all the more. I was a private investigator who specialized in spotting and outing cheating spouses.

Don't judge. Despite hours of boring surveillance work, it was often better paying and more interesting than insurance work.

That I'd missed all the signs with him—again—was a gut blow. It wounded far more than my pride. It cut down to the very core of who and what I considered myself to be—an ace P.I. with enough experience and know-how to spot the signs of a cheater without effort. Clearly I'd been deluding myself about that. Perhaps there were other things I'd been wrong about, too. This situation undermined everything about who and what I was—and for that, I could never forgive him.

"There is no 'we' anymore, Chaz. You burned that bridge and any other chance you might have had with me when you chose to lie and hide things from me."

He glanced over at me, brows deeply furrowed over his eyes, though he seemed more puzzled than angry. "Don't say that. I may not have talked to you about it, but I never lied. You forgave me for waiting to tell you about what I was. How is this so different? It's just a different aspect of the same beast."

"No, it's not," I said, fighting to keep my voice level. "It's nothing like that. It's true, before I knew what you were, I said some shitty things about Others. When I broke up with you, it was because I was pissed off at you for being manipulative and for hiding things from me. Acting like that makes you no better than Royce."

That shut him up. The lines etched into his face, particularly the deepening crow's-feet around his eyes, spoke of just how deeply I'd managed to wound him with that last comment. He hated Royce with a burning passion. Knowing that, I'd use it to the hilt. Maybe it was low, maybe it was unfair, and maybe it even made me a bitch—but at the moment, I was beyond caring. If it hurt him, I'd wield that knowledge against him, and gladly. Petty or not, at this point I was willing to do anything that might make him hurt the way he and his pack had hurt me.

"Royce," I hissed, leaning in to whisper in his ear, "never—ever—treated me with the disrespect you've shown me. Never hurt me like you did. Even with the contract and the blood bond. How's it feel to be lower than a leech?"

For the first time in his presence, I felt a thrill of fear for myself as Chaz raised his right hand off the steering wheel, clenching his fingers into such a tight fist that his knuckles popped. He'd never made such an overtly threatening move toward me before. I know his strength, so the move was sobering and had me withdrawing against the car door.

"Don't you *ever*—"

His fist came down, cracking the dash. I jumped, staring wide-eyed at the indentation he'd left in the plastic.

"—*ever* compare me to that leech again. We're *nothing* alike."

Only my fear of what he might do to retaliate kept me from speaking again. He huffed in silence for several minutes. Gradually, the tension eased out of his shoulders, and he resumed speaking, though his tone remained sharp and cutting.

"I never forced you into doing something you didn't want to do. Didn't change you, didn't harm you. Don't talk about me like I'm one of those . . . those monsters."

"Are you kidding me?" I exploded, unable to keep my temper in check, no matter the consequence. Some niggling sense of self-preservation kept me from telling him about the cuts Dillon had inflicted. Even now, enraged, I knew somehow things would go far more badly than they already had if he found out that I might have been infected with lycanthropy by one of his own. "What do you think seeing you and Kimberly fucking like bunnies was, Chaz? A walk in the park? Of course that hurt me, you selfish prick!"

He had the grace to redden. Some of the plastic steering wheel coverlet shredded when his fingernails grew into claws as his agitation got the better of him.

"She doesn't mean anything to me. She's just an outlet. You're the one I love," he insisted.

"Bullshit. I call bullshit."

"For God's sake—"

"Do you have any idea how hurtful this is to me? Do you even have a clue?"

"Of course you're hurt; you're always hurt whenever you find out something about me isn't *human* enough for you—"

"This isn't about that!" I shouted.

"Then what's it about, Shia? I told you what's wrong. I told you why I had to do it. I knew you'd freak out, just like you did when you found out what I was, and just like you're doing now. This isn't how I would've wanted you to find out, but it's too late for that now, and I don't know any words to say that will make it better. So what exactly is the problem here? What is it about, huh?"

"You! You lying . . . deceitful . . ." I sputtered off, too angry to continue.

"You know what? Fuck this. Get out."

I stared at him, some of my immediate anger edging over into confusion. "What?"

"You heard me. Get out of the car."

We were somewhere in the Bronx. Nowhere near home. We hadn't even hit Long Island yet.

"Are you kidding me?"

"No. I'm not dealing with your shit anymore." He cut through traffic in a few savage, jerking motions, and before I knew it, we'd pulled off I-95 and into a part of town I was completely unfamiliar with. He didn't bother to pull into a lot or find a parking spot, instead choosing to double-park at the side of the road. "Get out. Get your stuff and get out."

Numbly, I did what he said, hefting my purse on my shoulder as I slid out of the Jeep. He barely waited for me to pull my bag out of the back and shut the door before he pulled back into traffic to the accompanying honks and shouts of irate drivers as he cut people off and shot back onto the expressway.

I stood there between two parked cars for a long time, staring after him, not quite able to believe that he'd dumped me, literally and figuratively. The people passing by barely paid me a glance. Those who did quickly looked somewhere else and hurried on their way.

With a shudder, I hefted my purse higher on my shoulder and grabbed my bag, trying hard not to cry. That could come later, sometime when I was alone and curled up in bed with a pint or two of ice cream and enough chick flicks and alcohol to help me forget this weekend had ever happened.

That Chaz had ever happened.

There was a diner down the street, a real dive, but they might have a phone they'd be willing to let me use. I trudged the half a block to the storefront, dubiously taking in the glass fogged with dirt and cracked cement stairs leading inside. The place was empty save for a tired looking old lady with wispy white hair tied up into a fraying bun who was leaning against the counter, a cigarette hanging limply from her fingertips while she jawed with a cook over the serving counter. They both quieted, looking at me with wide eyes as I stumbled inside.

"Lawd's sakes, girl, you look like you done seen a ghost," the woman remarked, stubbing out her cigarette and standing straight. "Come in, sit down. You hurt? Need an ambulance?"

The mention of an ambulance made me jerk in response, terror at being discovered as a possible lycanthrope making my fingers fly to the cuts on my arm hidden beneath my long-sleeved shirt. She couldn't have seen. She couldn't possibly know. But the way the waitress looked at me, the concerned wariness in her dark brown eyes, filled me with a bone-deep terror that she somehow saw the monster I might be peeking out of my eyes.

"Jesus, girl, we don't bite here. Come in; sit down before you pass out. You gonna be all right?"

My throat tightened up at this unexpected kindness, and I shook my head. With some effort, I picked my purse and bag off the checkered tile, inching over to one of the tables by the window and setting my stuff down. My voice cracked when I spoke, so I had to clear my throat a couple of times before it came normally. "I'm sorry. Thank you. I'm just looking for a phone to call a cab, if that's okay."

The lady exchanged a look with the cook, one I interpreted as "no sudden moves, don't alarm the crazy lady." She gave me a smile, her teeth nicotine stained in places to a color that very nearly matched the chocolate hue of her skin. "Sure thing, sugar. You just have a sit right there. I'll call for you. You want anything while you wait? Some coffee, maybe a slice of pie?"

I gave her a watery smile, and she disappeared through a swinging door into the kitchen. A few minutes later, she came out bearing a cup of steaming coffee and a plate with a slice of warm apple pie. The scoop of vanilla ice cream next to it was already making a sugary pool.

"The cab company will send someone along in about twenty minutes. You just enjoy that now, and let me know if you need anything else."

I settled in to the comfort food and found it helped ease the nervous tension that had wrung my stomach into knots. Knowing I could curl up into a ball of misery in private at home soon also helped. My eyes burned from the effort to keep from spilling any tears, nothing I wanted to do considering how carefully the cook and waitress were watching me, despite that they'd resumed their casual chat behind the counter.

Already I was worried about strangers thinking I was something different. Something Other. If I went to the hospital, it would come out how I was injured. If anyone recognized me, word might get back to the newshounds who now kept such close tabs on me. Either would be a disaster.

But going to the hospital to get tested or vaccinated would be worse. The thought of what it might do to me to get the news that I was beyond treatment right on the heels of what had just happened with Chaz was terrifying. I didn't want to get the news that it was too late, that nothing could be done. I didn't want to be like Ethan, falling apart in a parking lot where anyone could stumble upon me and discover my secret.

I didn't want to be one of those statistics who disappeared.

Chapter 23

The cab stopped outside, bleating an impatient honk. I left a twenty on the table and gathered my things. The waitress waved her cigarette after me, smoke wafting from the cherry tip as she bid me good-bye.

The bags felt heavier, my reactions too slow. It took more effort than I cared to think about to drag my things out and approach the cab that would take me home. I'd have Sara pick me up in my car on the way into the office tomorrow instead of having the cab drop me off at her place where I'd left it. The thought of possibly running into her while I looked and felt like this was too much to bear. I needed to get my wits around a plan of action for the infection before I could handle talking to her or anyone else about it.

The cab driver got out of his car when he saw me struggling with the bags. It wasn't until he slid his hand over mine, pulling the heavier suitcase out of my grip, that I looked up and took notice of him.

He was eyeing me speculatively, slicked back hair showing a bad dye job with a few whitish roots that left his features unmistakable. His rounded, stubbly jaw and thickly muscled arms matted with enough hair to do a bear proud gave me a start. He grinned at me, though the expression was tempered with some concern.

"Fancy seeing you again," he said.

"You, too," I said once I swallowed back my surprise. How did this guy always manage to find me when I was on the verge of a breakdown? "You have the most fortuitous timing of any cab driver I've ever met."

He barked laughter at that, literally. The guy was a werewolf. A member of the Moonwalker pack, the largest one in New York, if not the whole country. They were "friendly rivals" of the Sunstrikers, and fiercely proud of themselves for being the ones responsible for making Others an accepted part of society. Mostly accepted, anyway.

"Economy being what it is, I can't offer a free ride this time. But I will lend an ear. Looks like you could use it."

His words dredged a smile from somewhere, and he returned my weak show of relief in kind before hefting up my suitcase and tossing it in the trunk. As I settled into the backseat, the scent of old fast food and musk swept over me. Familiar, but not as unpleasant as I remembered and expected. He pulled into traffic after I gave him the address and a few directions.

"So, you want to talk?" he asked.

I hesitated. My vision blurred with tears when my gaze settled on the sticker of the Moonwalker pack symbol plastered on the divider between the front and the backseats. If anyone would understand my most pressing problems, it would be my chauffeur-cum-therapist. Talking to this familiar stranger about what was wrong might very well lead to a solution to all of the problems whirring in my head. I couldn't think of anyone else who would be able to offer the unbiased insights or tempered sympathy this man could. And there was no chance of him subconsciously shrinking away from me as I feared Sara or my parents might once I told them what had happened.

"I . . . I'm not sure if you can help me . . ." I trailed off, unable to say it aloud.

"Can't help if I don't know what's wrong, sweetheart. You reek of Were, though it's not from my pack. Have something to do with that?"

I choked back the urge to sob, clenching my fists in my lap. He waited for me to get a grip on myself, flicking glances at me in the rearview every now and then.

"You might say that," I finally whispered, rubbing the moisture from my eyes with the back of my hand. "I might be like you next month."

"Like me?" He didn't get it immediately. Though, once the realization dawned, his eyes widened. "Oh! Oh, I see. Well."

He didn't speak again for a bit. I put my hand over my eyes, unable to stop the tears and unwilling to let him see them cutting a path down my cheeks.

"I take it by your reaction this isn't something you wanted."

I bit my lip, not wanting to let some careless, caustic comment fall out of my mouth.

"It's not necessarily a bad thing. You survived. Even if you are one of us now, you're not dead or badly injured. I'm sure whichever pack is responsible for it will take you on—"

"I don't *want* to be a Sunstriker!" I cried, slamming a fist against the Plexiglas hard enough to make it rattle. "That's just it. I'm not contracted to anyone in the pack, and I never will be! Even if I was, and even if I do turn into—" I couldn't say it. Saying it aloud might make it real. ". . . I don't want to be one of them. Not after what they did."

"All right, I believe you. Don't get yer knickers in a knot. Are you saying you'd rather be a lone wolf?"

My head thumped against the seat as I leaned back, unable to believe the absurdity of this conversation. The worst part was that it was completely serious. What I said now might mean the difference between my being accepted into the Other society and being hunted down by anyone with a permit to exterminate rogues next month. I doubted this friendly cab driver would give my name over to any authorities—or worse, White Hats—but once his pack leader found out, I could be in a world of trouble. I hadn't considered that when I first started talking, but now that the words had left my mouth there was no taking them back. He'd be obligated to tell Rohrik Donovan, leader of the Moonwalkers, that there might be a new wolf in town come the next full moon. For their own safety, they'd make an effort to draw me into their pack, just like the Sunstrikers had with Ethan.

Mouth dry, I croaked a few words, painful as they were to spit out. "No, that's not what I want. I don't know. I just don't want to be one of them."

His dark eyes reflected concern as he glanced at me through the rearview. I couldn't bear to meet his gaze, and soon looked away, scrubbing at the tears that wouldn't stop flowing. He pitched his voice low and soothing, and a sort of unwilling calm stole over me.

"Don't worry just yet. I don't blame you for being upset with the Sunstrikers if they're behind this. Could be Mr. Donovan wouldn't mind lending you a hand. The Moonwalkers owe you anyway; it shouldn't be any trouble for us to take you in, if it comes to that."

I nodded, not trusting my voice. At a red light, he twisted around to look at me, frowning as I withdrew and covered my face with my hands, peeking out between my fingers.

"Calm down, I don't bite," he said, giving me a forced smile. "Look, after I drop you off, I'll call Mr. Donovan and ask him to meet with you. Do you mind my giving him your address? He can help you."

"Okay," I whispered, not sure if it was. What would Rohrik Donovan be able to do for me? Hold my hand and tell me everything would be all right? That I had a place in his pack structure?

A violent shudder rippled down my spine, but the cab driver was no longer paying me any mind. His focus was now solely on the road and traffic before him.

"Wait—how did you know my name? And how did you know the Moonwalkers owe me a favor?" I asked, alarm driving me to scoot toward the door in case I needed to seek a quick escape. Rohrik Donovan was the one who'd told me as much, and if he was anything like Chaz, I couldn't imagine him sharing that information with just anyone in his pack. Their pride wouldn't stand for it.

He laughed. "Are you kidding? I'd be surprised if there was an Other in New York who couldn't recognize you on sight. Most of the humans probably know you, too, considering all the times you've been in the news."

I made a little choking sound in my throat, but he continued, ignoring it.

"Most of the dominant wolves in our pack know about Rohrik's promise. We're supposed to be keeping an eye on you and helping when we can. There wasn't much we could do to interfere with the Sunstrikers' keeping such close tabs on you. When you ran off into the park a few months ago, I arranged to run into you. This time? Pure coincidence, but it doesn't change anything. I've got my orders."

"Great. So you're stalking me now?"

"Not at all. Consider us a safety net. We're there to catch you if you fall. Like today."

That shut me up. My fingers crept back to the cuts on my arm, rubbing at the healing wounds through my shirt. Would it be so bad, being one of the Moonwalkers? Aside from Rohrik Donovan's being the one responsible for the Others coming out of hiding and announcing themselves to the world, I knew next to nothing about the Moonwalker pack. David Borowsky, the crazy sorcerer, had tried to use them to set himself up as the leader over all the Others in New York almost a year ago. Rohrik and I had fought; he walked away with a few bruises, and I got a stint in the hospital that lasted for months.

Oh, the Moonwalkers had made good on the promise to help me afterwards, but we hadn't had much interaction. Aside from a personal visit from Rohrik to apologize for smashing my ribs into itty bits, I'd had very little contact with any of that pack since I got out of the hospital.

The Moonwalkers and Sunstrikers had never gotten along. This cab driver had once referred to the Sunstrikers as a bunch of good-for-nothing show-offs. Chaz had never had anything nice to say about the Moonwalkers either, though his comments were usually far more disparaging.

I glanced at the ID card plastered between the seats to get the cabbie's name, something I'd neglected to do before. "Look, Mario, not that I'm not grateful for the help, but it's pretty freaking creepy that you guys may or may not be shadowing me. Are you the only one, or are there others in your pack watching out for me?"

"Mark Roberts has been helping you," he pointed out, making me blush at having forgotten the obvious connection—my accountant, the balding father of three, who had given me cut-rate deals on my corporate books and personal taxes ever since I saved the Moonwalkers. "He likes you, you know. Talks about you once in a while when the pack gets together. There are a few others, but I don't think it's my place to discuss this with you."

I made a noncommittal sound in answer and turned my attention outward, staring out the window at the passing cars and buildings. It wouldn't be much longer before we'd reach my tiny apartment in Terrace Heights. My lease was up in a few months. Recalling that also brought up memories of plans made over wine and candlelight to move into Chaz's much bigger brownstone. The thoughts were jarring and painful, and I might very well have started crying again if I hadn't been so exhausted by my ordeal. It was too soon to think about moving again, too soon to be making plans that didn't involve a future with that lying son of a bitch.

My returning anger warmed me to my chilled core. I'd have to be very careful of my choices over the next few hours. I would meet with Rohrik Donovan and get a feel for what he was like and what his plans were for me. Since the supernatural grapevine would no doubt be buzzing with the news of my infection before long, as soon as my meeting with Rohrik was over I'd call Arnold and swear him to secrecy. I couldn't risk his accidentally slipping the news to Sara or my parents. That would be followed by a call to Royce to see what, if anything, this might do to change or void our contract.

It was the first time I'd thought of the vampire in a while, other than as a tool to use to hurt Chaz. Royce was older than dirt, and had a streak of possessiveness. He might be tempted to do something to take revenge on the Sunstrikers.

Then again, if I was lucky, he might have come across a cure for lycanthropy in all the years he'd wandered the Earth.

Either way, I needed to talk to him. Somehow he'd known that something bad was going to happen on this trip. Even Jack had known. I needed to dig deeper and find their sources, and see if I could use them for my own ends. I wouldn't ever let myself be hurt like this again.

"We're here."

I'd been so deeply engrossed in my thoughts, I hadn't noticed that we'd arrived. I dug my house keys out of the bottom of my purse while Mario went to the trunk for my suitcase, pulling out a cell phone and dialing with his free hand as I led the way. I half-listened to his end of the conversation as he gave a brief account to Rohrik of what had happened and where to find me.

Once upstairs, Mario stopped at the doorway to my apartment, setting my bags down. He made me promise I'd open the door for Rohrik when he came, and not do anything "rash" (a kinder word for "stupid") in the meantime. I settled before my computer with a cup of coffee as I contemplated what I would say to the Moonwalker pack leader when he arrived, and waited.

Chapter 24

Rohrik Donovan looked more like a construction foreman than a seasoned werewolf pack leader. Though it hadn't been that long since the last time I'd seen him, I detected a little more salt than pepper in his short hair this time around, and there were more laugh lines around his eyes and mouth than I remembered. When I opened the door, he was looking casual in jeans and a plain white T-shirt, his dark brown eyes widening slightly at my no doubt frighteningly pale features.

I stepped back to let him in. He hesitated at the threshold of my apartment door, and I belatedly remembered the seal keeping out any Others I hadn't keyed to it. He didn't protest as I took his hand and pulled him inside. The magic barrier Arnold had installed for me, after some nasty vampires had tried to break in, grudgingly let him pass; I could feel it sticking to his skin and clothes like invisible glue as I drew him through it.

"Ms. Waynest," Rohrik spoke first, cautious, unsure. His deep voice was soothing, mellow, but with the rougher edge of a Jersey accent and a smoker's husk. "It's good to see you again."

"You, too," I replied, gesturing for him to take a seat. "Coffee?"

"Yes, please. Black, one sugar, if you would."

Heathen. What's coffee without real cream?

I got him his drink, refreshed my own, and we settled across from each other at the table. The silence stretched too long, neither of us quite knowing where to begin or what was safe to say. It felt uncomfortably like a stare down, so I looked away first. He cleared his throat and tossed the opening salvo.

"Mario tells me you've got a problem we might be able to help you with. I'd like to know what happened, if you don't mind telling me."

I sipped my coffee to buy time and compose myself. My voice still wavered despite my best efforts to stay calm while relaying my story.

"I'm sure you remember Chaz. We were making plans for the future—our future—together. Part of that plan was for me to meet the rest of his pack and go somewhere I could get to know them without interference. We rented some cabins upstate. We thought if I could handle seeing the pack as they really were, maybe I could handle being a part of it someday. Chaz didn't know, but I brought a contract with me. I signed it, but never got up the courage to show it to him."

"You planned to be one of the Sunstrikers?"

"Maybe. I don't know. I was more interested in showing good faith and commitment to Chaz than being furry—no offense."

He nodded, thick hands cradling the coffee mug as he lifted it to his lips. "None taken. Go on."

"I caught him with another woman. Another Were. After I found them together, I ran back to my cabin and had to get a couple of the other pack members out who were on the verge of shifting. It's a long story, but I didn't get their chains off in time, and one of them scratched me."

I didn't say anything else after that, uncertain, not knowing what else he'd need to know or what I'd be comfortable enough to tell him. We barely knew each other for all that I'd saved his life. I wasn't comfortable speaking about Chaz's betrayal yet, though I'd no doubt be railing and ranting about it as soon as I had a chance to wrap my wits around all the crazy twists and turns my life had taken in the last twenty-four hours.

He stared at me evenly across the table, the chocolate hue of his irises darkening. I tensed, but he gave no other sign of apprehension; his fingers curled loosely around his mug, and the set of his shoulders remained relaxed. It both relieved and bothered me that he wasn't more upset about my predicament.

"So you've been injured, possibly infected, outside of a contract. Have you informed any authorities?"

"No," I said, mollified that he was more interested in the technicalities than the dirty details of Chaz's infidelity or what had led up to the scratches on my arm. "I wasn't sure what to do at first. I only just got home. I'm afraid to go to a hospital for the vaccination shots."

"Don't bother," he said, holding up a hand. "It's not worth it. The chances of the shots stopping the infection from spreading are far lower than they would have you think, and it will only endanger you if your name goes on a list of possible lycanthropes. We've lost three of our newest pack members since January; it wouldn't do to have you become a statistic, too."

Chilled, I nodded and hid my discomfited grimace by taking another long sip of coffee. I very nearly choked on it at his next words.

"It could be war between the Moonwalkers and the Sunstrikers if we take you in. I'm not sure that I can risk it."

I grabbed a stray napkin from the middle of the table and blotted my lips, coughing my breath back so I could speak. "Why? Chaz burned his bridges with me when he cheated on me. Why couldn't you take me?"

Rohrik met my gaze, his own reflecting a great deal of regret in the face of my confusion. "You may not have been contracted to him, but Chaz was grooming you to be a part of his pack. He wouldn't take it kindly if we offered you a place in our ranks after he'd spent so much time and effort on you. Werewolves are very territorial, Ms. Waynest. He'd see it as an unforgiveable encroachment if you joined our pack instead of his. We outnumber the Sunstrikers by a great deal, but they are still the third largest pack in the state. Relations between us are already quite strained, and I can't see how this would improve matters."

I carefully placed my coffee down in front of

me, rubbing at my burning eyes with both hands. Not that long ago, I'd have sworn I'd rather be dead than furry. Now I was upset because the werewolves wouldn't have me. Funny how these things turn out.

"Okay." I paused to compose myself before continuing. My life was turning into one long comedy of errors. If I kept up at this rate, I'd be a homeless werewolf begging for spare change from the tourists in Central Park before the month was out. I needed to come up with a plan. "I see what you're saying. I know this is a risk for you. But I'm willing to use every resource I have to back you up, too. If you'll help me, I have friends in The Circle, in another Were pack"—if the Nightstrikers could even be called as much— "and I can also ask for help from Alec Royce. I can bring a lot to the table, even if it's only temporary. If I am infected and you really don't want me to stick around, then just help me get through the first time or two so I don't hurt myself or someone else when the change comes. Please? That's all I'm asking."

Maybe it was the helpless despair to my tone, or the "please" I tacked on at the end. Rohrik reddened, rubbing the back of his neck and glancing away.

"I can do that much. I can't promise we'll keep you in the pack, but we'll help you through the change and with sorting out how your new needs will fit into your lifestyle."

New needs? There was a thought that didn't bear much scrutiny. It was my turn to look away, fingers tightening on my mug as I thought about Chaz's talk of "needs" in the car.

"How soon will I know . . . ?"

He would have made a good doctor. He didn't flinch at my question, remaining calm and level as he listed off all the things that made the blood turn to ice in my veins.

"Without blood tests, you won't know for sure right away. Symptoms don't usually appear until seven to ten days before the next full moon. You'll crave rare or uncooked meat. You'll find your temper snapping at things that at any other time would be insignificant. Some environmental triggers, mostly scents, may make you feel nauseous or uncomfortable. As it gets closer to the full moon, you'll develop a sensitivity to loud noises and may run a fever. Bright lights will hurt your eyes. The first change is painful and disorienting, so don't wait to contact me if you start showing symptoms. Too much stress, and you might change before it's time. Do you still have my number?"

Unable to speak around the lump lodged in my throat, I nodded.

"Good. There's no reason to be alarmed. We'll be here to help you. It's better this way, I think. You'll see what it's like to be in a normal pack. The Sunstrikers are an unstable bunch, so I can't say I'm terribly surprised at what's happened. You do have my sympathies. If there was a way for me to keep you on as one of us, I'd do it. Perhaps once you are strong enough, you can even start your own pack. We'll support you if that's what you choose to do."

Calling the Sunstrikers unstable was like calling Chernobyl an unexpected and unfortunate occurrence. Words were insufficient for expressing how screwed up it all was. I could appreciate Rohrik's attempt at politeness, but it wasn't enough to calm the sudden rage I felt at his carefully worded consolations. The Sunstrikers would pay for this. Every last one of them.

"Thank you, Rohrik," I said, extending a hand across the table. "I appreciate the offer, and I'll think about what you've said. I'll call you once I know for sure."

He clasped my hand in both of his own, warm, calloused fingers engulfing mine in a reassuring grip. "Don't be afraid to call on me if you need someone to talk to. I know this must be stressful for you. If the wait becomes too much, let me know, and I'll see if I can arrange for some tests to be done by someone who won't betray you to the authorities."

"Thank you," I whispered, slowly drawing away. He let me go, pushing back from the table and rising with a deep sigh.

"I'm sorry there isn't more I can do. Get some rest. Contact me when you've had a chance to think things over, and I'll brief you on some of your legal options for how to deal with the Sunstrikers. I've met a few decent attorneys who would likely love to take on your case."

My lips peeled back in something that might have been a smile. The lack of expression on Rohrik's face led me to believe it wasn't as cordial as I'd meant it to be. "Thank you again. I'll be in touch."

He nodded, giving me one last look that spoke of calculation as much as concern, before seeing himself out. I remained at the table for a few minutes after he was gone, mulling over what he had told me and the offers he had made.

Waiting three weeks to find out if I was infected was going to drive me around the bend. Until then, I'd somehow have to keep it a secret from my family, Sara, and the media. I'd have to consult Arnold while making it crystal clear that he was not allowed to tell anyone. I'd have to contact Royce, too. Not only to find out how the hell he'd known that I would face trouble while on vacation, but to find out if and how my new "condition" might change things between us.

Whether this altered or voided my contract with Royce was a question I wasn't terribly eager to have answered, but was something I needed to know. Certain aspects of those papers gave him rights to all of my stuff, including my interest in H&W. I needed to make sure I wasn't putting Sara at risk. If she needed to buy me out to escape him, I'd need to let her do it before any of this went public. Before Royce could do anything to stop me.

The thought put my stomach in knots. Vampires and werewolves did not get along. Would Royce consider me his enemy now?

That thought once would have frightened me. Now, it filled me with an empty sort of sadness, not what I expected to feel upon realizing that we might be playing on opposite sides of the supernatural sandbox. I'd used his name to hurt Chaz, but in truth the vampire had been a better friend to me than the Sunstrikers ever had. Considering his needs, Royce might even have a doctor in his pocket who wouldn't mind doing some off-the-books testing.

That was probably nothing more than wishful thinking on my part. The bond we shared had faded but never completely broken. My ability to view him as nothing more than a callous beast had been skewed after drinking his blood. I still felt he was a prick at times, but he no longer frightened or repulsed me—which was exactly why I made such a strenuous effort to avoid him. Thanks to the bond, it was too easy to see him as a man, not a monster. If I allowed it, I'd be no more than another puppet dancing to the tune he played.

I'd put off calling him until later. Much as I dreaded it, I needed to tell Arnold first. He needed to hear it from me instead of through his connections in the supernatural community.

The big question was whether he would do as I asked and keep my new condition a secret from Sara.

With no small measure of trepidation, I got the mage's number from an old e-mail stored in my computer, picked up my cordless, and dialed him.

Chapter 25

Arnold picked up after a couple rings.

"Arnold, it's Shia."

"Hey, how was the trip? Are you home?"

His cheerful greeting made me feel even worse for what I was about to say. Gripping the phone tightly, I wandered over to the window and peered between some cracks in the perpetually drawn blinds. Ever since the paparazzi had decided my personal life was of interest, I'd needed to be extra vigilant about keeping the interior of my apartment closed off from prying eyes and long-range cameras.

Which was a sudden, frightening reminder that Jim Pradiz had been intent on a story at the beginning of my trip. Had he caught wind of anything at the lodge? Followed us back to the city?

"Shia?"

"Sorry," I said, shaking my head and gripping my free hand into a tight fist. "I've got a situation—"

"Oh, hell. You didn't break my computer, did you?"

I paused. Tragic as the loss was, his busted computer wasn't what I was worried about at the moment. Time to use some evasive tactics.

"That's not what I'm calling about. Are you alone? Sara's not with you, right?"

"No, she's on a job. I'm at home. What is it?" The alarm in his voice was palpable. Little I could do about it at this juncture. "I can keep a secret, Shia, but I can't promise she won't find out some other way. She's a good P.I."

"I'm not just talking about Sara here. *No one* can know this. Not your coven, not Sara, not my family—*no one.*"

"Yeesh, what'd you do? Blow up a building?"

"I'm not kidding around. They absolutely cannot find out from you under any circumstances. Understand? I need your word."

"All right, I get it. I'll keep it secret, whatever it is."

I examined the bloody crescents my nails left in my palm before speaking, the words coming in a rush. "Last night, one of the Sunstrikers scratched me while turned. I may be one of them next month—I might be infected. There's no way to know yet. Not for sure. I can't let my family find out, not until I know."

It felt a bit like running a marathon to get all that out. Aside from my somewhat heavy breathing, the silence dragged between us.

I couldn't stand it. "Jesus, Arnold, say something."

"Christ," he breathed, and I gathered from the shuffling and scraping coming through the line that he'd settled—perhaps *collapsed* is a better word—into a chair. "Are you sure? You—I—have you gone to the hospital or made an appointment to get tested yet?"

"No. I spoke with Rohrik Donovan, and he didn't recommend it."

"Rohrik Donovan? No shit." He paused. Exploded. "Jesus Christ, Shia, how did it happen? Are you okay?"

"No," I said, fighting the tears that suddenly threatened. His concern was shattering my careful control. "I mean, I'm not hurt too badly, but I might be a fucking *werewolf* next month. I'm not okay. There's nothing that could ever possibly be okay about this. Fuck, Arnold, you don't even know the half of it."

"What else could there be? I mean, this isn't the end of the world—you're not dead—but this isn't the greatest way to end a vacation. Does Chaz know?"

"Fuck Chaz!" I cried, slamming my palm down on my computer desk, sending papers spilling to the floor. "The fucking bastard was cheating on me, okay? The whole freaking pack knew he was doing it. Why didn't I know, Arnold? How did he get away with it this long? He's been screwing that . . . that *whore* for who knows how long, and—"

"Whoa, whoa, whoa! Slow down. Chaz was *cheating* on you? With who?"

I snarled something unintelligible before slumping into my office chair, rolling across the plastic floor mat until one of the wheels stuck on the carpet. Now that the shock of being potentially infected had worn off, my anger was coming back in force. I spat out the words, rubbing hot tears off my cheeks with my knuckles as I vented.

"That bastard has been sleeping with some other Were named Kimberly. They met at his gym. I can't *believe* he would do this to me—"

"Shit, Shia, I'm sorry. Do you want me to check the archives and see if there's anything The Circle might be able to do for you?"

"You have a spell to make Chaz's dick fall off?"

"No." He barked unsteady laughter, though it tapered off soon enough into a more serious, professional attitude I'd only encountered in him once or twice before. "No, but we might have one to cure lycanthropy. I know of ways to suppress the change after the fact, so we might have an antidote on file, too."

That sobered me. I rubbed the palm of my free hand against my jeans, then noticed I was leaving bloodstains behind from where my nails had dug in and stopped, clenching my fist on my knee instead. The cuts didn't hurt, not yet, but I didn't want to ruin any more of my clothing after all I had already lost this weekend.

"Yes, please. If there's anything that can be done to stop it, I'll do it. God, Arnold, I don't want to be one of them. I don't want to be an Other. Not this way."

"Hey, I don't blame you or anything, but speaking from experience here, it isn't the end of the world. Whatever happens, I'll help you get through it. Let's focus on the positive for the moment. You said you won't know for sure if you're infected right away, right? Well, you might not be. Don't write yourself off yet."

I closed my eyes and tilted my head back, placing my hand on my forehead. Arnold was right.

That didn't make it any easier to swallow or set aside, but he was right, nonetheless. "Okay. I'll try not to freak out any more than I already have."

"Good. This probably isn't the right time to ask this, but what are you going to do about Chaz?"

Good question. My eyes popped open, my gaze shifting toward my bedroom as though called. An idea was forming, one I wasn't about to share with the mage.

"I'm not sure yet. Keep that under your hat, too; let me tell Sara. I need some time to get myself together before I discuss it with anybody."

"Okay." He didn't sound convinced. "This might sound stupid, but don't do anything to provoke him. He may be in the wrong here, but you could get hurt if you go after him for revenge."

"I know. I'll be careful."

"No," he said, tone sharp. "Don't be a cowboy, Shia. He's got no reason to play nice anymore if he thinks you're out to get him. The Sunstrikers don't have a great reputation for playing by the rules. If he gets the idea that you're going to report him or a pack member to the authorities for assault, he might do something to ensure the sentence never gets carried out."

My blood chilled, fingers tightening on the phone. "What do you mean? What are you talking about?"

He sighed, the sound crackling through the receiver. It did nothing to reassure me. "Maybe it's nothing. I never said anything before now because he was your boyfriend, and it wasn't my place, but the Sunstrikers have a reputation for playing dirty. Nothing lasting, nothing that would stick in court, but that might be because no witnesses ever stuck to their guns or survived long enough to see the witness stand."

"Are you telling me I was dating the werewolf equivalent of a mob boss?" I squeaked.

"Maybe," he replied, all seriousness. "I can't say for sure. There's a supernatural grapevine, and nothing I've heard on it about them has been any good. Whenever I saw Chaz with you, he displayed perfectly good behavior, but it may have been a front. I hate to say this, but he was probably using you for something. You know I never trusted him during the time you were looking for the Focus. I wasn't lying then; he probably sees you as a stepladder to something he wants. Maybe it's a tie to Royce, or maybe it's nothing at all. He might still try to play you somehow when he thinks you've cooled off."

"Oh, that's freaking fantastic. Just peachy keen," I snarked, thinking once again about how Chaz had talked of his "needs." Now that I had some perspective, there wasn't much doubt in my mind that he'd been intending to talk me into being his next alpha bitch. That, or a broodmare for his kids. Either one would most likely have suited his purposes. "I'm going to kill the son of a bitch. One way or another."

"Don't do anything stupid," came the pointed reply. "Think long and hard about the consequences before you rush headlong into a fight. He's got, what, fifty or sixty other werewolves at his back?"

"He couldn't stop the cops. Not if he didn't want a war on his hands. He'd be screwing things over for all the Weres, not just himself or his pack."

"You don't seem to get it. They might not care.

If they have nothing to lose, why not fight it? And take you down with them."

I paused. Considered and discarded any idea of discussing my violent train of thought with Arnold. The mage was far too cold in his calculations; right now, I needed someone with a temper that matched mine. Someone who would agree with what I was saying, back me up, and, best of all, not tell me to stop once I started down the path of revenge.

"Okay. You're right. I won't do anything about it for right now." No, not right now. Later was another story.

"All right. Anything else I can do?"

"Not for the moment. Just keep quiet about everything, and let me know if you find a cure."

"You got it."

I had another task to see to before I could do what I was thinking about. The rolodex beside my monitor held all the numbers that had been in my cell phone. Luckily I'd gotten past my inability to keep my life organized and implemented the system of copying all the numbers in my phone as a security measure after losing my second-to-last cell phone to Max Carlyle.

Part of me still worried the crazy vampire had collected the contact info from it and might seek to use it against me some day. It had been a couple months, but that was no time at all to a creature who's seen the passing of several millennia. He could strike at any time, which I'd done my very best to think about as little as possible. That didn't mean I didn't have the occasional niggling feeling of panic when something reminded me of the psycho vampire or what his plans for me had been. Plans that might not have changed, only been delayed.

As they say, you're not paranoid if they really are out to get you.

Royce's card held every number, address, and e-mail he'd ever given me, written in my cramped chicken-scratch so it would all fit. My usual hesitation to contact him had been replaced by a hesitation to tell him what had happened to me. Thankfully, that would most likely be put off for a while. It was only midafternoon. Though I'd seen him up and about during the day, chances were the vampire was resting. I'd leave him a message, and no doubt he'd return my call as soon as night fell.

As expected, his phone went immediately to voice mail. I waited for the beep, and then left a curt, perfunctory message with little more than my name, home number, and a semi-politely worded request for him to call me back as soon as he got the message.

After I hung up, I rose and headed to my bedroom. Tucked away in the bottom drawer of my dresser lay my hunting gear, arranged just as I'd left it. I ran my fingers over the handles of the three silver stakes, the belt they were attached to lying quiescent. The spirit inside would wake after sunset, the same spirit that hated all things Other. Whoever it had been, it had once hunted creatures of the night. Years of practice added to information collected from all who had worn it resulted in a formidable and deadly weapon, as it passed all that anger and experience on to the current wearer.

Maybe it would have some advice for me.

Chapter 26

After showering and bandaging my hand, I took what I intended to be a short nap. Instead, I ended up sleeping the remainder of the afternoon and most of the night away, and woke up to my message machine blinking. I'd slept right through someone's trying to call me. With a groan, instead of snuggling under the covers as the rain pattering against my window urged me to do, I rolled out of bed. I had no idea what time the sun would rise. Panic drove me to move fast, hurrying to the dresser in the desperate hope that I hadn't missed my opportunity to speak to the belt before dawn.

With shaking fingers, I pressed my hand to the coil of leather, praying the buzz of life was still in it. I was rewarded with a mental blast of impatience; I hadn't taken it out in weeks, and it was not happy that I'd been ignoring it.

With no little trepidation, I picked the belt up and settled the side imprinted with the swirling brand of magic runes against my skin. The tongue adhered to the rest of the black leather, sealing it to me until sunrise. The voice of the spirit inside instantly berated me, and I took the lashing in silence.

'Why have you been ignoring me? Do you have any idea how boring it is to have no one to talk to for so long? Your panties aren't great conversationalists, I'll have you know!'

"Hey, I never stuck you in with my underwear," I protested, settling down on the bed. The belt didn't want me to sit; it wanted me to move, to *run,* to let it feel all the glorious sensations of having a body again. It radiated eager agreement at my absent thought of making some coffee. It loved my morning staple almost as much as I did. "I need your advice."

'As long as you drink some coffee, I'm all ears.'

I complied, heading to the kitchen and letting all my angry thoughts return. The sensation of the belt examining and absorbing the memories of my time with the Sunstrikers this past weekend was not unlike the dainty prickle of a spider creeping along my skin. Except that this spider was crawling around inside my skull. Talk about creepy.

"Do you see?" I asked, taking a sip of java heavily medicated with cream and sugar.

After a blissful wash of pleasure, the belt spoke. *'I'll talk. Keep drinking.'*

I did what it asked, rolling the drink over my tongue, enjoying the artifact's reaction almost as much as my much-needed caffeine fix.

'You have a right to be angry. Perhaps you're starting to understand why I've always been so eager to rid

the earth of these monsters. Now you are seeing them as they truly are.'

"They're not all evil," I said, obligingly quieting when it broadcast a scolding wave at me.

'I don't have much time before the sun rises, so let me speak. You have every right to wish a plague upon these monsters, particularly if they have made you into one of their own. I do not have the power to tell you; I'd only sense it once the disease has progressed to the point of no return. If you are one of the moon-chasers, once you turn you won't be able to use me again. I don't work for anything other than humans or magi. If you are serious about your desire for revenge, you've only got a limited amount of time to use me for that purpose.'

"Okay. Let's say I do want to do it. Let's say I want to use you to do something to the people who did this to me. What's your advice?"

The belt was quiet for a long time, collecting its thoughts. It was still there; I could feel the occasional burst of emotion from it as odd reflections of my own. It could make me move when it needed to, but only when I was frozen by indecision or not carrying out a necessary action to deal with a threat. For now, it was busily coming up with an answer, and taking far too long to do it.

'Can't make that decision for you,' it said, the echoing voice trailing off. It was gathering its strength before saying more. *'Werewolves make dangerous opponents. They have superior senses of smell and hearing, which means it is next to impossible to sneak up on them. However, they are all intensely allergic to silver, and with me to augment your skills you should be able to match their speed, if not their strength. Only an alpha like your ex might have the speed to outmatch you in*

hand-to-hand combat. If you are willing to take the risks inherent in fighting something with greater reach and strength, we may be able to take him down. I can formulate a plan to do as much during the day. Do you want to proceed?'

I thought about it. It listened in, seeing everything I saw, feeling everything I felt, knowing my answer before I spoke aloud. "I'm not sure yet. Let me know what you think up. I'll come to you as soon as I get home from work tonight."

'Don't try anything during the day,' it warned, voice fading. The sun must have been rising behind the thick thunderclouds outside. *'Stay clear of them all, even the Moonwalkers. They come offering peace, but you saw where trusting one of their kind got you.'*

"I'll be careful," I promised, lightly touching the leather even as the tension holding it together faded. The belt loosened around my waist, signaling that the spirit was gone for the day. "Very careful."

Bolstered by coffee and the promise of assistance, I wandered over to listen to my voice mail, sipping my coffee as the messages played.

Sara had left one around 8:30 last night that she was home and she'd pick me up on her way in to the office at around ten this morning. My brother Mike left one asking if I was back yet, why I wasn't picking up my cell, and asking me to call him as soon as I got the message. He sounded agitated, but he'd just have to wait until I was in a better frame of mind before I called him back. Chaz had left one, too, but I savagely slammed the delete button as soon as I recognized his voice.

Then came Royce's voice, late, past midnight, pleasant and smooth as it always was.

"Ms. Waynest, I'm sorry I missed your call. I trust you got my message before you left for your vacation, though I do hope nothing untoward occurred during your time out of town. If you still need to speak with me, I'll have my cell phone on me the rest of the night. Call me anytime."

I had to hunt for the phone buried under the covers somewhere on my bed. I'd been so dead to the world I hadn't heard it ring, even though I'd somehow shoved it under my favorite pillow. Settling cross-legged on the bed, I picked at a loose thread on my nightshirt as I listened to Royce's phone ring, not quite sure whether or not I was hoping he'd bedded down for the day.

Just as I was about to hang up, he picked up.

"Ms. Waynest. You called?"

"Yeah, I did," I said, hating my sudden bashful stammering. Last night, thinking nothing but angry thoughts about Chaz and the Sunstrikers had done plenty to boost me with false courage. Now, though it was necessary that I speak with him right away, I was regretting ever calling the vampire.

"Well then. What can I do for you?"

"I—I'm sorry. I need a sec to get myself together," I admitted, leaning forward to balance my forehead against my palm.

He made a sound of frustration, faint but unmistakable. "I do hope you don't consider me responsible for whatever may have happened while you were out of town. I have little control over the Were population, and did not have enough time to sufficiently prepare—"

"Royce, shut *up*," I demanded, though my heart leapt into my throat once the words left my lips. Telling him off wasn't a great way to start off this conversation, but neither was letting him go on about how much he hoped he hadn't been implicated in something he had no control over. "I'm sorry. Actually, no, I'm not sorry. But I need you to be quiet and listen to me for a minute. Can you do that?"

"Very well," he said, wariness undisguised. He knew as well as I did that, while the belt would do well against werewolves, it had always been intended for vampires. I knew his daytime resting place, too. He had good reason to bear me a measure of respect, even if it was due to an unspoken threat I'd never carry out against him. "What did you want to tell me?"

"I'm going to say some things to you in confidence. I need your word that you'll keep this to yourself."

"You have it. Speak freely."

If nothing else, I trusted the vampire to be truthful. He might bend and reshape the facts to suit his whims, but he was never completely dishonest with me. "Okay. First, I need to know something about our contract. I need to know what it might mean for us if I turn Were."

There was an understandably long pause. I bit my lower lip to keep from saying anything until he answered me.

"That depends. Did you sign a contract with someone else?" His voice was deceptively mild;

I was sure there was a great deal of emotion underlying the statement, no matter how calm he sounded right now.

"No."

"Then it means nothing. You are still wholly mine."

I had to fight back a sudden, violent shudder at that statement. It took a silent count to ten before I could continue.

"So that means if I become Were, everything that's mine stays mine?"

"Yes. When you die, your belongings will be turned over to me to manage as your estate. Turning Were does not change that clause, though it would throw a great number of things into question and might involve a lengthier, more expensive probate process. However, that shouldn't happen unless you sign another contract. If you are considering it, I would advise against doing so. The legal liability alone—"

"I haven't, and I won't," I said, voice harsh, breaking with the strain. "Don't assume anything here, Royce. It's not what you think."

He quieted, considering my words. I knew the moment he must have realized what I meant. His anger was immediate and intense. "Who is responsible for this? Have you reported them to the authorities yet?"

"I haven't, and I'm not sure I will."

"If it was Chaz, I can understand your reluctance. However, consider the implications of failing to uphold your obligation to report an incident like this. With the attention paid to you by the media, it won't go unnoticed for long."

"It wasn't Chaz," I said, voice cold. The mention of the media dragged out a deep, abiding sense of hatred for the direction my life was now hurtling, no matter how much I wished it otherwise. "I asked you to keep quiet about this because the reporter tailing me—hopefully—doesn't know yet. Neither does my family."

"I see. I'd like to know exactly what happened. Are you certain you are infected?"

I rubbed at my forehead as I thought about what to say. How much to tell him. What he might use against me later.

"It's not certain. I was scratched on Sunday night by one of the shifted Weres. I've had a conversation about it with Rohrik Donovan, and he told me I won't know for sure for maybe three or four weeks."

"I see."

"Royce, how did you know something bad was going to happen out there?"

"It's not something I can risk disclosing over the phone. Next time we meet, I'll go over it with you."

"That's not very helpful."

"I'm sorry that I can't do more for you right now. Please believe I didn't expect anything like this to happen," he said, some of the cold anger draining out of his voice. Instead, he seemed resigned. "I knew there was a possibility you might have been hurt by one of the people seeking revenge against the Sunstrikers, but I never considered that Chaz would be so careless as to put you in a position to become infected. Our conversations had led me to believe that wasn't in his plans for you. I apologize for my lack of foresight."

"Hey, you just apologized to me twice in less than a minute. You're creeping me out here."

His laughter was a shadow of the usual ironic tones I was used to hearing from him. "It's unusual, yes. You're one of few people I've had good reason or desire to apologize to in quite some time. I suppose I should be getting used to it by now."

"Okay, no pity parties allowed. I'm the one who's supposed to be upset about all this."

"Ms. Waynest—Shiarra—I feel some measure of personal responsibility for your well-being. I did as much as I could for you without forcing you to remain by my side. This is not what I would have chosen for your future."

If not for the sincerity with which he said it, I might have taken offense at his assumptions that he had any right to plot some fate for me. Knowing Royce, it was a bit hard to be angry at him for saying he was sorry he hadn't turned me into a vampire instead. He hadn't made it a secret that's what he wanted from me, after all.

"It's too late to be sorry. It wasn't something I wanted, but there's nothing to be done about it now. All I'm asking is that you stay quiet about this. I may have more questions later. I suppose it depends on how things turn out."

"That may be so, but it might not be too late to do something to change your future. If you are willing to take the risk, I could make you a vampire instead."

Chapter 27

"What?" Master of the witty comeback, that's me.

"It's possible the infection hasn't spread enough to prevent the change into a vampire instead. It would be risky, but you could become one of us if you wish. You'll need to make the choice quickly, though, for I can't guarantee it would work. The longer you wait, the less likely the change would take hold."

I rubbed my forehead with the heel of my hand, scrunching my eyes closed as a stress headache bloomed. "Run that by me again."

His voice seemed to reach me from a distance, echoing through a wall of shock that had settled comfortably between me and reality. "It may not be too late for you to make a choice. You would be far better off if you were one of us. Immortality alone would be an immense benefit over the reduced lifespan of a Were. Think about it, at the very least."

". . . Reduced lifespan?" For whatever reason, that cut through my haze and brought with it a fresh rush of terror. "Please tell me you are saying that in comparison to the life of a vampire."

"I'm afraid not. Their increased metabolism helps them heal faster, yes, but it also means their bodies age far more quickly. Though this is certainly not true in every case, and I'm sure there have been no hard scientific studies on the matter, in my experience they do not last much beyond forty, perhaps forty-five years of age."

More surprises Chaz had never shared with me.

"This is too much. I'm sorry, Royce, it's—this is just too much. I need to go."

"I understand. Think about my offer. I'll check back tonight."

I hung up without saying good-bye. My mouth felt like it was stuffed with cotton, and my eyes positively burned with strain, aching in waves that pulsed in time with my now pounding headache. My hands shook, and I struggled to keep from giving in to the looming panic attack.

The choices laid out before me were terrifying. No matter which way I looked at it, there seemed no right answer.

Sit back and do nothing? I might or might not be infected. There was a possibility nothing would happen to me. Arnold might even be able to do something about it; he'd promised to check to see if The Circle had any spells that would cure lycanthropy.

Then again, if I was infected and there was no cure, I could look forward to life as an outcast from Were society, disowned by my family and crucified by the media. Oh, and shaving who knew how many years off my expected lifespan.

If I took Royce's offer, I'd have an eternity to look forward to of drinking blood, never seeing sunlight, and watching my friends and family gradually die off, one by one. I'd be no more than a monster preying upon people to survive, hiding behind a human mask.

I'd never been particularly religious, despite my mother's efforts. Popular opinion was that vampires and werewolves had no immortal souls; if they ever had, the soul fled the body once they turned. Either way, in Mom's eyes, I'd be treading the path of the damned.

Sick did not begin to cover how I felt.

I stayed that way on the bed, empty, drained of life and unable to do so much as shed a tear, for quite a long time. It wasn't until nearly noon that I realized how late it had gotten and that Sara had neither shown nor called. I checked the office to see if she'd forgotten to pick me up and gone in without me. The answering machine greeted me instead of Jen's cheerful voice. Frowning, I called Sara's cell next, my concern deepening as the call went straight to voice mail—which was completely full and wouldn't accept any new messages.

Not wanting to deal with what that might mean, I tossed the phone down and headed for the shower. That should help me wake up a bit. Perhaps Sara's phone would be turned back on after I got out.

Twenty minutes later, I was clean, refreshed,

and didn't look quite so much like I'd just risen from the dead. My temper wasn't improved, but that was par for the course.

When I stepped out of the bathroom wrapped in a towel, Sara was sitting on my bed, gray faced. She looked as bad as I felt; her blond hair, normally salon-straight and perfectly coiffed, was tangled and unbrushed. Her clear blue eyes were bloodshot, while her skin had taken on an ashen pallor under the late summer tan. Even her clothes, usually perfectly pressed, were rumpled, the buttons on her shirt done up unevenly.

"Jesus, Sara, you look like shit."

What would normally have gotten a similar crack out of her didn't come off quite as I'd expected. She burst into tears.

"Holy hell, what's wrong?!" I rushed forward, but she held up a hand to stop me, wiping at her eyes with the other. She still didn't say anything. Frustrated, I backtracked, grabbed a box of tissues from the bathroom, and settled down beside her on the bed. As she took one of the tissues I offered, I noticed the papers crumpling up under my butt; I'd sat down on a newspaper.

I rose just enough to pull the papers from under me, staring at the headline screaming off the first page of today's news.

NEW YORK'S WEREWOLVES DON'T PLAY BY THE RULES
By JIM PRADIZ

MANHATTAN (Oct. 6) – A dangerous trend has surfaced in New York's werewolf community.

Local packs have come under intense scrutiny by government-funded regulatory bodies; recent investigations into the actions of the Sunstriker and Ravenwood packs have produced evidence that some of these werewolves don't adhere to federal guidelines of gaining signed authorization from their victims prior to exposure to the lycanthropy virus.

Evidence is mounting that many of these werewolves have chosen to work outside the bounds of the required contracts that legalize intimate contact between humans and Others. When the Other-Citizen Amendment to the Constitution, Article XIV-1(B), was passed on November 12, 2001, it was determined that no intimate physical contact would be permitted between Others and any human who had not yet signed and filed an agreement giving their full consent to potential injury or death at the hands of their Other-citizen sponsor.

It has become apparent that New York's werewolves do not always honor this legal requirement. Instances have been documented of some of these creatures having potentially infected and even turned humans without a legally signed and filed contract in place.

Deputy Chief of Police Alberto Rodriguez made a statement regarding the accusations. "We have received reports of unlawful activity in the Other community. Rest assured, this situation is under investigation. All I can say at this point is that anyone considering friendship or close connection to an Other-citizen should be very wary of the potential consequences."

Calls for comment to the leaders of the Sunstrikers and Ravenwoods have not been returned. Rohrik Donovan, leader of the Moonwalkers and lauded for his involvement in Other-citizen rights activities, refused to comment. Donovan is best known for his work to spearhead progressive changes for Other-citizens to help them be more accepted by our society.

This reporter has found in the process of undercover investigation information that victims of potential or confirmed infection outside of a contract include:

- Trish Booker, the CEO of Fortune 5,000 company Gen-U-Con, Inc.;
- Reed Thompson, a student at NYU;
- Ethan Peyton, an EMT;
- Patrick Driscoll, an attorney;
- Aurora Vacchio, an actress; and
- Shiarra Waynest, local private investigator.

(See photo spread, next page.)

Deputy Chief Rodriguez confirmed that there may be other victims based on witness statements and evidence at hand, but that no arrests have yet been made. Several suspects have been detained for questioning.

Per public records, Waynest and Booker were contractually bound to vampire Alec Royce prior to exposure to lycanthropy in-

fection. No records were found of contracts
lawfully filed involving the victims and the
werewolves identified in the incidents, or
documentation indicating a connection with
or an end to their obligations to the vampire.

Comments from such anti-werewolf groups
as Mothers Against Others and the White
Hats have been unanimous: "Something must
be done to stop these creatures from spreading their disease."

I stared down at the spread. Turned the page.
Stared at the pictures.

No wonder the reporter hadn't bothered me
since that brief meeting at breakfast. He'd
snapped pictures of me clutching my injured
arm, one of the werewolves visible as a huge presence looming nearby. Jim must have set up camp
somewhere outside, waiting patiently for someone to do something stupid enough to merit a
spot in his story, which he'd clearly been planning to print regardless of what happened over
the weekend. The other victims pictured were
caught in similar poses, looking as frightened and
shocked as I did as they clutched at what were obviously fresh wounds from the werewolves looming in the background. How he'd managed to
capture the photos wasn't my concern.

With that picture of me to act as the proverbial
icing, he had neatly ruined every chance I had of
keeping my problem a secret.

Though my reaction was delayed by shock, it
didn't take long for the enormity of having my

picture and name attached to the article hit me. The papers fell from my nerveless fingers, scattering on the floor as I sank back onto the bed. Sara was watching me with watery eyes, the tissue clutched over her mouth.

I closed my eyes and bowed my head, saying nothing. My whole body shook with the effort of containing my fury. The need to find an outlet was sudden and intense. The desire to take out the belt and use it for the hunt was greater than anything I had ever experienced, even eclipsing the memories of craving and withdrawal from Royce's blood. If I wasn't careful, I might lash out at anyone at this point—even Sara.

"They've been calling the office," she said, hushed, uncertain.

I paused before speaking, afraid of what might spill out of my mouth if I wasn't careful. "Who?"

"Police. Reporters. Political activists. You name it. I gave Jen the okay to turn the phone off. They've been calling my cell, too."

My neck creaked from tension when I turned to her. For her part, she held her ground, not flinching at the look I gave her.

"It won't be long before they start knocking on our doors," she said, ever so gently placing a hand on my arm. She wasn't afraid of me; she was concerned. That brought with it a breath of relief, brief and ephemeral as butterfly wings. "Do you want to stay with me until the worst of this blows over?"

I looked around the tiny bedroom, at the pictures hanging on the wall, and the tchotchkes lined up on my dresser. My gaze zeroed in on the picture in the middle. My whole family gathered in the backyard, with Sara and Chaz and Arnold, taken at my younger brother's birthday party earlier this year. Arnold had been pretending to be my boyfriend that day; Chaz hadn't liked it, but he'd been civil enough about it. That day had started the chain of events that led to my getting back together with him, back when I thought he was a decent guy. When I thought that breaking up with him had been a mistake.

If not for him, I wouldn't be in this mess. Sara wouldn't be looking at me with a mixture of pity and horror.

I wouldn't have to worry about how long it would take before my parents or brothers saw the paper.

"I don't know," I finally replied, the heavy weight of the statement making my voice raw. "My dad has probably already seen this. He always reads the paper in the morning. Did he call the office? My cell was broken on the trip."

"I haven't heard from him or your mom yet. I turned off my cell when I figured out yours was off, too. I'm sorry I didn't come earlier, but I needed a little time. . . ." She trailed off, voice faint.

I offered a weak smile, which she didn't return. "Thank you."

"For what?"

"For not judging. For talking to me about it. For offering to let me stay with you. Shit, Sara, I don't know. For being my friend."

She leaned over to put her arm around me,

plucking up the box between us and pressing a tissue into my hands. Only then did I realize that tears were spilling down my cheeks.

"Fuck going into work today. Do you have any alcohol?"

Chapter 28

After I got dressed, we spent the next few hours alternately packing up some essentials and crying over ice cream and coffee liberally spiked with Bailey's and some of the aged whiskey I'd tucked in the back of the fridge, saved for a special occasion. Sara asked some tough questions I didn't know how to answer. When I explained that I'd sent Arnold on a mission to find a cure, she nodded and said nothing, though I could tell she was hurt that I'd told her boyfriend before her.

We decided to wait a few hours for the alcohol buzz to pass out of our systems before leaving for her place, passing the time in planning and arguing. I gave her the no-holds-barred account of what had occurred over the weekend. We ranted and railed about Chaz's infidelity together before easing off into a subject that was, in its way, even tougher for me to face than my plans for dealing with the Sunstrikers.

Sara thought I should come clean to my parents

about everything that had happened, including why I'd hidden from them that Chaz was Were. I thought that was crazy talk. My parents were no doubt both furious with and worried about me. I was not in the frame of mind to deal with my mom's hysterics, and likely wouldn't be for quite a while.

Finally, the two of us came to an uneasy peace; we'd figure it out later. We went back to packing.

A pounding on the door jerked me out of my funk. Sara shot me a look from across the room, hands paused over the books she'd been skimming on my shelf.

I got up from the table where I'd been sorting through some papers and peered through the peephole in the door. There were two men I didn't recognize outside. When I pulled the door open, leaving the chain on, one of them held up a badge for inspection.

"Ms. Waynest? I'm Detective Terry Smith, and this is Detective Yarmouth."

Police. The perfect end to a perfect day. I unlocked the chain and opened the door all the way, gesturing them inside. "Let me guess. You guys saw the morning paper."

The officer smiled at me, his eyes a flinty gray that reminded me too much of Max Carlyle. I looked away and edged over to the kitchen table, settling into a seat. The officers remained standing, both of them eyeing their surroundings. Smith shared a look with the other detective once he spotted Sara across the room.

"Ah, Ms. Halloway is here, too? That's good. Saves us a trip." Detective Smith tucked his badge away and pulled out a pad and a pen, glancing between us. "We can keep this short and sweet, if you like. Is there anything you'd like to tell us about the evidence Mr. Pradiz presented in the paper today?"

"I think it speaks for itself," I stated sourly, rubbing self-consciously at the cuts on my arm. "I'd like to press charges, too."

"We'll get to that. Can you identify the Other-citizen responsible?"

"His name is Dillon. Charles Hallbrook can tell you where to find him."

"Thank you. We'll follow up on that. In the meantime, we wanted to let you know that we'll be examining the documentation and photographs that Mr. Pradiz collected and plan to proceed accordingly. We'd appreciate it if you would keep this out of the press as much as possible as the investigation is still pending. We don't want to bias every potential juror in the county."

"It's a little late for that."

"You can prevent any more details from being leaked."

I nodded, fiddling nervously with a napkin. Though they hadn't questioned me about it, I had no doubt they'd find out about the hissy fit I'd had, the property I'd technically stolen and destroyed, along with all the other stupid crap that had happened this weekend.

"Ms. Waynest, Ms. Halloway, we believe there may be some danger to your persons and wanted to suggest you find a safe place to stay until the worst of this blows over. We've had problems in the past with disappearing witnesses; we don't want that to happen to you."

"Great," I said hollowly. Lovely. Arnold's earlier words were now confirmed by an irrefutable source. Just another reason to feel inadequate as an investigator and wronged by my decidedly *ex*-lover. I didn't have time for self-pity, and I forced myself to pay attention to the rest of the conversation.

"She'll stay with me," Sara said, her tone brooking no refusal.

"That may not be wise, ma'am. You may be called as a witness, too. We need both of you to stay somewhere safe until the trial is over."

"Are you taking us into protective custody?" I asked, straightening in alarm. "A witness protection program or something?"

The officer rubbed the back of his neck. "Due to budget cuts and a lack of foundation in this aspect of the case, we haven't been able to get the approval rushed through yet. For the time being, until we can, we strongly suggest you get out of here and find a place to stay where you won't be found. A hotel might do the trick. Don't tell any friends or family where you are. If you can afford it, take some time off from work. And stay in touch with us." He offered a business card, which I barely glanced at before stuffing it in my pocket. "We can call you in when it's time, or when the approval to put you under official protection goes through."

"This isn't an official visit, is it?" I asked.

Smith reddened, sharing a significant look with

Yarmouth before answering me. "No. Can we trust you?"

I blinked. "Excuse me?"

"Can we trust you?" he repeated, darting a furtive look at Sara.

"We can keep a secret, if that's what you're asking," Sara replied, puzzled.

Yarmouth kept his voice low and conspiratorial. We had to lean in to hear him properly, he spoke so quietly. "In his way, Jim did you a favor. Earlier today he sent us copies of all the material he had gathered, along with some extra info on your connections to the Sunstrikers. This is our case, but someone's been doing their best to sabotage it. We've lost a few witnesses in this investigation already. We can't afford to lose any more. All of this is completely off the record; we were never here. And since that's the case, I can also tell you that you may want to hurry; there are a few other officers from a different bureau planning to speak with and possibly detain Ms. Waynest. Stay out of any places where your information might be traced. No hospitals, no credit cards, no cell phones. Get it?"

Sara and I shared a look. This wasn't good news—not that I'd had much of that the last few days anyway, but this made things even more difficult and convoluted than they already were. Funny to think that the reporter had been looking out for me, in his way, even if it took destroying my personal life to do it.

"Thank you, officers," Sara said. "We'll get back to you as soon as we've found a place to stay."

They nodded, heading for the door. "Don't tell

us where you are. Just let us know you got there safely and check in every few days."

"Will do," I promised.

As soon as they were out the door, I leapt into action.

"Damn it, Shia, where are we going to go?" Sara asked, following me into my room. She slammed her palm against the wall, gritting her teeth as she spotted the picture of Chaz I'd been glaring daggers at earlier. "I can't believe he'd stoop so low. We can't go to my house, or my sister Janine's, Arnold's, or your parents' place. I'm not camping out at the office, and I can't leave the dogs behind. Where the hell are we going to go? How are we going to get any work done?"

"Let me think a minute," I replied, though a hazy idea was already forming in my mind.

I didn't have enough cash to pull off a disappearing act until this blew over. Sara might, but most likely she kept the bulk of her money in the bank, which meant any transaction could be traced and lead authorities—or the Sunstrikers, if any of them were savvy or connected enough— right to us.

If the cops were that sure there would be retaliation for being a victim or a witness or whatever the Sunstrikers thought of me, I wasn't going to sit around and wait to be found. Undoubtedly, they'd eventually come across me if I stayed in the city. No matter what, I'd make it as tough on them as I could. If they came looking for a helpless human, then I'd do my best to pull together all the firepower I could muster. Since we couldn't go to my family or Sara's for help, and had little money, our options for running were extremely limited.

That left us with only one place to go that might be (relatively) safe.

Sara watched in confusion as I tore through my closet, shoving things around—until I found the body armor made to ward off vampire and were-wolf attacks buried in the back. I tossed it on the bed, soon followed by my combat boots, trench coat, matched guns, extra ammo, and the hunter's belt. Next came the Amber Kiss perfume I'd hidden under the sink in the bathroom, designed to make me smell less like food to Others. I wrapped the fragile vials in a towel and placed them carefully on top of everything else.

Sara eyed the piles curiously but said nothing. All of it was shoved unceremoniously into a duffel bag slung over my shoulder. She followed as I grabbed my purse off the table and, as an after-thought, plucked my rolodex off my desk and tossed that in my duffel as well.

She gave me a look when I tucked the mostly empty whiskey bottle into my duffel, too.

We trekked down to my car, tossing everything in the back. Sara got into the driver's seat without asking, and I didn't question it. Jingling the keys, she glanced at me. "Any ideas yet?"

"Yeah. Let's go pick up some stuff for you. I think I know where to go from there."

It didn't take long to get to Sara's cute little brick number tucked away in one of New York's most excellent examples of upper-middle-class suburbia. Her dogs, Buster and Roxie, had their paws up between the slats of the white picket fence, tails going a mile a minute as they barked a furious storm in greeting.

Sara threw together a suitcase with enough clothes and necessities to keep her going for a week or two. She made a few calls, including one to Jen telling her to take a couple of paid days off, which made me cringe. I'd pulled in a lot of dough doing that job for The Circle last year, but reserves were running low, and there was no guarantee we'd be able to pull off working any jobs until the worst of this mess was over. Aside from which, I wasn't sure how I'd be able to operate now that my face had been plastered on a leading newspaper, no doubt to follow soon on the Internet. That was sure to hamper my undercover work, just as the media coverage after the incident with Royce and Max Carlyle had resulted in a couple of jobs where my cover had been unwittingly blown by curious bystanders and, in one memorable instance, the mark himself recognizing me.

That was a problem for later. For now, I had Sara at my back. Depending on her was something I'd normally rail against, but for now I was willing to make an exception. There were too many variables and too many immediate troubles to let my pride get in the way of our safety.

The dogs were a bit of a problem. I wasn't thrilled with the idea, but we put the backseats down and let the dogs ride in the bed of my SUV. They kept shoving their heads between the seats and slobbering on me until I opened the back windows so they could stick their heads out instead.

Sara let me take the wheel this time. As I headed

toward 495, she cleared her throat, breaking what I came to realize had become an increasingly tense silence between us.

"I take it you've got an idea of where to go now?"

I noted the angle of the sun before answering her, tightening my grip on the wheel. "Yes. You're not going to like it."

She snorted, waving at the traffic around us. "This isn't exactly how I envisioned spending my day, Shia. I suppose it beats doing more surveillance on the Riker case, but we're going to have a lot of pissed off clients and demands for refunds soon if we don't come up with a plan. Hiding somewhere for months or years until this trial is over doesn't strike me as a great way to keep the business going. Plus, I'm not sure how we're going to pull off staying hidden while keeping the company's doors open."

"I have an idea," I said, keeping focused on the traffic ahead. "We just need to last a month outside of the office. Until I know for sure what will happen to me."

When I glanced over, her skin had taken on a touch of that sickly pallor she'd had earlier. She audibly swallowed before answering me. "Okay. Until then?"

"Until then, we stay with Alec Royce."

Chapter 29

Sara spluttered, something that I'd never seen her do before. It was comical enough to make me laugh, even given how shitty my mood had become.

"Are you joking? What the fuck are you thinking?"

"No, I'm serious. He owes me for saving his life. He's no more dangerous than waiting around my apartment for one of the Sunstrikers to come finish what they started, and more likely to be able to protect you if I start changing." Sara sobered, but she still looked ill, and she fidgeted nervously with her lap belt. "You're not contracted, and as long as you hold your ground, never will be. His place is practically a fortress, and every vampire in it is prepared to defend it. With John and Max gone, it's probably the safest place for us to hide without having to leave the state."

"But what about you? You're contracted to him. He might not want you around if you're . . . if you . . ."

"No," I said shortly. "He might not. I already talked to him early this morning, though. He's also got some ideas on how to handle this mess." Ideas I wouldn't share with Sara until I'd made my choice.

She nodded, fiddling with the strap of her purse now. I was tempted to slap at her hands to make her stop, but her worry was understandable. She was rarely this nervous; I was more used to seeing this kind of behavior out of her neurotic sister, Janine.

"He lives by Central Park, too, which is Moonwalker territory. The Sunstrikers don't come by here often, so as long as we don't stray too far we should be fairly safe."

"Has Royce agreed to this?"

"I haven't asked him yet."

She quieted again, and the tension in the air crept up a notch. I was too on edge not to react; the words spilled out of my mouth before I could stop myself. "For fuck's sake, Sara, he's not the Antichrist. He's been the most decent man— creature—whatever, that I've dealt with since the shit hit the fan. I'm sure he won't mind helping us out here."

"That's funny, coming from you," she said, too flatly for me to take offense. "A couple months ago, you would've cut off your own hands before driving to see him. What changed?"

"Fuck if I know," I snarled, fingers tightening on the wheel until the rubber Tinkerbell cover slipped off. I scrabbled at it until it snapped back into place, cursing under my breath. Then slammed on the brakes when I realized the guy in front of me had come to a sudden stop, prompting more cursing and a one-finger salute from me.

"Do you need me to drive?"

"No!" I shouted. After a few deep breaths, I managed a much calmer reply. "No. Sorry. It's been an incredibly shitty day. Why am I telling you this? You already know."

"Getting in an accident won't make it better."

"I'll be careful," I said, settling back and rolling my shoulders to help ease out the tension. "Sara, really, I'm sorry. I'm not thrilled about this either, but it's the best idea I can come up with on short notice. Maybe we can find someone else to stay with later. At least for now, he's someone who can provide us shelter and protection."

"Never thought I'd hear those words used in conjunction with a vampire."

"Pulling out the fancy lawyer-talk on me, eh?"

A short laugh escaped her, though I could tell she hadn't meant to let it slip. Some of her nervousness was easing off. "Yeah, yeah. Don't make me go all devil's advocate on you."

If she knew the real reason I thought staying with Royce was a good idea, she'd have been wrestling me for control of the wheel. For now, I relaxed and followed the path burned into my memory from the day I'd first visited Royce's home.

He owned a small apartment building half a block from Central Park that housed the closest and most trusted or valuable members of his "family," plus the humans he'd once offhandedly mentioned were closest to being turned by him or one of the other vampires in the building. I'd met most of them during my stay while the bond between us wore off, though I'd made no special effort to get to know them. I wasn't even sure I remembered all of their names; unless they were guarding me, they were the least of my concerns at the time.

If I was lucky, there would be space for Sara and me to stay for a while. A couch to crash on, at the very least. Royce had often extended the offer to me to return to his side, though I'd made efforts to ignore it—until now. Hopefully he wouldn't mind my dropping in and wouldn't have a problem with Sara, or her dogs, tagging along.

I was lucky enough to find parking directly across the street from Royce's home. We left the dogs and the bags in the car while we went to test the waters and find out if we were welcome to stay.

The apartment building didn't look anything like you'd expect from a vampire den. With the white shutters and brick façade, not to mention the roses entwined through the iron-and-brick fencing surrounding the property, it looked more like a bunch of families with kids should be calling the place home. That it housed over a dozen vampires, and another dozen human servants, was enough to make me shiver once we passed into the shadow of the building.

Though the sun was still high in the sky when we arrived, I wasn't surprised a vampire was pulling guard duty, seated in the shadows at the back of the windowless foyer. He looked up from the paperback he was reading, puzzlement reflecting in his gaze before he rose from his seat at the table covered with in-baskets for tenant mail. I recognized his angular, handsome features, and took his offered hand.

"Shiarra, I remember you. Good to see you again."

"Hi, Wes. This is my business partner, Sara Halloway."

The vampire took her hand as well, and she did an admirable job of hiding her uncomfortable flinch at his touch. Wes's pale blue eyes locked onto her throat, and I was sure he'd detected her heart rate speeding up out of what I hoped was fear.

Like most of the vampires in the building, Wes was (pardon the pun) drop-dead gorgeous. With his killer physique, short blond hair, and neatly trimmed goatee, he looked like he would've made a handsome and dashing hero for the latest Hollywood summer blockbuster. Or maybe he would've played the part of a pillaging Viking warrior who left mayhem and murder in his wake. I cleared my throat to pull his attention off Sara and held my ground despite the fact that his pupils had taken on a reddish tint.

"We're here to see Mr. Royce. I know he's probably resting, but—"

"You never fail to surprise me," Royce said, cutting me off. Sara and I both jumped, not having heard him as he settled into a comfortable lean in the doorframe leading deeper into Alice's rabbit hole. Scars or no, he always cut a fine figure. The ancient vampire hadn't bothered to put on a shirt, his hands pocketed in his fashionably faded jeans, leaving his toned chest and corded arms bare to view. If he hadn't scared the crap out of me, I'd have been eating up the view with my eyes and damn the consequences.

Wes inclined his head to Royce, taking a step back from us to resume his station at the table.

"I suppose you've come because you need my assistance with something."

"Yes," I agreed, putting myself between the vampires and Sara as surreptitiously as possible. She reached for my hand and I took hers, hiding my misgivings at the way she was trembling by presenting as calm a front as I could manage. "I'm sorry to put this on your plate, but the police seem to think that Chaz and the other Sunstrikers might not be too pleased with us thanks to an article that ran in today's paper. They suggested we get gone until we're approved for a witness protection program."

"So you came to me," he stated flatly, frown lines appearing between his black-as-pitch eyes. "I'm not in the habit of doing favors like this, Ms. Waynest. The legalities of my involvement would be questionable, if it is as you say. Unless you have something new to offer?" His gaze flicked to Sara, back to meet mine.

"Shia, forget it, let's go," Sara whispered. The urgency in her voice only made me more determined.

"Don't involve Sara in this. Whatever you want, take it from me. All I'm asking is for you to give her a safe place to stay until the trial is over and it's safe for her to go home. If I can stay for a little while, too—"

"Are you sure you want to offer me anything I ask for?" Royce drawled. He pushed off the doorframe, moving with all the sinuous grace of a panther, stalking toward me on bare feet. I didn't flinch when he ran a fingertip over my cheek, testing the heat that no doubt rose from the blush marring my skin. "That could be dangerous. Very, very dangerous . . ."

Sara's nails dug into my wrist, dragging me back to reality.

"Within reason, you perv. Don't touch me." My demand would've been more impressive if my voice hadn't been shaking so badly.

He threw back his head and laughed, giving me an excellent view of his extended canines. Wes was rolling his eyes behind the paperback he'd resumed reading.

"Oh, you are a treat. All right, enough with the dramatics. No need to worry, Ms. Waynest, Ms. Halloway. You are welcome to stay, and have my word you won't be in any danger while you're with us," Royce said. He slid past me to take Sara's free hand, the one that wasn't clinging to mine in a death grip. He brushed a kiss over her knuckles, smiling that wicked, winsome smile that had won him a place on the cover of innumerable fashion magazines. Her blush was as clear as her unease. "Mr. MacLeod will no doubt be pleased to see you again."

"Oh, he's here?" she stammered, drawing back. I stared blankly at this exchange. Since when did Sara know anything about Royce or his people?

"Indeed. It just so happens that one of the apartments on the first floor is available. Your timing is convenient, as I was about to have some tenants reassigned. For now, I'll have Ryan and Louis help you get your things from the car. If you're planning to bring those dogs inside, see that you keep them quiet. Many of my people are asleep for the day and won't appreciate being woken by excessive noise."

"Oh," she said faintly, her grip finally loosening on me. "Oh, all right. Thank you. I'll see what I can do."

"Wesley, if you can see to that?" At the Viking-esque vampire's nod, Royce turned his attention to me. "Ms. Waynest, might I have a word with you?"

Sara looked like the proverbial deer in head-lights at being left alone. Come to think of it, I wasn't thrilled with the idea of separating either, but now wasn't the time to be ticking off the vam-pire. I gave her hand one last squeeze, passing her my car keys and leaving her with Wes. He was busying himself with an intercom set into the wall, telling someone named Julio to kick Louis's lazy ass out of bed.

Royce pointed out the apartment that I'd be sharing with Sara for the next month, then led the way to the stairwell at the far end of the build-ing, saying nothing as we headed up to the third floor. On the way, a yawning guy who could have modeled for Calvin Klein ads in his spare time passed us, giving Royce a nod and me a curious look on his way down the stairs. His chiseled fea-tures looked familiar, but I couldn't remember if that was Ryan or Louis, one of the human ser-vants catering to the vampires in the building.

Sara would fit right in with all the pretty people

here. I felt like the redheaded stepchild from hell, particularly with my hopelessly frizzy hair, utter lack of any curves where they counted, and the scars on my face, stomach, and arm acquired in my "adventures" over the last year or so.

Not that I was really worried about fitting in with a bunch of vampires and their servants. Yeesh.

When we reached the top floor, Royce let me precede him into the giant, wide open room with its Greek statuary of long-dead gods lit by tiny spotlights. All the windows were, of course, shuttered for the day, leaving the space in a semblance of twilight. The little lights helped brighten the room by reflecting from the mostly bare hardwood floor, giving the illusion of walking on a carpet of stars.

There was a girl seated cross-legged on one of the chaise lounges in the middle of the room, a stack of books to one side of her, typing furiously on the laptop balanced between her legs. She was effortlessly lovely in that way that some girls manage to pull off. The smooth, clear skin that needed no makeup to the grace infused in the simple motion of absently sweeping long auburn tresses out of her eyes made her a vision of quiet, calm beauty that was right at home amidst the statuary. She glanced at us briefly then did a double take, fingers pausing over the keyboard.

"Jessica, will you excuse us, please? I need a moment alone with Ms. Waynest."

She shrugged, packing up her laptop. "Sure. I'll come back for the books later. Let me know when you're ready."

He drew her to him when she rose, cupping her cheeks as though she were made of the finest, most fragile porcelain. I was admittedly shocked at the—dare I say it—tender way he kissed her. She rose on tiptoe to meet him, and I looked away, feeling far too much like a voyeur, even though they weren't doing anything terribly inappropriate.

When they broke the kiss, she gave me a cheery smile and a wave, practically skipping out of the room. She was far too . . . too . . . *nice* to be so intimate with someone like Royce. The way his eyes followed her as she left the room spoke of hunger, but not the kind that lusted for blood. He wanted something else from that girl, something less tangible. The implications made my head, already hurting, reach whole new levels of what-the-fuck.

"She will be John's replacement in due time," he remarked, blinking and turning his attention to me. Though it didn't surprise me that he hadn't found a replacement for his turncoat flunky yet, that he wanted a woman—a human woman—to take the place of the dead vampire was entirely unexpected. I wasn't sure what expression I had on my face—maybe incredulity—but Royce was amused by it. His smile widened, and he gestured to the chaise. "Please, sit."

Once I did, he chose a seat facing me, settling back in the cushions and propping his feet up. He was far too relaxed and cheerful for my peace of mind. I wasn't used to seeing him this way—not at all.

He saved me from having to explain myself by

resuming the persona I was more familiar with. Royce-at-home was not the same as Royce-at-the-office, and the disparities bugged me for no reason I could readily put my finger on.

"Now, then. To business. Knowing you, I don't dare assume that you came with the intention of allowing me to turn you."

I nodded, biting my lower lip. Whatever he expected in payment would most likely involve my opening a vein—which wasn't something I was terribly excited about doing. I'd thought he wanted me for other reasons, but his actions with Jessica made me question his motives on levels I hadn't previously thought to explore.

"If you turn Were, I can't have you stay here. Sara can remain, but you would present too much of a hazard to my people. I have properties upstate, but I usually require some form of exchange when I offer shelter to those who come to me. I know the state of your finances. You have few reserves to call on, and fewer friends to back you or trade in that most valuable commodity, information. Despite what you have done for me in the past, I would call our debt to each other even by now. That does not leave many options. What do you intend to offer, Ms. Waynest?"

"I'm not sure what you want. You've already got willing donors, and I don't even want to think about you bumping uglies with somebody—least of all, me."

He chuckled at that, folding his hands behind his head and giving me a wicked smile. "Are you sure? You've never once thought about it? What it might be like?"

"Don't play games with me," I said, more harshly than I intended. At his sardonic look, I swallowed hard, and my voice shook, but I somehow managed to meet his gaze levelly. "Clearly you've got Miss Sunshine to fool around with. You don't need me for that."

"That all may very well be true, but you have not yet answered my question. I expect an answer, Shiarra. My patience is not limitless."

I closed my eyes and clenched my hands in my lap to hide how they shook, praying I was making the right decision this time, that I wasn't plunging into an abyss from which I might never return. Despite his threat, Royce waited for me to gather myself enough to answer him, unmoving, not speaking, intent upon my response. I gathered my courage and gave him what he was waiting for.

"Keep Sara safe, and let her go when it's time. None of your people can touch her or even talk to her about a contract. Arnold is searching for a cure for lycanthropy, so there's a greater chance I won't turn Were. In exchange for offering us sanctuary, I'll be yours on more than paper."

His black eyes were pitiless cold pits when I met them. His voice was low, smooth, as empty of emotion as his eyes. "Explain."

Though I wanted to hide away, to flinch from him, to escape this life and start over somewhere new, I had no time to come up with a better solution. The words spilled from my mouth, hollow, dry, like someone else was saying them. I needed to remember to breathe or I might very well pass

out from the strain of offering what shreds were
left of my soul to this monster on a silver platter.

"I won't fight you, I won't try to seek vengeance,
and I won't try to avoid it like I have in the past.
I'll submit to a blood bond, and offer my blood
to you willingly. It'll be yours to take whenever
you want."

Chapter 30

"No."

I blinked, the haze of shrieking terror clamoring in my mind receding at his unexpected response. "Excuse me?"

"I won't take what isn't offered freely. You're selling yourself out of some misguided sense of obligation. You do not want me or what I have to offer, and I won't accept the blood of a donor who doesn't truly desire to be in such a position. Not when my survival is not dependent upon it. Despite what you may think, and regardless of how other vampires may operate, that is not how I choose to treat those who have contracted themselves to me. It's too intimate an act to ask so much of another."

I sat there for a long moment, too stunned to speak. Royce had never given me the impression he wanted anything but to have access to parts of me I'd never thought I'd be willing to give him. That he'd essentially pointed out I'd be reluctantly whoring myself to him—though not in as many words—was enough to set me to blushing furiously, running my palm down my face as I tried and failed to come up with a reply that wouldn't make me look like an even bigger fool.

"Might I make a suggestion?" he said, once it became clear I was too embarrassed to speak. At my hesitant nod, he continued. "Perhaps an offer of friendship is in order. We have not had much opportunity to get to know each other outside of life-threatening events."

I gradually lowered my hand from my face, staring at him blankly. He was as still and calm as before, lounging, relaxed and sated, in the cushions, much like he'd been placed *just so* to model how truly appealing he could be.

To say I was thunderstruck would be like calling the sky blue. Next obvious observation, please.

He spoke softly, in a light and pleasant voice, as though we were chatting over tea. "If that doesn't suit you, I often need people to cover various functions at my businesses—catering, kitchen work, security—any of which you might be able to assist with if you're needed on short notice. For as long as you're here, if you can help with those activities when asked, and perhaps during those times when your potential condition is under control, I would consider that acceptable."

"Royce," I said, further embarrassed at being choked up by tears, "I don't—I'm not—"

"You don't need to sell yourself to me," he stated quietly, unfolding so as to lean forward in one smooth movement and take my hand in his. His fingers were cold but reassuring nonetheless. "When you're ready—and only then—I will gladly show you that being beholden to me is not as terrible as you imagine it to be."

I lowered my head, hiding my tears from him with my free hand. Of all the things I'd ever expected him to be, generous was not one of them. This was not the first time he'd extended an offer of friendship, though I'd thought during previous times that his version meant friends with some really icky benefits. His insistence in the past had led me to believe that he would stop at nothing to have me under his thumb. My naïveté and paranoia had often led to my embarrassment before, but never anything on such a spectacular scale.

The strangest thing yet was that he moved from the chair he was on to settle next to me, wrapping an arm around my shoulders and drawing me against his chest. Any other time, I would've been clawing at the walls to escape his touch. Now, I gave in to all the pressure of the last few days and truly wept, twisting to cling to his bare shoulders, my entire body shaking with the torrent of emotions fighting to escape me. Though his skin was cool, I felt no lingering sense of doubt or terror at being pressed so close to him. He did no more than hold me, lightly running his fingers through my hair, even as I buckled under the weight of worry and stress. He was my anchor in that moment, a pillar of cold strength, holding me close and keeping me from being swept away entirely.

I'm not quite sure how long I cried. By the end of it I was exhausted, chest heaving as I gasped in a few last hitching, sobbing breaths.

"All right?" he asked, pausing in his soothing motions.

"I think so," I whispered, voice raw. Though I'd cried until there were no more tears, I wasn't totally empty. There was enough sanity left to me to worry what he must think of me, and what could possibly have prompted me to hold him so tightly. "Thank you."

He loosened his grip on me and dipped a finger under my chin, tilting my head up. At first, he said nothing. Instead, he lightly ran the pad of his thumb under my eyes, carefully wiping away the moisture gathered there. His smile, usually wicked and hinting at all things dark and devious, was surprisingly kind. "What are friends for?"

I choked out a little laugh, wiping at my eyes myself. Unbelievable. I'd just cried all over *Alec Royce. The* Alec Royce. One of the oldest vampires in the United States. The same guy who had once tried to kill me. Even if the attempt hadn't necessarily been made under his own volition, it was one hell of a strange way for our relationship to turn. Who'd have thought the monster had a heart?

"Why don't you go ahead and clean up? The bathroom is through my bedroom in the back."

I nodded weakly, and he helped steady me when I stood up. He left me alone to put myself back together, shutting the door behind me.

I took a few minutes to rinse my face, gathering my shattered pride back into a semblance of what it had been before I broke down. A few minutes later, after washing the worst of the signs of my breakdown from my face, I emerged to find the vampire sprawled on the futon in his bedroom tapping away on a laptop. He looked up, the clear concern in his features tugging every last string tied to my heart.

"Better?"

"Much," I replied. My eyes were still red in the mirror, but that would fade with time. "Thank you, Royce. I'm sorry about—"

"Don't," he admonished, waving a hand at me. "You've been under an extraordinary amount of pressure. Don't apologize for it."

"Okay," I whispered, chastised.

"I need to get some things done, but I'll speak with you tonight before I go to the office. For now, why don't you go downstairs and get settled in. Try to rest. I'll have someone stop by later to fill you in on how we do things here."

I nodded, heading to the door. He stopped me before I got far.

"Shiarra?"

"Yes?"

"Don't blame yourself for any of this. Regardless of how events turn out, you will always have a place with me."

I needed to get out of here before the waterworks started up again. I nodded and hurried away, padding quietly across the empty expanse of the room with the statuary and dashing down the stairs. When I reached the foot of the stairs, Wes was peering down the hall. He shrugged and turned away when he spotted me, resuming his post.

I entered the apartment I was going to share with Sara for the next month or so, taking it in

at a glance. Clean, furnished, and tastefully—
if sparsely—appointed. A bookshelf holding a
number of German titles and a few pieces of art-
work added a touch of hominess to an otherwise
painfully plain room.

The dogs didn't greet me at the door like I expected; instead, they were cringing at the far end
of the room, huddled shivering like they were
afraid they were about to be eaten by monsters.
Come to think of it, that might not have been too
far off the mark if Sara and I hadn't been guests
in this vampire-infested sanctuary.

Sara peered out of the inner hallway, her face
too pale. She let out a sigh of relief on sighting
me, pressing her hand to her chest. "Jesus, you
about gave me a heart attack. Everything okay?"

"Yeah. Had to set some things straight, but it
looks like everything will be fine."

Her blue eyes searched my face, judging the
truth, and finding it better to let my little white lie
go unchallenged. "Aside from the lack of windows, this place is pretty nice. I picked the room
on the right. We've both got our own bathrooms
and closets. Everything is already furnished.
Looks like it was a couple of guys who lived here,
though. The girly mags and lotion in the dresser
were a dead giveaway."

A giggle escaped me despite myself. Then I remembered that someone, probably the mute
vampire, Mouse, had told me that the two men
who had lived in this apartment before Max Carlyle came to town were killed in the fight in the
basement. That sobered me quick enough.

"Just toss them. I don't think their owners will be coming back for them."

"Aye, love, ye may want to put some gloves on 'afore you handle that stuff," said a chipper voice from behind me. I glanced over my shoulder—and then turned around, blinking down at a woman who barely came up to my shoulder. "Good tae see ye again, lovey."

"Hi, Clarisse," I said, smiling wanly at the tiny vampire. I edged out of the doorway to give her room to come in. She flounced into the room, bright green eyes the color of Easter basket grass glittering with curiosity and excitement as she took in Sara and the dogs at a glance. She was wearing silk pajamas an eye-rending shade of lavender that somehow worked with her porcelain features and her curly black hair that trailed all the way to her hips when unbound, as it was now. "This is Sara, my business partner. Sara, this is Clarisse. She's one of the house guards. Don't ever take a bet from her."

"Ooh, lass, ye ruin all my fun," she pouted, setting her hands on her hips. Despite her tiny size and disarming looks, the vampire was formidable. Like Royce and Wesley, as well as a number of other vampires in the building, she was very, very old, which meant she didn't always need to rest the entire day. It was little wonder she had come to investigate. Eminently curious as she was, those Shirley Temple dimples distracted you from the dainty fangs that now peeked from behind bright red lips, and gave no hint as to the enormous strength in those tiny fingers.

"I hope ye two don't mind my stopping by. I

heard the hubbub when Ryan started complaining and came for a look-see."

Sara, for her part, took it all in stride. She shushed Buster when he gave one sharp, authoritative bark—warning Clarisse not to approach. The dogs whined nervously in their corner, but obeyed, staying (mostly) quiet while Sara took Clarisse's outstretched hand. She blinked at the vampire's cold, firm grip, but exhibited no obvious alarm.

"Are ye contracted, lass?"

Sara blanched, glancing at me before answering the vampire. "No. No plans to be, either."

"A shame. Ah, lovey, ye never know, ye might change yer mind 'afore ye leave."

"Right, thanks, Clarisse," I hurriedly interjected, ushering her toward the door. "Hey, maybe you could tell Mouse and everyone we're here later. We need to get some rest. Long day and all that."

"Oh? I smell a bet coming on." Her eyes took on a dangerous twinkle, and I groaned. It was the same look she got when about to start a wager on who would sleep with whom in the household, or win the next round of *American Idol.* "Not to fear, lass. I'll tell everyone to leave off until tonight. 'Til then!"

"'Til then," I replied, ushering her out the door and locking it behind me. Followed by running my palm over my face for what felt like the fiftieth time today.

"Er, Shia?"

"What."

"What the hell was that about?"

"Clarisse is going to start a betting pool in

the house on who's going to get you to sign a contract. Just ignore it; maybe it'll go away."

Sara paled, nodded, and rapidly walked away. "I'll be in my bedroom for the rest of forever. See you later."

I shook my head and followed her example, heading to my own room. I was grateful to see Louis and Ryan had brought all of my bags in and set them down at the foot of the bed so I wouldn't have to drag anything out of my car. The scent of vampire was nigh overpowering in the room, though, and I was a bit annoyed that there were no windows—not even in the bathroom—to vent the place.

The whole household would know we were here by nightfall. There were a few people I wouldn't mind seeing again, but getting reacquainted with them was going to be interesting with Sara here. Royce would undoubtedly stick to his word and let all of his vampires know she was off-limits but, until he did, I'd have to keep a very close eye on her.

Chapter 31

I did manage to get some rest before nightfall. The constant stress had exhausted me more than I'd realized until my head hit the pillow. Waking up smothered by the smell of vampire wasn't pleasant, but the high thread count sheets and cushy mattress did a lot to soothe my ruffled feathers. The scent of food gradually penetrated my sleep-fuddled haze, drawing me out from under the covers. I threw on some fresh clothes and shambled out into the living room.

Sara was talking quietly but animatedly with Clarisse, Mouse, and a couple other people I recognized, but couldn't remember the names of. They gestured me over with welcoming smiles, and I was very pleased to see the pizza boxes on the table between them. After snagging a slice, I settled down on the arm of the nearest couch, inclining my head to our visitors.

The girl was one of the two Asian donors who lived in the building, though I couldn't remember if this one was Ivy or Joy. The big guy seated next to Mouse was someone I'd met once, briefly, when I was under particularly heavy strain of the bond to Royce. All I remembered about him was that he'd also appeared pretty stressed at the time; now he seemed more relaxed, sprawled in his chair like he owned the place.

Sara, perhaps recognizing the way my eyes crinkled as I tried and failed to remember the names, smoothly filled me in.

"Hey, Shia, you've met Mouse, Christoph, and Ivy, right? Now that you're here, Ivy's supposed to give us the lowdown on how things work around here."

"Good to see you again," Ivy said, smiling brightly at me. I returned the expression, if a bit more wanly, and she hooked a thumb at the kitchen. "There's a notepad and pens on your fridge. We get groceries delivered once a week. Write down anything you need, and turn it over to Timothy by Thursday night, and he'll place the order in the morning. Mouse can introduce you if you haven't met him yet. He's a bit shy.

"I'm sure you noticed we don't have windows. The vent systems are good, but if you smoke, take it outside. Use the fire escape at the end of the hall to chill in the courtyard. We barbeque out there in the summer, too. Let's see, what else . . ."

Christoph spoke up, scratching the back of his neck. "If you don't want everyone and their brother trying to bite you, make sure someone claims you fast."

Mouse and Clarisse gave him disapproving looks. He shrugged. "What? It's true."

Ivy rolled her eyes then continued, ticking off

each rule on her fingers as she went. "Right. Anyway, no visitors without clearing it through whoever's on guard duty first. That includes pizza and other food deliveries. If you're on the roster to work, you'll find your name posted on the notice board in the gym on the second floor. Never leave the house through the front door without a partner; if you can, restrict your movements to the tunnel system in the basement. Someone will get you keys later. If you need a tour of the tunnels, ask Mouse or Ken; they know the place better than anyone. Oh, laundry's done in the basement, too. Give dry cleaning to Ken on Mondays.

"Since you've got dogs, if you want to walk them, don't take them to Central Park. It's restricted to the werewolves, so we're not supposed to bug them. Territory issues or something."

"That's very important, you know," Christoph said, in the tones of one deeply offended.

"Pipe down, lovey; no one's going to bother the Moonwalkers," Clarisse said.

Mouse started to scribble something down on a notepad she'd brought, but threw her hands up when Ivy continued on a completely different topic.

"Alec said for you to pay him a visit once you were up. He's working in his office upstairs. I'd knock first; Jessica was supposed to be spending some"—and here she added air quotes, rolling her eyes again as she did it—"quality time with him."

"Er, ew, thanks," I muttered.

"What?" Sara asked, brows arching. "What am I missing here?"

"They're probably fucking," Christoph said, placidly enough. Mouse and Ivy simultaneously smacked him on the back of his head, and he cringed, grabbing at his thick, curly hair. "Ow, ow, ow! All right! Enough!"

Sara made a face, then glanced at me. "Aside from the gross-out factor, that's not as bad an answer as I was expecting. You ready to brave the lion's den?"

I waved my pizza slice at her. "Let me finish eating. Not that I have much of an appetite after that lovely visual."

"I know, right?" Ivy grinned at me, and I soon found myself smiling back.

Christoph, Mouse, Clarisse, and Ivy excused themselves with invitations to swing by and say hello after our meeting with Royce. They were planning a movie night in someone's apartment at the end of the hall on the second floor; we promised to join them as soon as we were done.

"This place isn't so bad," Sara remarked once they were gone, reaching for a slice of pizza for herself. The dogs, braver now that the vampires had left, edged close to the table in hopes of being fed some scraps. Sara and I obliged them by tossing them bits of pepperoni and sausage that they eagerly snapped up. "I thought it was going to be all creepy and full of cobwebs or something. Nothing like this."

I shrugged, swallowing the food in my mouth before replying. "Don't be too surprised. Royce isn't Dracula. He's got better taste."

She coughed on her pizza, then gave me a weak grin. We finished the rest of our food in companionable silence, then headed up to Royce's room on the third floor.

I knocked and waited for an answer, ready to run back down the stairs if necessary to avoid any confrontation with Jessica. The idea of being in her presence after what Christoph had said downstairs and her little display with Royce during the day was a bit too much for me just then.

"Come in," Royce called, his voice echoing across the expanse of what I was coming to think of as the Statue Room.

We went together, and this time the windows were open, allowing a cool breeze to waft through the room, stirring the gauzy white curtains. The spotlights had been dimmed, casting barely any illumination, giving the place a creepy vibe it hadn't had during the day.

"I'm in the office. Come on back."

Shivering, Sara and I looked at each other, exchanging glances before pressing onward to the black pit of the office. The only light to be seen was a bank of computer screens displaying the logo for A.D. Royce Industries.

Royce was hidden in the shadows, seated before a computer at the far end of the room. He glanced at us over his shoulder, an indistinct form in the dark gesturing for us to come closer.

"Both of you take a seat. I've got something to show you."

We complied, though I had no clue what this was about. He tilted the nearest screen so we both could see, and played a video from a news Web site, the anchor's face grim as she relayed her story.

"A terrible tragedy rocked Manhattan today

when the body of award-winning journalist Jim Pradiz was discovered by police officers following an anonymous tip. According to sources, he was found in his home, dead of multiple animal bites and stab wounds. Involvement of Other-citizens is certain, though it was not immediately clear if Mr. Pradiz had been contracted at the time of his death. Though Detective Bobby McNeill, who is leading the investigation, stated it is too early to speculate and that no autopsy has yet been completed, he did admit that there is strong evidence of a connection between this tragedy and the investigative work done by Pradiz on local werewolf packs just prior to his death.

"Mr. Pradiz was best known for his Pulitzer Prize-winning editorial piece covering the introduction of the Others to our society in the wake of 9/11—"

Royce stopped the video and turned to face us, folding his hands in his lap. I dragged my eyes off the screen to face him, making a conscious effort to draw my hand away from my mouth and put it back in my lap.

Sara cleared her throat a couple times before managing a hoarse, "Wow."

"Mr. Pradiz's death leads me to believe that you two are in more danger than I had originally estimated. I foresee difficulties ahead with the trouble the Were packs are stirring up. For your own protection, until I have a better idea of their plans and the effects of their actions, I need to ask you both to remain restricted to this building. If you are traced here, it could endanger not only you, but the others in this building. I won't have that. You both must exhibit due care for our protection and security, as much as your own. Agreed?"

Sara nodded gravely, but I wasn't happy with his pronouncement. It put too much of a damper on my plans. "For how long?"

"Just until I get a better grasp on the movements of the packs. Rohrik Donovan will be taking an interest in this, I'm sure. I can request his assistance to determine what the Sunstrikers and Ravenwoods are up to, and check with my sources with the police so I can plot a course of action. For now, you're safe as long as no one knows you're here." He turned to me, his eyes glittering unnaturally in the dark. I suppressed a shiver, and met his gaze without flinching. What he was asking of us meant that, if he or one of the other vampires did something to harm us, no one would ever know. Though he spoke sense, we were essentially trapped in a building full of predators, with nowhere else to run.

"Shiarra, I'll have someone move your car to a storage lot, so your presence should go unnoticed as long as you remain inside."

That helpless anger I'd successfully clamped down on earlier was back with a vengeance. I was raging at being trapped, hating that Chaz might have been involved in the death of the reporter. I held my knees to keep from digging my nails into my palms again. There was no way to know for sure, not yet, but something deep down told me that Chaz knew about it, even if he hadn't participated in the act of murder. Whatever he and the other Sunstrikers were up to had to stop. Others' lives, including mine and Sara's, depended on it.

After a few deep breaths, I calmed down enough to think of a coherent answer to give Royce.

"All right. No movies, no malls, no clubs. What about walking Sara's dogs? They can't stay inside all the time."

"Someone else in the building can take them out when needed. Ivy offered to be your host while you're here, so you can check with her about who is available."

Sara nodded. Even in the dark, I could tell she'd gone pale, though there was no lack of determination in her voice. Either she hadn't realized the depth of the pile of shit we'd landed in, or she was much better at coping with swimming in it than I was. "We'll be careful. I need to make some calls, tell my sister and my boyfriend that I'm okay. A couple of police officers paid us a visit before we came here, too. Do you have a phone I can use?"

"There should be one hooked up in the kitchen of your apartment downstairs. You're welcome to use it, as long as you bear in mind that you cannot give out the number or tell anyone where you are."

"Not even Arnold?"

Royce frowned, considering the image of the reporter on his computer screen before responding. "It may not be wise. Chaz is aware of his connection to you, and, through you, to Shiarra. If the Sunstrikers put pressure on him, despite his best intentions he might let something slip."

"He would never do such a thing!" Sara said. Her quiet vehemence didn't sway the vampire.

"Even the most stoic can break when the correct leverage is applied, whether by torture or a threat to loved ones. You cannot be certain that he would be able to withstand whatever the Sunstrikers might attempt to do to him."

The sick feeling that washed over me at the statement left me wanting to protest, to say that Chaz would never do such a thing. The sorry thing was, I didn't know *what* Chaz—or the other Sunstrikers, for that matter—was capable of anymore. That any of the werewolves might stoop to such tactics was utterly reprehensible, but clearly not out of the realm of possibility considering how Jim Pradiz had died.

Royce continued, not waiting for us to recover from that gut blow. "Arnold's connection to you also puts him in some measure of danger, so it may be for the best if he were to go into hiding as well."

Sara said nothing. I cleared my throat and asked her unspoken question. "Could he stay here with us?"

"I won't abide keeping a mage in my home, and I sincerely doubt he would wish to stay here even if I extended the offer. I'm sure The Circle must provide safe houses for their own when needed. Unless he is willing to relocate until the Sunstrikers have been taken in hand, I can't condone telling him that you will be staying here."

We thanked him and rose, making the trek across the Statue Room in solemn, somber quiet. He stayed in his office, the sound of keys rapidly being tapped on the keyboard trailing after us. It wasn't until we were on the stairs and headed back to our apartment—what a strange concept, "our" apartment—that Sara said anything.

"You should call your parents."

"I know."

She nudged me with her elbow, and I looked at her, pausing on the stairs. Her concern was clear, and I had a hard time meeting her gaze. After a bit of hemming and hawing, I caved. "I'll call them; I just don't want to. Mom's going to have a cow, and Dad will probably chew me a new asshole. Thing is, they'll be *right*. I've hidden a lot from them, and I'm not looking forward to explaining why I never told them Chaz was Were. Mikey called and left me a message, too, so I think he may have found out. I'm not too excited about talking to him either."

"You want me there when you do it?"

"No." I sighed. "How about you call Arnold, Janine, and the cops, then head upstairs for that movie? I'll call Mom and Dad after you go. I have the feeling I'm going to need some alone time afterward."

She gave my shoulder a squeeze. That simple touch was enough to remind me why I needed to stick to my plan. Sara didn't deserve to be dragged into my mess. It was up to me to make this right.

Chapter 32

Sara made her calls, and I waited in the living room until she was done. The call to Detectives Smith and Yarmouth didn't take very long. She let them know we were safe and had a place to stay. That she'd heard about Jim, and no, we didn't have any information on what had happened other than what was in the news. Yes, she'd check in with them in a few days.

The call to Arnold was similarly brief. He'd already packed some things, having planned on going into hiding since my phone call to him. He knew where Royce's home was and would be careful to keep any visits to a minimum. We broke the rule about not giving out the phone number so he could get in touch with me if he found a cure.

Next, she called Janine. That took longer, since Sara's chronically neurotic sister didn't quite grasp immediately that being in hiding meant not telling anyone where we were or how to reach us. Sara kept her voice calm and soothing, letting Janine know that it would be a while before she'd see us again, but that she promised to stay in touch.

I swear, Sara has the patience of a saint. I would've hung up on Janine by the third repetition.

I listened in on Sara's end of the conversations with half an ear. Most of my attention was focused on figuring out exactly what to say to my parents and my brother. Needing a little comfort, I whistled to Buster and Roxie who were lying down on the rug a few feet from the couch. Though I called them, the dogs wouldn't come to me, shying away from my touch. It was most likely from the heavier scent of vampire on my skin. Realizing that did nothing to improve my mood.

As soon as Sara was done, I got my rolodex and settled down in front of the phone, staring at it as though it might make the phone calls for me. She paused on her way out the door, peering at me over the counter of the breakfast bar.

"You sure you don't want me to stick around?"

I gave her a grim, cheerless smile. "Yeah. This is something I have to do on my own. Thanks, though. I'll be up to join you in a little while if this doesn't take too long."

Sara's look made it clear she knew I was lying through my teeth. Rather than call me on it, she nodded slowly and turned away. "Don't forget you've still got friends, Shia. We're here when you need us."

I didn't say anything as the door shut quietly behind her. Her words smacked a little too closely of what Royce had said to me, making the lump in my throat too hard to speak around. I muttered a quick prayer under my breath, then picked up the phone and dialed my older brother, figuring whatever he had to say to me was no doubt the lesser of two evils. My hands shook badly enough that I had to redial twice to get the right number. It didn't take long for him to pick up.

"Mike here."

"Hey, it's Shia."

"Shia? Jesus Christ, where have you been?! I've been trying to reach you for three days! Are you okay?"

I cringed, covering my eyes with my hand. "I know, I'm sorry. I'm fine. Sort of."

"I saw the paper. Who did it? I swear to God, I'll kill them with my bare hands—"

"Mike!" I cried, cutting him off. Yeesh, he was more like me than I liked to admit. Being brash and hot-tempered must be a signature Waynest family trait. "Don't do anything stupid. They're Others. It's too dangerous."

He growled something I didn't quite get, then resumed in a reasonably normal tone. "Where are you? Mom and Dad have been worried sick."

"I can't say. Sara and I are hiding out for a while. We're safe."

As safe as we could be surrounded by vampires, that is.

"Damien said he stopped by your apartment today and the door was unlocked. Looked like everything was okay inside, nothing missing that he could tell." That gave me a chill. I distinctly recalled locking up behind me. While theoretically the lock could have been picked, the only other person who had a key to my apartment was Chaz.

If it was him, when would he have stopped by? What would he have done if he'd found me there?

"Police have been looking for you, too. They called the family. Are you going to need someone to rep you in court?"

"Maybe. You offering?"

"What are big brothers for? I'll protect you if you need it. Pro bono and everything."

I chuckled. "You sure the rest of Graves and Pearson are going to appreciate that? This might be a bit heavy for them."

"Doesn't matter. You're family. The partners can take a hike—I've been thinking about opening up my own office anyway. Enough of that, though. Tell me what happened."

I did. As tempting as it was to keep mum about some of what I'd done the past few days, I didn't pull any punches. He stayed quiet, asking a couple clarifying questions, but otherwise not interrupting as I explained to him my relationship with Chaz, what really happened at Damien's birthday, how I ended up contracted to Royce, and why that had so much to do with what happened this weekend. I told him about Chaz's infidelity, the Nightstrikers, the Cassidy family, even what I did to destroy Chaz and Kimberly's things after I found out he was cheating. Basically, everything Mike might need to know to defend me in court.

He made a faint sound—a mixture of worry, disgust, and anger, all balled up into one—when I told him that I'd been scratched and potentially infected with lycanthropy by Dillon.

It took a while to get it all out, and by the time I was done, I felt about a million years old. The emotional gamut left me high and dry, too wiped out to be prepared for his response.

"Wow. Mom's probably going to kill you when you tell her."

That set off a fit of giggles. Which quickly devolved into guffaws. Soon, I had tears streaming down my cheeks, and it wasn't entirely thanks to the uncontrollable laughter that exploded from me at Mike's observation.

Once I managed to get myself back under a semblance of control, Mike spoke up. "You sure you're going to be all right?"

"Yeah," I gasped, choking back a last chuckle as I wiped a few tears from my eyes with the back of my hand. "Jesus. Mom is really going to have a fit."

"Do you want to tell Damien, or should I?"

My younger brother avoided the news like the plague. Unless my parents had said something to him, he probably didn't know a thing about what was going on with me yet. "I'll call him later. He should hear it from me."

"Okay, no problem. If you get pulled in for questioning by the authorities, call me before anyone else. Got it?"

"Got it. Thanks, Mike. I owe you big time."

"I'll keep that in mind. Hey, if you turn furry, don't tell Angela. She's been riding my ass to go to one of those Were-run restaurants for the last two months. I think she's got it bad for them."

I laughed again, a bit more normally this time. "Okay. Tell her I said hi. I'll call you later in the week."

"Take care. Love you, sis. Stay out of trouble."

"No promises."

Feeling a bit better knowing my big brother had my back, I didn't have such a hard time dialing my parents' number. Though I'd gotten lucky last time and only had to leave a message after disappearing for a few weeks during the aftermath of Max Carlyle's visit, this time my dad picked up the phone.

"Waynest residence."

My heart sank at the hoarseness of his voice. He'd started smoking again, something he only did when truly stressed.

"Hi, Dad."

There was a long beat of silence. Too long.

"Dad?"

"Where are you?"

I cringed. He was not pleased. Not at all. "Hiding. Safe. Dad, I'm really sorry I didn't call sooner, but there's a lot of bad stuff happening right now. I need to explain—"

"I don't want an explanation."

I hesitated, uncertain what to say in the face of his cold wrath. "I'm sorry."

"Were the papers right? Have you been infected?" He said the last word like it was something dirty. Maybe it was.

"I was scratched. I don't know if I'm . . . like that . . . yet."

He went quiet again for a while. I didn't say anything, waiting tensely for him to speak. When he did, it was brusque, bitter, and exactly what I was terrified of when Sara argued with me earlier about making this call. She didn't know my parents like I did.

"You're not welcome in this house. Do you understand me? I don't know what you are, or what you've become, but you're no Waynest." He spat out that last as if I were some *thing,* some wretched beast too disgusting to behold. I didn't say anything. Couldn't say anything. "You broke your mother's heart. I won't let that happen again. You hear me?"

"Dad, please—"

"Don't call me that!" he roared, making me flinch. "You're not our little girl anymore. Don't call this house again!"

He slammed the phone down, cutting the connection. I slowly lowered the phone from my ear, staring down at the plastic while shock settled in like an old friend, here to stay.

At first, I didn't move. I know I was crying. Wetness trickled down my cheeks, fat drops of moisture falling to spatter on the linoleum. I could see them fall, but couldn't feel it. Couldn't feel anything but cold numbness, seeping from my head to my toes, spreading over my limbs until the phone slid from my deadened fingers to land with a sharp crack on the floor. One of the dogs barked once at the sound, but they didn't come to investigate.

I slowly slumped down to my knees, my back resting against the cabinet, as the weight of what my father had said truly hit me.

The man who taught me how to ride a bike, who took me to the hospital when I broke my arm falling out of a tree when I was little, who gave me my first car, who held me when I cried after being dumped at my senior prom, who told my mother

I was a big girl who could make her own decisions when I decided to be a private investigator—no longer wanted me in his life.

I wrapped my arms around myself and huddled on the floor for a long time, alone, doing what I could to hold myself together so I wouldn't shatter from the loss. It wasn't working very well. Waves of sick grief rolled over me, crushing everything, stealing away my breath.

It was a very long time before I could bring myself to get back on my feet and keep moving like there was something left of me to save.

Chapter 33

I've held up to a lot in my day. Psychotic magic-users, crazy vampires, and cheating boyfriends are no walk in the park. Being bound by blood to a vampire, losing myself to him, and then having that closeness ripped away from me in the agony of withdrawal was quite possibly one of the most physically and emotionally painful experiences I've ever had.

None of those things prepared me for being disowned by my father.

Once the immediate edge of shock wore off, I didn't take the time to consider what I could do to fix it. I didn't pause to consider the consequences of my actions. I didn't stop to think holy-hell-what-am-I-doing?

Instead, I went straight to my room and donned every last piece of hunting equipment I owned. A few drops of Amber Kiss perfume would ensure my scent would be dulled to supernaturals, while the body armor would protect me from claws and fangs, giving me a fighting chance at surviving things no mortal should ever have to face. My guns went into the shoulder holster, soon hidden beneath my trench coat, a replacement after the last one was shredded in a fight for my life.

The belt came last. Though in the course of my breakdown it felt like it had been a long time since the sun went down, it wasn't quite midnight yet. There were a lot of hours left to the night.

A lot of hours left to hunt.

The belt knew what I wanted.

On silent feet, I left the apartment. No one was in the hall. Whoever was on guard duty did not notice my stealthy exit.

Instead of trying to sneak past whoever was on watch at the front door, I headed to the back of the hall and took the stairs two at a time, pausing on the landing of the second floor. The sounds of heavy music, a car chase, and laughter came from the last door on the right side of the hall. The door was open, and I could hear the under-tones of a few voices beneath the soundtrack of mayhem; the party was in there. Sara would be with those people, enjoying herself, safe for now in the shadow of the vampires who had seen fit to take us in. I'd have to pass by that open door to reach the window at the end of the hall, right above the roof of the foyer. There was a chance I might be seen by one of the vampires old and fast enough to stop me, even with the benefits granted by the belt.

It was a chance I'd have to take. If I stayed here, Royce and the other vampires wouldn't let me do what needed to be done.

I ran—fast—faster than I could ever remember

running before. The doors to either side of me were nothing but blurs, and all I did to protect myself was cover my eyes with my arm at the last moment, right before I leapt through the window.

Glass shattered with a sound so sharp it hurt my ears, so newly attuned to the quieter sounds of the night. Sheer momentum was carrying me much farther than expected. I was airborne.

For one heart-stopping moment, I was terrified.

Then, the utter *rapture* of the belt kicked in, reminding me that—with its help—I was now something more than human.

We flew, reveling in the wind making our hair stream, cutting through the material of the body armor as a cold caress, making the trench coat flare behind us like dark wings. As light as a bird, we landed on the roof of a car parked in front of the building, using it as a lever to leap off before it could be crushed under our weight.

There were shouts and cries from behind me, but I didn't stop running.

The hunt for those who had wronged me was on.

Please turn the page for an exciting sneak peek of the new H&W Investigations novel, coming soon from Zebra Books!

Days left to full moon: 24

My fingertips pressed against the cool stone of the ledge, helping me balance as I crouched on the balls of my feet. The heavy winds choked with smog and tainted with the stink of the Hudson threatened to push me off the edge of the apartment building's roof if I wasn't careful.

People bundled against the cold moved five stories below me, oblivious, never thinking to look up. Hours had passed since I'd fled Alec Royce's apartment building with nothing but murder on my mind. It had taken me a while to find my current perch. I'd been waiting up here for nearly an hour after first checking inside the apartment, and my mark had not yet shown. Strain burned in my calves, but I remained as I was, held in check despite my desire to rampage through the city, destroying everything in my path until I found my targets.

'You are so impatient,' a voice whispered in the

back of my skull, tinged with an edge of laughter. *'Just wait. He has to come home sometime.'*

I growled, the sound reverberating deep in my chest.

'Touchy.'

"Shut up," I snapped, running my fingers through my hair to shove the errant curls out of my eyes. "If he doesn't come soon, I won't have enough time to do anything. The sun will be up in less than an hour." I'd been counting on Dillon being home so I could destroy the bastard before he hurt someone else. Or at least beat him into new and interesting shapes to make him think twice before infecting another uncontracted human.

'Maybe he spent the night with someone. Or left for work before we arrived.'

I didn't say anything, a pang of doubt giving me pause. The belt wrapped around my waist was the source of the voice in my head; a voice that would be banished once the sun rose. Aside from providing moral support and snarky commentary, the first rays of morning light creeping over the horizon would take with it all of my enhanced skills and senses, leaving me frail and human again. Though most of the time I hated what the belt did to me, I couldn't afford to be without its help while facing down an angry werewolf.

'Then wait until tomorrow night to face him. Use the day wisely; get some rest and food to build up your strength, and use those P.I. skills of yours to track him down.'

I nodded, turning away from the street and huddling into my trench coat against the cold.

Now that I'd had a few hours for my ire to cool, I found that I was suffering from a wintry, calculating hatred instead of the heated, unthinking rage which had driven me here to begin with. Despite that the wait was really weighing on my nerves, it had given me plenty of time to think about what I was going to do once Dillon showed his face, and what I would do about the other Sunstrikers who had driven me to hunt them like the cowardly dogs they were.

In the space of a few days, my entire life had turned upside down. Not that it had been particularly normal to begin with, but my now very ex-boyfriend Chaz had been cheating on me. He'd also been running some kind of werewolf mafia ring right under my nose. Though I had no solid proof, I was sure his pack had something to do with the murder of Jim Pradiz. Not that I'd liked the sleazy reporter, but it was terrifying to know that the werewolves were willing to stoop so low to silence him.

To top things off, one of the Sunstrikers had scratched and quite possibly infected me with the lycanthropy virus. It would be weeks before I'd know for sure if I was going to join the ranks of the terminally furry come the next full moon. Clearly, thanks to the murder of Jim Pradiz—which the Sunstrikers were somehow connected to, I just knew it—I would never be one of that pack whether or not they accepted me. It was entirely possible that they were out to kill me, too.

Thanks to Chaz's pack, I was on the run from a bunch of murderous werewolves, the police, and half the media in the state. The last straw had been my father telling me point-blank that I wasn't his little girl anymore. Being disowned from my family for my involvement with the Others had been a gut blow I wasn't prepared for. Recalling the raspy, accusing tones of my dad as he forbade me from ever coming home to him and Mom again made my eyes burn, but I'd cried my last tear over his pronouncement hours ago. I had work to do to make sure that the people involved with bringing this load of misery down on me and my family paid for everything they'd done. My resolve only firmed as I paused at the edge of the roof above the rusting metal framework of the fire escape that would lead me back down to the filthy alleyways and web-work of New York City streets below.

Considering it was Chaz and the rest of his pack's fault that everything—my life, my livelihood, my family, and possibly my humanity—had been taken from me, I was not in a forgiving mood.

'That's an understatement.'

The droll "tone" of the belt had me grinning, though it was more a feral baring of my teeth than an expression of agreement. Stone chipped under my fingers as they tightened on the cornice molding on the edge of the roof. I absently flicked blood from my fingertips before dropping lightly down to the fire escape. It clanged dully at the impact, the sound rattling through the framework. I barely gave it time to finish shuddering before I leapt over the side, my already-healed fingers catching on the rail as I propelled myself down to the level below. Ladders and startled faces in windows passed in a blur, my body moving with the grace and surety of an Olympic gymnast and my stomach edging up into my lungs as I gained speed. Soon, much too soon, I was airborne.

Before I knew it, I was in a feral crouch on the alley floor, hair in my eyes and trench coat billowing around me like one of those clichéd action movie heroes and the last echoes of my landing ricocheting off the alley walls. An inhuman feat I wouldn't have been able to accomplish a few weeks ago without breaking my legs, even with the belt's help. Something about giving in and letting the belt take over had done something to change how we worked together; it augmented my strength, speed, agility, and stamina to a far greater degree than the first time I had worn it. Not to mention made me heal minor injuries nearly as quickly as a vampire. I wondered if that's what it felt like to be an Other.

Adrenaline burned in my veins, but I didn't give in to the belt's siren song or half-hearted pleads for violence. Instead, I shoved my hands in my pockets and edged out of the shadows, past the dumpsters, and into the trickle of pedestrian traffic in the city street.

Clenching my fingers around the vial of Amber Kiss perfume and the box of ammo I'd shoved in my pockets didn't hurt, though flakes of dried blood and shed scar tissue from cuts received and healed on my way down from the rooftop rubbed off in the process. I didn't want to think about what I had become, or what I would be once I saw my quest for revenge to its end.

'If not for the vampire, you wouldn't be in this mess,' the belt whispered. *'You should plan to remove him, too.'*

"Aside from the fact that he'd kill me if I tried it, Royce didn't do this to me," I muttered under my breath. "Don't push me."

A woman walking next to me glanced over, arching a silver-studded brow before ignoring me. That was the most attention I'd received from any of the sea of pedestrians all night. Not that I was complaining.

'He may not have infected you, but he's the one who brought you back into Chaz's sights, and he's also the one who keeps involving you in supernatural business. You wouldn't have been bitten by vampires—'

"Enough!"

I nearly shouted the word, and this time I did merit a few stares from early morning strollers, late night revelers sloshing their way home, and a handful of people in power suits on their way to the office. Ducking my head and popping up the collar of my trench coat, I sped up the pace, growling under my breath. I would've snarled something nasty back at the belt, especially since it was laughing at me again, but I was attracting too much attention as it was.

In fact, only yards away from me, a black-and-white was cruising past. I couldn't help but watch over my shoulder as it went by before realizing how conspicuous that must look. I drew out of the press of the foot traffic to pretend to consider buying a magazine at a nearby news stand. My stomach did a turn at the headline on one of the local rags: "New York's Hottest Vampire Sponsoring Charity Concert!" There was a picture of him on the cover of the latest issue of some financial news magazine, too. I twisted away, scowling. No matter how far I ran, it seemed Alec Royce would follow me everywhere.

Oh, great. When I looked back, the cops had pulled into the alley I had just come from, flicking on their search light as they parked.

That was my cue to hightail it. I needed to be less conspicuous with my actions if I was going to carry out my plans without landing up dead or in jail before the month was out. Abandoning my feeble ruse, I turned and took to a brisk walk in the opposite direction from Dillon's apartment building.

I needed to figure out where to go once the sun came up. After the stunt I'd pulled, there was no way I was putting myself back under Royce's watchful eye. Knowing the vampire, he'd chain me up in the basement or something to keep me from escaping again. Going home was out of the question, as was Sara's house and my parents'. Arnold might let me crash, but he'd tell Sara, which meant the vampire would know where to find me. I didn't want that.

Not to mention that I didn't have any money to get myself to my theoretical daytime hiding spot. In my headlong rush to escape Royce's building, I hadn't taken any necessities with me but my hunting equipment. My duffel with my clothes and my purse had been left behind.

Assuming I survived long enough, I needed to work on my ability to plan ahead.

Thrilling Suspense from
Beverly Barton

_After Dark	978-1-4201-1893-3	$5.99US/$6.99CAN
_As Good as Dead	978-1-4201-0037-2	$4.99US/$6.99CAN
_Close Enough to Kill	978-0-8217-7688-9	$6.99US/$9.99CAN
_Cold Hearted	978-1-4201-0049-5	$6.99US/$9.99CAN
_Dead by Midnight	978-1-4201-0051-8	$7.99US/$10.99CAN
_Dead by Morning	978-1-4201-1035-7	$7.99US/$10.99CAN
_Don't Cry	978-1-4201-1034-0	$7.99US/$9.99CAN
_The Dying Game	978-0-8217-7689-6	$6.99US/$9.99CAN
_Every Move She Makes	978-0-8217-8018-3	$4.99US/$6.99CAN
_The Fifth Victim	978-1-4201-0343-4	$4.99US/$6.99CAN
_Killing Her Softly	978-0-8217-7687-2	$6.99US/$9.99CAN
_The Last to Die	978-1-4201-0647-3	$6.99US/$8.49CAN
_Most Likely to Die	978-0-8217-7576-9	$7.99US/$10.99CAN
_The Murder Game	978-0-8217-7690-2	$6.99US/$9.99CAN
_Silent Killer	978-1-4201-0050-1	$6.99US/$9.99CAN
_Sugar and Spice	978-0-8217-8047-3	$7.99US/$10.99CAN
_What She Doesn't Know	978-1-4201-2131-5	$5.99US/$6.99CAN

Available Wherever Books Are Sold!

Visit our website at **www.kensingtonbooks.com**

Romantic Suspense from
Lisa Jackson

See How She Dies	0-8217-7605-3	$6.99US/$9.99CAN
Final Scream	0-8217-7712-2	$7.99US/$10.99CAN
Wishes	0-8217-6309-1	$5.99US/$7.99CAN
Whispers	0-8217-7603-7	$6.99US/$9.99CAN
Twice Kissed	0-8217-6038-6	$5.99US/$7.99CAN
Unspoken	0-8217-6402-0	$6.50US/$8.50CAN
If She Only Knew	0-8217-6708-9	$6.50US/$8.50CAN
Hot Blooded	0-8217-6841-7	$6.99US/$9.99CAN
Cold Blooded	0-8217-6934-0	$6.99US/$9.99CAN
The Night Before	0-8217-6936-7	$6.99US/$9.99CAN
The Morning After	0-8217-7295-3	$6.99US/$9.99CAN
Deep Freeze	0-8217-7296-1	$7.99US/$10.99CAN
Fatal Burn	0-8217-7577-4	$7.99US/$10.99CAN
Shiver	0-8217-7578-2	$7.99US/$10.99CAN
Most Likely to Die	0-8217-7576-6	$7.99US/$10.99CAN
Absolute Fear	0-8217-7936-2	$7.99US/$9.49CAN
Almost Dead	0-8217-7579-0	$7.99US/$10.99CAN
Lost Souls	0-8217-7938-9	$7.99US/$10.99CAN
Left to Die	1-4201-0276-1	$7.99US/$10.99CAN
Wicked Game	1-4201-0338-5	$7.99US/$9.99CAN
Malice	0-8217-7940-0	$7.99US/$9.49CAN

Visit our website at **www.kensingtonbooks.com**